The
Nine Lives
Of
Antoine Montvoisin

ANGELA ELLIOTT

For Jacob

Prologue

The year 1658 began with a violent north wind and freezing temperatures. No one could remember a colder time. In Paris the River Seine iced over and the occupants of the little houses and shops built on the bridge they called the Pont Marie took to praying for deliverance from the inclement weather in the small church of St. Andre-des-Arcs, where on Sunday the 17th February the chalice containing the 'blood of Christ' had to be held over a lit candle to thaw it.

Walking back from church that morning, Antoine Montvoisin, a haberdasher whose shop stood close to the Île Saint Louis end of the bridge, felt a tickle in his beard and wondered if the wind had changed direction. Antoine was a stocky man, with a round face and belly to match. He specialised in fine silks and sumptuous Italian velvets, but the cold snap had put paid to customers and he was struggling to make ends meet. To make matters worse, his savings had been depleted considerably by the purchase of a large house on the Rue Beauregard, at the insistence of his wife, Catherine, who refused to live on the bridge a moment longer than was absolutely necessary. Swaddled in a thick wool coat and wearing a fur around his shoulders and a hat pulled down over his rather large ears, Antoine peeled off a glove and tested the air. Yes, the wind had changed. The thaw would come soon.

Four days later, as he lay in his cot in the shop atop the bridge's second arch, Antoine heard the frozen river crack.

When he looked out of the window he saw black water forcing its way through the white ice. As he'd lived on the bridge for the best part of his life, he thought little of it, other than it would be nice to feel warm again, and set about making an inventory of his stock. He knew if he didn't pull in more custom he'd be out of business soon. He thought he might branch into jewellery. To do so he'd have to off-load some of his slower moving items. The brown fustian for instance and the rough felt from England. He knew a man who would take both and give him a fair price.

For several days Antoine rummaged in his back room, oblivious to the thawing ice outside. He came upon a box of buttons, nestled between a bird's egg blue cotton and a greying linen. Nary a button had a fellow to match. As a boy he'd used them as counters, lining them up and ranking them by size. He emptied them onto the table. It was going to be hard to part with anything much. Antoine scooped the buttons up, deposited them back in the box and set it on the shelf. His stomach growled. He'd treat himself to a nice quail's egg. Yes, that was what he'd do, then he'd open the shop and see if the thaw had tempted anyone onto the bridge. At which point, said bridge gave a shudder and then another and another. Antoine steadied himself against the wall. Two shudders in a row wasn't normal. Three, unheard of. The shelves started to wander across the room. The topmost bolts of fabric toppled. Cursing, he bent to retrieve them. A great cracking sound came up from the depths and a gulf opened up in the floor. Antoine fell backwards, his feet pushing hard on the remaining boards. The box of buttons disappeared into the yawning watery maw, as did the silks, the velvets and his entire stock of gold ribbon. To save his livelihood or his life, that was thing. The walls began to quake. Any moment now and the entire shop would simply disappear. Antoine flung open the door and ran.

The scene that greeted him outside wasn't much better. The island end of the bridge had completely collapsed into the river. Not a single shop was left standing, save Antoine's own, itself now teetering on the brink of complete annihilation. A woman folded like an empty sack and plopped into the water before he had a chance to do anything other than stand and stare. Her screams were lost in the watery roar. An old man, tears rolling down his face, wandered haphazardly back and forth. A child bellowed for a mother who would never again hold it close and tugged Antoine's coat. Downstream, bodies were tossed this way and that like bobbing corks. The shop shed the bottommost corner into the river, followed swiftly by rib upon rib of wood until all collapsed and was washed away. Antoine picked the child up and ran, not daring to look back until he reached the houses along the waterfront. He couldn't bring himself to think about how many had died, nor about how bloated and unrecognisable they would become on their progress to the sea. The water lapped around his feet, reminding him to find dry land. He carried on up into the city streets at a slower pace, his chest hurting, his head pounding.

By the time he reached the Tavern of the Dun Cow, the child had stopped screaming and lay dead in his arms. Antoine pushed back against a wall and sank to the ground. Who in their right mind would choose to live on a bridge? Terrifying, untrustworthy structures. Right there and then he swore never to set foot on one again.

Chapter One

The idea to reopen the shop had started as a memory. Antoine had been ambling along the Rue Beauregard, kicking up stones and wondering how to fill his day, when a hawker passed him with a tray of iridescent silk ribbons and his mind had flitted straight to the shop on the Pont Marie. Good God, but he'd been born into the business. Not in *that* shop, true, but certainly *a* shop. Catherine couldn't deny him his birthright. He'd open anew, that's what he'd do. He told her so at supper that evening.

"It's only right. I'm a marchand-mercier after all." Since the flood he'd done little more than run errands and garden.

"Haberdasher, you mean," Catherine said.

They'd been eating in silence up until then. She with dainty sips from the side of her spoon. He with great gulps.

"I'll have to sell the house. Find somewhere with rooms over. Perhaps I'll even take on an apprentice. I can't carry on like this. Gardening and errands. Haberdashery is in my blood."

"I thought you were a marchand-mercier?"

Antoine shrugged. "Either way, I was born to it."

"Huh, " Catherine grunted. "Over my dead body."

"The best place is the Rue Saint-Honoré. It's where everyone goes."

"You're mad. You can't afford that."

"I'm not suggesting for a minute that I... Look, Paris is awash with merchants. Have you seen those houses going up outside the city gates? The road to Montmartre is a nightmare of stinking outhouses."

"You needn't think I'm moving to a tumbledown shack on the Montmartre Road."

Tumbledown shack? What on earth was she talking about? "More people means more business. It's common sense."

"I don't want to move."

"But why?" To Antoine, it was all possibility and very little pain.

"My life is here and my clients know where to find me."

"Your clients. Damned fortune telling. What about my clients? What about the business I lost in the flood?"

"My mother lives in the next street. She would miss me."

"Where on earth do you think I'm suggesting we go? Paris isn't that big."

"Well it won't be close. The Rue Saint-Honoré is... is streets away."

On and on she went: the expense this, the distance that. Antoine gazed out of the window at the tumbling roses and drifting lavender. It had been a stupid idea. What had he been thinking? Sell up and move? Catherine was right, he couldn't afford the Rue Saint-Honoré. So where? A garret over a tiny *chemiserie*? He couldn't do that to her. He loved her with all his heart. She was happy in this grand house. She'd made a life here, and she was a good fortune teller. A *very* good fortune teller. He remembered how desolate he'd felt when he'd lost the shop. No, he couldn't take the house away from her. He couldn't.

***

Catherine wondered why she hadn't thought about poisoning Antoine before. It was the perfect solution. The house was bought and paid for. She had money of her own and a lover. What use did she have for a good-for-nothing husband? She certainly wasn't going to let him sell everything. She'd worked too hard for that. Her reputation was at stake. What customer would come to her to have their fortune told if all she had to offer was a pokey room above a shop? No, she'd poison him and that would be an end to his nonsense.

That evening, as the light faded and the stars came out, Catherine took down her mortar and ground up extract of snapdragon, pennywort, aqua cymbelaria and two drops of a madman's spittle, and topped it off with a sprinkle of arsenic. Then she mixed the poisonous mess into Antoine's bedtime goblet of wine and watched him drink every last drop down. Poor unsuspecting fool. She kissed his forehead and sent him up to bed like she would a child, telling him she'd be up in a short while. Two hours later, Catherine peeked round the bedroom door, fully expecting Antoine to be stone cold rigid, his lips blistered, and his eyes glassy, but instead he lay snoring like a baby.

Impossible!

Catherine growled and threw the door wide open. How dare he still be alive? She wasn't the best poisoner in Paris for nothing. She'd killed plenty of men in her time. Goodness, but she specialised in husbands. What would people say if they heard she'd failed to kill her own? She hovered over Antoine, her silk-slippered feet tapping furiously on the floorboards, her teeth clenched. Oh, but she couldn't bear to look at him any more: his flabby belly rising and falling, his lips fluttering obscenely with each snort. He had to die. He had to. There must have been something wrong with the arsenic. Or the madman's spittle. Perhaps he hadn't been truly mad. That could be it.

Antoine grunted, balled his fists, rubbed his eyes, licked his lips and fell back into snoring.

Disgusted, Catherine sneered, "Cats know not how to pardon." Then she bent low and whispered in his ear, "I'll kill you if it's the last thing I do."

Chapter Two

Three days after the attempted poisoning the idea for the shop came to Antoine again. He was lying on his belly in the garden, shears in hand, one eye screwed up to snip the tops off a few obliging blades of grass. It was a damned good idea and if he thought about it long enough he was sure he could remember some of his suppliers' names. So what if things were difficult at first? He wasn't afraid of hard work. The corporation for haberdashers wouldn't dare deny him admittance. For goodness sake, Montvoisin, marchand-mercier had been known city-wide for quality and fair prices – and hadn't he watched the Pont Marie being built? Yes, yes, it was true; he'd been very small; a child, and yes, the bridge had been destroyed in a flood, but forget about that. It was nothing…

…well, it wasn't nothing. He hadn't stepped foot on a bridge since, nevertheless, Montvoisin marchand-mercier had been a force of nature, and would be again!

Antoine snipped.

The grass yielded.

Oh the memories.

"Now this is Lampas," his father had said, late one evening. He'd held up a candle and stroked the patterned fabric. "It's similar to brocade. It has a silk main warp and a linen weft. It takes time to create something of this quality. The person who weaved this is creating a story;

each piece of cloth like a new life written on the firmament. Can you see it boy? Can you?"

Antoine had been barely twelve years old. He'd stood there in warm, sweet candlelight, in thrall to the twisted threads and the tale they told - in and out, in and out; writhing tender-coloured filaments. He danced with them and his mind took flight. He was a bird soaring high over the city. He was a cloud, a rainbow, a bolt of lightning. His father brought him back to earth.

"Warp and weft are very different," Montvoisin Senior said. "Ah, but I am one and my petite Mignonette is the other."

"Do you mean Maman?"

Antoine had torn his gaze away from the storied textile to stare at his mother, grading cotton at the cutting table. Madame Montvoisin had been a dark-haired, brown-eyed beauty, who'd lived for gossip and inflicting pain on her son. Although Antoine learned how to judge her moods, hiding in forgotten corners to avoid the worst of her rage, she'd always find him. One morning he upset a box of buttons. Perhaps the very same buttons he'd lost to the flood. It was possible. Desperate to avoid a beating, he'd crawled nose to the floor, fingers exploring frantically, eyes roving this way and that until a pair of feet interrupted his progress.

"What devil made you, eh? As God is my witness, you will suffer for your sins." His mother had grabbed him by the ear and, with her eyes empty of love and her lips pursed in disapproval, had thrashed him so soundly he hadn't been able to sit down for a week. There was no rhyme or reason to it. Madame Montvoisin had just been made that way.

Tears filled Antoine's eyes and the grass blurred; a green ocean in every sob. His father had turned to the bottle. His mother? Ah, his mother had died when he was fourteen; a blessed release and a curse, all in one. It was only then that Antoine had found joy in the bridge-wide world of middling merchants and noisome peddlers: the baker and his flour-dusted apron, the poultry dealer and his feathered hat, the cobbler and his leather jerkin with the silver buttons, one of which had once popped off and gone down between the bridge's giant stones, so that it winked and shone like an eye from out of the blackness between - and then there was the idea of being moored, bankside to bankside, with the swirling tannery-tainted, cadaverous river below, and the smoke-filled sky above. It was all gone. The bridge had been everything. Absolutely everything, until the flood. Antoine groaned. He still loved the river, but the flood had given him nightmares for years. Still did. Now as then, bridges were untrustworthy things.

Like mothers.

Like wives.

Antoine raised his eyes heavenwards. True, the same sky flew overhead, but now he lived in a landlocked house. Still, at least he had the garden. That first year after the flood he'd planted a verdant swathe of aromatic herbs: basil, hyssop, dittany, fennel and mint beneath insectivorous-barked apple trees. He'd salted the beds with bulbs brought in from the far distant city of Amsterdam and included peonies and marigolds, primroses in the spring and raspberries in late summer – and then there was the green and glorious grass. Glorious, but lumpy. The uneven surface annoyed him so much he spent hours in contemplation, observing it this way, walking it that. He'd flatten a particularly irritating section, to find it, the next morning, punctuated by fresh earth.

Antoine inched forward and came up against a small eruption of soil. No one would buy the house with lumpy grass. No one.

"Damned moles!"

He raised his head above the offending hillock and scowled at the undulating sward. The kitchen door banged and Catherine rounded the corner of the house and left via the garden gate.

Now where was she going? Where? To the constant stream of guests she was all charm and smiles, but to Antoine, nary a glance, and certainly not the kind of smile that crinkled her crow's feet and lit up her eyes: the kind of smile he'd dreamed of all his life. Mostly, she just scowled at him. Or complained. Or threw things.

Like mother, like wife.

Antoine stabbed the shears angrily into the ground and struggled to his feet.

"Damned moles."

It wasn't that he had anything in particular against the innocent little creatures; it was just that they were messing up his grass and he couldn't have that. The grass was sacred. The whole garden was sacred... yes, that was it... sacred to the memory of his despicable, unloving mother. Not that she deserved it. Not at all.

The sun hung low over Paris; twilight threatened. Antoine went into the house and came back out with two bulbous bottles of rough wine clasped by their necks between the grimy fingers of one hand. What to do about the moles? That was the thing. A man couldn't sell a house with molehills littering the garden. Positioning himself on the bench by the kitchen door, he lay his spade across his lap and set one of the bottles down, so as to swig from the other. He had a powerful thirst on him, did Antoine. He could drink wine like water. The sky turned a delicate shade of pastel pink. The swallows dipped and wheeled. The light faded and with it some of the day's warmth. The house sat at the edge of Paris, where the dark countryside met the intestinal streets. A distant industrious cacophony hung in the air, like the echoes of an ancient civilisation.

Antoine gulped down the contents of the first bottle, belched and started on the second. Soon, his head nodded, his chin rested on his chest and the bottle slipped from his grasp. It rolled beneath the bench, the last dribble of wine dampening the stones. A beetle tried the air with raised antennae, detected the liquid treasure and tested it with fossorial legs. The night air wafted cool around the snoring gardener and it wasn't until women's voices pierced his befuddlement that Antoine came to. He sat in the dark, wondering if his imagination had the better of him.

"There's no room for another. Take it to La Lepère."

Was that Catherine?

"I can't do that. Please take it. I'll pay whatever you want."

Antoine squinted. Two shadowy figures, one short and voluptuous, the other thin and tall, moved towards the end of the garden. Ah, yes, the garden – the moles. That was it, but where had the afternoon gone? What time was it?

"Give it here then," said the shorter shadow.

Antoine wished he could work out what was going on, but the moon was not being kind; behind clouds one minute, out the next, and really, his wife's business was none of his. He was tempted to go back to sleep, and yet, as soon as the mysterious visitor had gone, he cleared his throat and bellowed out into the gloom, "What you got there my dear?"

Catherine flinched and attempted to hide something in her skirts.

Now what was that all about? Hiding something? But what? A mole?

Antoine made his way across the garden, using the spade as a walking stick.

"It's none of your concern, old man." Catherine turned her back on him.

"Ah, but you have something." He followed her as she tried to avoid him.

"Nothing. I've got nothing. You go to bed now." She flapped him away with her free hand.

"You found a mole?"

Curiosity killed the cat, but not Antoine. That sentiment would come to haunt him later, but not now. For now, he grabbed and Catherine pulled away.

"I said, go to bed."

Too late, a bundle of uncertainty slipped from her hands and fell into a neatly kept row of hyssop.

Antoine shouted, "Darned thing'll be off down a hole now, wreaking havoc with my grass. You should have just given it to me."

He raised his spade, ready to deal the death blow to the poor creature. As he did so, the moon came out from behind a cloud and illuminated the contents of the bundle: a tiny dead baby lay swaddled in its winding sheet, its eyes black and empty. Antoine recoiled, horror and anger itching at him in equal measure. His mind whirled and clacked, creaked and spun. His stomach churned and leaped. His bowels threatened to empty, but thankfully held on. He remembered the conversation he'd woken to earlier; the business about 'no room for another' and managed to turn away as a stream of vomit shot out of his mouth. It sprayed the trunk of the apple tree. He hadn't felt this worked up in... well... he'd never felt this worked up.

"No room for another?" he bellowed. "There are more?"

"Of course there are, you fool," snapped Catherine. "What do you think your precious molehills are?"

Chapter Three

Antoine sat up all night at the kitchen table, musing over his terrible discovery. The garden lay beyond the pile of dirty plates; beyond the hazy leaded window; beyond the path hugging the house.

The garden was full of dead babies.

Full.

Well, not the vegetable plot or he'd have turned a corpse over with his spade, but certainly the grass, which he'd tended with loving care, in the garden sacred to the memory of his cold-hearted mother. How in God's name could he sell the house now?

The flutter of an unexpected memory; there and not there: his mother's fingers round his neck, feet dangling, his eyes standing out like stalks until she let him go and he collapsed in a heap. So long ago. The memory ghosted; a wisp of nothingness.

Very well, so perhaps the land had once belonged to the church, and perhaps it contained other bodies, older and deeper than the little molehill babies. Every blade of grass a green memorial. Fitting really. The church was right next door, and certainly it might account for some of the visitors: sad-eyed merchant women, lost looking courtiers, highborn mistresses. Oft-times they filled the garden with their weeping and wringing of hands. Lord, but the city was a veritable hotbed of sickness. Death stalked even the healthiest of people, and it surely explained the money for the novenas. Every couple of weeks Catherine would come up with a purse of coins and tell him to run to the Abbé Davot. Antoine didn't have much to do with the church and even less with the superstitious nonsense of saying prayers for the dead, when no one *he* knew had died. Not recently, at any rate.

He took a swig from his bottle. The wine was vinegary - should be thrown away, or drunk down fast.

Oh yes, it was all starting to make sense. The babies. The burials. The prayers. Catherine had opened a cemetery and not told him. Nothing new there: she was a law unto herself was dear Catherine, but a cemetery? No, no, no. She couldn't, could she? But how? How had he let this happen?

Dawn lent its soft light to confuse the shadows. Antoine squinted through the window at the uneven, dew-covered grass. He upturned his palms; as rough as old wood; knotted and peeling. He rubbed them on his chest and remembered the way silk thread had felt when tested between finger and thumb. Yes, haberdashery was in his blood alright and it had made him a rich man. Well, relatively rich, until the flood that was…

The flood. Damn the flood.

That was then. This was now. Now he had nothing but a heart full of sorrow. He sucked in a long slow breath and let it out with a sonorous sigh. He was a marchand-mercier. Always was, always would be. Don't forget that. Don't forget. Go to the corporation in the morning. Pay your dues… but what with? He had to sell the house first and that was easier said than done.

The bed creaked in the room overhead.

Footsteps sounded on the boards.

If the church had paid Catherine for the use of the garden, then he wanted his fair share. It was *his* garden, after all. It was *his* grass. This business with the moles had irked him and he wasn't used to being irked. Unhappy yes, irked no. Unhappiness was nothing new. It had stalked him all his life. Irked though was something else. Didn't he deserve love? Hadn't he given Catherine everything? Yes, everything, and she had rewarded him with this. He had to stop being a mole of a man. He had to make a stand. He *would* open another shop and he'd use the money owed for the rent of the garden to pay his corporation dues. Antoine's zeal took him up from his seat.

The stairs groaned.

He sat back down.

If he questioned Catherine she'd lie; she'd fill his mind with half-truths and desultory promises. She'd ever been a duplicitous and manipulative woman. He loved her, but he couldn't trust her – not one bit.

The rustle of petticoats.

She was almost on him. Her, or the maid, or his daughter, Marguerite.

God, a house full of women, and not a decent, love-filled smile between them. Well, perhaps his daughter. He pondered. Did a baby, who must be born out of and with love, only learn to hate later? And if it never learned to hate, would it not feel love easily and without fear? What of the babies in the garden? Born in love or hated from the moment of conception? It would take a better man than he, Antoine Montvoisin, to work it all out. A priest might have the answer. Yes, a priest. All right then, he'd ask Abbé Davot. It was as simple as that. Antoine abandoned his post at the table and made off for the church next door.

Catherine pushed the door open and stood in the empty kitchen, queen of all she surveyed.

Chapter Four

Antoine took the short cut over the lichened wall. He snagged his breeches and cursed. There was always something: his mother, the flood, the babies and now his breeches. He felt for the tear and put his finger straight through it into his pasty flesh. Could things get any worse?

The church door stood half open. He slipped inside and waited for a moment while his eyes adjusted. Thin shafts of incense-dusted light filtered through the high mullioned windows. The great pillars of the nave rose to the clerestory: the high vault a chamber of whispering echoes, where stone cherubs played amongst intricate decorations and a secret gallery lay hidden in deep shadow. The tap tap tap of Davot's claw-like footsteps on the flagstones raised the hairs on the back of Antoine's neck. He hopped from foot to foot. He was about to turn tail when came the words, "Monsieur Montvoisin. To what do I owe this pleasure? You wish to make a confession?" Davot stood in the aisle, arms open wide, as if about to embrace his visitor. Antoine took a step back. The priest's left eye twitched. Antoine's also, in ungodly rapport. Better say what he had to, and quickly. The night's tortured rumination had frayed his nerves, and now he'd torn his breeches. The twisting, frustrating annoyance of it all.

"I've come about the graveyard."

"Graveyard? You want a plot? There isn't much room." Davot's bushy black brows knitted. Momentarily, Antoine felt his eyebrows come together. No. No. He warded the priest off.

"Not the one here. No. The one next door, in my garden. They have to be buried somewhere, but they're messing up my grass. Yes, messing it up." There, he'd said it. He felt a little better. It was good to get things off your chest.

The priest scowled.

Antoine hesitated. Should he turn tail, but no, he'd come to find out what was going on and find out he would.

"You've been paying Catherine to use the garden and I want to know how much. It's a private garden. Private."

"Private?"

"Yes, private, and it's full of little babies no more than a few hours old. Perhaps even… unborn." Horrified, he put a hand to his mouth. For certain they were in the ground, so they must have been born, but had someone done away with the contents of each woman's belly before…. before… Not his Catherine, no, not her. She wasn't capable. She couldn't do it. She was a good woman - a good woman with a fierce desire for money, and here, he'd gone and told this…. this… raven.

The priest nodded, as if he knew all. "Even fools are thought wise if they keep silent."

"Silent? What do you mean, silent?"

The morning threw its bright promise through the open door. Carefree birdsong drifted in and ghosted a chirruping echo. A cold draft whistled around Antoine's nether regions.

Davot's top lip curled. No sweet song from the raven. "I have not come to bring peace, but a sword."

A sword? Antoine fidgeted. Menace hung between them. Yes, that was it: menace. Damned priests. Damned church. He should never have come.

"A man's enemies will be the members of his own household." Davot took a step forward. Antoine, a step back.

Escape. Escape now. The door's open. The morning's bright and beautiful. No need to linger in this gloomy church. Go home!

"Whoever would love life and see good days must keep their tongue from evil and their lips from deceitful speech."

The priest's piercing eyes skewered the remains of Antoine's nerves. The ex-haberdasher ran. Outside, the sunlight dazzled him. He pressed himself in close to the church's golden stone wall and waited for his heart to stop pounding, thump on insistent thump. The babies in the garden would take some thinking about.

Chapter Five

The morning after Antoine's garden discovery, four days after the attempt on his life, and some six after his great 'idea', Catherine prepared her mother's breakfast, crossed the street and took the short cut through the alleyway between crumbling walls splattered with shivering sunlight. Uppermost on her mind was how to get rid of her annoyingly alive husband; a man who now wanted to turn them out of house and home and go back to the life of a haberdasher. Very well, let him see where it would get him. Dead, that's where. Dead. Should have done it a long time ago. Should have done it right after that damned flood. And you know what? It was all her mother's fault. Oh, yes she had a lot to answer for.

As a young man Antoine would walk through the riverside lanes on his way to the thread merchant. His route would take him past Madame Deshayes's door. On the day he'd worn a finely tailored red jerkin and jaunty hat, she'd followed him with great interest. He seemed like a fine upstanding young man; the kind of man her daughter would do well to court. When she discovered he lived in a shop on the Pont Marie with his ageing sot of a father, Madame Deshayes couldn't wait to tell Catherine.

"The old man trades jewellery as well as fabrics. He's got money hidden somewhere. I know he has. Reel the son in. Dispatch that drunk of a father and take what's yours.

When you've taken all you can from your sniveling husband, kill him off. Yes, yes. Kill him off."

All these years later "kill him off" still rang in Catherine's ears. She should have done it right after the flood; before Antoine had moved into the house on the Rue Beauregard with her. That would have been the right time. She stepped over a puddle of early morning urine, lifting her petticoats with one hand, and balancing the platter on the other.

Oh yes, Antoine had served his purpose. She had no need for a husband with ideas that might well bring them to destitution. She could put the poison in his wine. That might work, only she couldn't be sure he'd be the one to drink it. Marguerite's young man, Romani, was always lurking around, and he was as partial to wine as any. Perhaps in the supper then? No, that would be difficult without poisoning everyone else too. Lure him with sweetmeats? Perhaps, but it seemed like a waste of good food. There was always the salt beef; as foul a meat as any and almost all gone. She could easily palm the remains off onto Antoine. Poison that and no one would notice. Still, it didn't feel right. Choices, choices. Perhaps it didn't matter what she put it in. Dead was dead. Of course, if she hadn't married him in the first place then she wouldn't be having this problem. Oh yes, it was all her mother's fault. Telling her how, if she didn't find herself a husband, she'd end up walking the streets like a common whore; a pathetic creature with nothing to look forward to but bird bone charms.

At the end of the alley a horse laboured by with its cart load of vegetables, its owner walking in its wake. As Catherine started forward she met a cloud of hovering flies and a pile of dung. If there was one thing she hated, it was flies. A thought came to her. *Ruptoire* would do it: quicklime and pearl ash, vine shoots, beanstalks, all macerated and boiled up. Attracted flies like nothing on earth, it did, and it would pierce the intestines of anyone who ate it. One dose would do it. Just one dose. No one would guess he'd been murdered - and that was the trick of it; to make it look like an accident. Catherine flicked the flies away and sighted the door to her mother's lodging house.

"Marry a rich man. Someone with prospects. A merchant with plenty of customers." Catherine parroted out words she'd heard a thousand times. "From them will come your trade. The wives you see, the wives. They will want lovers. They will want rid of their husbands. They will want rid of their babies. They will want and want and want and you will give it to them… for a price."

Catherine rapped on the door. Nothing. The old lady was still abed and the rest of the lodgers too, by all accounts.

"Maman?" Still nothing. Catherine let herself in. The place smelled of stale urine and burned onions. Three old souls lived here, not a one related to any other. In the house next door lived the pot-bellied curmudgeon of a landlord. Catherine climbed the stairs, the toes of her shoes catching in her petticoats and threatening to bring her down. At the top she paused to listen to the house groaning, age-full and festering. She lifted the latch on the door to her mother's chamber and entered.

Light sliced through the shutters here and there revealing a crumpled coverlet and an array of petticoats strewn across the floor. The air was thick with the sour aroma of sweat, dirt and excrement. Last night's fire lay cold in the hearth; a scattering of ash like burned bones. Catherine placed the plate down on a table by the window and threw open the shutters. The sudden light made her squint. Over in a chair by the fireplace a bundle of rags moaned.

Catherine shook her head. "Maman, I've told you time and again, I can't be clearing up after you. Did you even go to bed?" She gathered the coverlet from the bed like she had once with so much fabric in Antoine's shop. She'd been young then. So young, and her head full of romantic nonsense. She'd listened to her mother, but the practicalities of marriage had not struck home until it was too late.

Madame Deshayes rubbed her button nose and her wrinkled face uncurled to display a toothless maw. "Yes, course I did. What you got there?" She nodded at the plate. "Fetch it here." Her fingers were crooked and gnarled, her nails like cats' claws.

Catherine flung the coverlet down, picked up the plate of food, and thrust it angrily at her mother.

"It's not hot. If you want it hot, you have to come to the house." Even then, it wouldn't be that warm. No one ever sat down to eat as soon as the food was ready in the Montvoisin household, and certainly not together.

"Haven't got time." The old lady tucked in greedily, gumming each morsel until drool ran down her chin. "Got someone coming. Wants me to weave her a spell, she does."

"Of course you do. You'll choke, eating like that."

Right on cue, Madame Deshayes gagged and motioned wildly, casting about for something to drink, the coughs coming in volleys, her eyes tearing with the effort. Catherine snatched up a jug of day-old ale from the dresser and held it to her mother's lips until the coughing turned to splutters and then to throat clearing and grunts.

"You killed him yet?" The old lady pinched away her tears.

"Not yet."

"Why not?"

"He's making it difficult." Wasn't he just? Catherine sat down on the bed.

"Huh. Losing your touch. I'd have done for him by now if it was me."

"I'm sure you would."

"He could learn a thing or two from your father, could that man of yours."

"He's dead, Maman."

"You just said you were having trouble with him."

"Not Antoine. Papa. Oh, for goodness sake." The old witch was impossible.

"Send him to me."

"He won't come."

Mother looked at daughter with innocent eyes, as if new born. "My daughter will be here soon."

"I'm your daughter."

"Have you killed him yet?"

"Not yet."

"Got someone coming. Wants me to weave her a spell, she does."

Catherine groaned. Round and round the mulberry bush the story went. The old lady was worse today than she'd been for a long while.

"I'm here Maman. I'm here. What spell do you have for me today?"

Chapter Six

Antoine knew of nowhere better to hide and think than the Court of Miracles. This ramble of old houses, dingy courtyards and dubious twisting thoroughfares occupied but a tight couple of acres two streets to the south of the Rue Beauregard. It was said the area got its name from those who by day, on the more salubrious streets of the city, feigned a variety of diseases in order to fleece the better heeled Parisians of their hard earned cash. By night, when the fakers returned to their slums, they shook off all pretense of illness and were thus, miraculously 'healed'. Antoine didn't care how it had come by its name, only that it felt as remote as the bridge once had.

He entered the Court of Miracles beneath the sign of the fan-maker, followed the barrel-vaulted alley with the overflowing, gastral conduit, and soon came upon his regular haunt: the cellar of Monsieur Fagioli, an Italian crook of a wine merchant with a penchant for fat women and stinking sausages. A foetid miasma hung in the air like the sulphurous fumes of hell. The wine cellar issued up an easy hum. Installing himself between barrels and benches, and with recourse to jug after jug of Fagioli's wine, Antoine soon fell into a stupor. With the fog of drunkenness lying heavy on his brow, he dreamt of dancing girls and acres of silk that wound round and over and under their naked bodies. Several hours later, Fagioli rested his hand on the dreamer's shoulder and it was enough to wake Antoine from his boozy slumber. He rubbed his eyes. The slit window, high on the wall above, let in little of the late afternoon's grey gloom.

"What time is it?"

"What time? Time to go home. You got a nice fat wife waiting for you."

Antoine belched. Fagioli's lip curled. He removed his hand and wiped it on his apron.

Misery rose in Antoine's caw. "I can't sell the house now. Not when my garden's a cemetery."

"A what?"

"Who will buy it? Who?" Antoine winced. The world was now a blur of dancing bottles and a whore with more than her fair share of breasts. He half wished she'd swing his way so he could take a closer look, but then... he waved his hand... maybe not. A pain rose beneath his breast bone. Argh, but it hurt. He rubbed his chest.

Fagioli shrugged. "It's up to you." He wiped the table with a wet rag, smearing it with sticky wine.

Antoine closed his eyes. It was warm here. Warm and... He drifted and dreamed and drifted some more. The pain nudged at him. She never smiles. She taunts. She nags. She demands. Please smile. A glimmer. Then everything would be alright. Then he'd know she loved him.

The very first time he'd met Catherine she'd offered to read his palm. She'd wandered into the shop, a sly grin on her face; a smile of sorts, but not the right kind. Smitten, Antoine had charmed her with a promise of great fortune, a big house and beautiful garden. He told her: "When my father dies, I'll be a rich man." By then his mother had passed away and he and his father had been rubbing along in an uneasy and increasingly drunken alliance.

"It's not yours then?" said the then young Catherine.

"Not yet, but it will be. I'm a master marchand-mercier. I can marry whoever I want." The corporation had strict rules forbidding apprentices from marrying, but since he'd been made master he was free to do as he pleased. Catherine had run her fingers through his fine dark curls and kissed him full on the lips. She wasn't as plump then; voluptuous, but not plump. Antoine had seen possibilities.

"I have the gift, you know," she'd said.

"The gift?" Antoine grunted in his sleep, seeing bows atop parcels and cascading flowers.

Fagioli nudged the barmaid. "One too many."

The barmaid circled the cellar with her jug of wine. She stopped in front of Antoine, but he paid her no mind. Far away, he nuzzled the place behind Catherine's right ear. Her skin was so soft, and her scent so delicious; like dusty linen; like his mother – a mother who'd hated him, though he'd tried to win her love – oh, but he'd tried so hard, and now it was too late.

Too late.

"I read the stars. I consult with the spirits," said the illusory Catherine.

"And what do they say?" Antoine mumbled.

A whiskery old grandfather, sitting at the next table in Fagioli's den, stroked his beard and gave the dreamer a grave look. Imprisoned by his alcohol-fueled memories, Antoine sank deeper, ever deeper. In his mind's eye, he caught Catherine up and whirled her round. Gold thread spun out from a spool to form a ship's rigging, as a mast thrust through the ceiling and linen-white sails unfurled. A bolt of iridescent blue silk sailed overhead, like the skies of high summer. The lovers steadied themselves against the bulwark as gold-filled coffers overflowed at their feet. They were set on sea-bound course up the wide River Seine.

"Your father won't live long. He's old. He drinks." Catherine's eyes glinted gold.

"Everyone drinks, but yes, he drinks too much. I've told him it'll be the death of him, but does he listen?"

Fagioli's cellar dwellers watched in amazement as Antoine suddenly stood up and shouted out 'does he listen' before collapsing back into his seat.

In the land of nod, silk ribbons, snaking long, wound round Catherine's arms, mooring the gold-digger to the masthead.

"There's more where that came from," said Antoine. A fat tear ran down his face and then another. He thumped Fagioli's table. A man shouldn't have to suffer so. It wasn't fair. It wasn't right. A man should have his wife's love. Come to think on it, his mother's too. He opened his eyes. Ship becalmed, the whiskery grandfather swam into view.

"What d'you want?" The pain in Antoine's chest rose to greet his throat. He swallowed it down. So much water: river, flood, and tears.

"Nothing at all," replied the grandfather. "Absolutely nothing."

"I bought her the house. She wanted to tell fortunes. Said she couldn't do it on the bridge. She didn't need the garden as well. That was special. That was mine."

The grandfather nodded, sagely.

"I looked for it, I did. But I never found it."

"What was that?"

"Not a glimmer, not a spark, not any kind of love. No smile, you see. No smile. Cold eyes, she has. Cold." Antoine raised a finger and pointed it vigorously at his right eye. "I love her though. I do. I love her more now than ever."

"And why's that then?"

"I don't know. I suppose…"

"She filled an empty space in your heart?"

An empty space left by his mother's death. Why did love make itself known so sharply through grief? Antoine let out a small cry and clutched his chest, right where it hurt him the most.

The barmaid slammed a fresh jug of rough wine down with the words, "Always a mistake to marry for love."

Trembling, Antoine ignored her and poured himself a mug of courage. The grandfather had hit the nail on the head: he'd had an empty space in his heart and Catherine had filled it. He supped his wine. It tasted foul. The priest had said to keep his mouth shut, but he couldn't. The garden babies had been born before their time. Wasn't there a statute or something about the unbaptised? Hadn't the law-makers decreed that every pregnancy must be declared? Wait. Born before their time? Mon Dieu! Antoine stood up, sending the mug spinning. It wasn't right. Babies were sacred, precious little bundles of joy. God, but he wished he'd been able to save his own son. So long ago and yet still the pain knifed through him; endless years of tortured hurt. Tiny little thing he'd been; hands like perfect pink scallop shells; robin's egg blue eyes. They'd called him Balthazar. Died in his sleep Catherine said, but had he? Had he?

What an idiot he'd been. He ran to the door, knocking a stool over, tripping on the grandfather's outstretched foot. What a stupid… drunken… He stepped outside. A cantering horse almost mowed him down, but due to some as yet unrealised ability on Antoine's part to survive any and all predicaments unscathed, it did naught but cause him to fall back into Fagioli's arms. Twenty or so armed foot soldiers thundered past.

"What the…"

"De La Reynie." Fagioli pushed Antoine behind him and shut the door fast.

"Who?"

"The new Lieutenant General. They say he has the ear of the King. The Minister Colbert appointed him to police the city. Clean. Clear. Secure. That's the motto of the gendarmerie."

"The what?"

"The gendarmerie. Come to clear out the old Court of Miracles and make it safe, or so they say. Make all of Paris safe. Well we don't want them in here."

"We don't?"

"We don't. Have another drink." Fagioli, set the mug upright and poured murky wine into it. Antoine stared into the unfathomable depths. He didn't understand why Fagioli was so afraid. So the gendarmerie wanted to clean up the old Court of Miracles. They wouldn't close a wine cellar. Even one as grim as this with its greasy tables, floor awash with sticky beer and assortment of reprobates. A knock shuddered the door in its frame.

"Open up." The voice was low pitched, but loud.

Fagioli dropped the jug. "That's torn it. The game's up. Ssh, don't say a word. Not a word." He put a finger to his spittle-flecked lips. Fagioli must have done something very wrong to be this afraid, thought Antoine.

The grandfather cocked an eye at the haberdasher. "You in trouble with the law?"

"Not me. No." At least, he hoped not. Perhaps the babies in the garden, but that had nothing to do with him. No, this was all down to Fagioli. He'd infringed some ancient law or other; served tainted beer or poisonous sausages. They certainly smelled bad enough. It couldn't just be about cleaning the Court of Miracles up. Where was he, anyway? Antoine searched the gloom. There he was, opening up a trapdoor in the corner. Antoine crept close, wondering what lay beneath. A fusty smell rose from the depths. Antoine took a step back, and then another.

Fagioli hissed, "Come on now gents, into the hole. Careful now."

Assorted crooks tripped and cursed and disappeared into the nothingness below.

"You too," said Fagioli. "Hurry up. Get down there." But Antoine wasn't going to do anything of the sort. He wasn't going to hide in a stinking cess pit. Dead babies or not, he had nothing to fear from the gendarmerie. Let them do their worst. He was a master marchand-mercier. The corporation had his details. They knew who he was. He had nothing to fear. Nothing.

Someone banged on the door fit to tear it off its hinges. "Come on. We know you're in there."

Fagioli slammed the trapdoor shut and hurried to the door, shouting, "I'm coming. I'm coming." He threw back the bolts and a contingent of gendarmes burst in, and pinned those remaining above ground to the far wall. Antoine felt the point of a short sword on his cheek and smelled the man's rotten breath. He cast about for an escape route and noticed that the whiskery grandfather hadn't moved. The old man's rheumy eyes twinkled with amusement as the gendarmes upended a bench and destroyed a table. Down came a barrel. The staves split and wine swirled across the floor.

Fagioli took up position over the trapdoor and cried, "Please, take what you want... have a drink... a sausage... I'm a good man. I beg you. Please. Stop. I beg you."

A stool flew at Antoine. He ducked and it splintered against the wall. A voice cut through the cacophony.

"Enough!"

Lieutenant General Gabriel Nicolas De La Reynie strode through the mess. He cut an impressive figure: tall, and well-muscled, with an angular face. He could have been a gentleman upon a game of hunt your sweetheart, or a cruel dictator with a ready passion for torture.

"Who's the owner of this hovel?"

Antoine tried to melt into the wall at his back. His hand passed over a splinter; a piece of chair embedded in the wall and now in his palm. Dead babies, hole in his breeches and now a splinter in his hand. What more? The barmaid buried her head in his chest. Her touch roused a long-dormant desire. Antoine resisted the urge to stroke her dark curls. He should have hidden in the cess-pit below.

"I... I am. Me. At your service, kind sir." Fagioli bowed nervously.

"We sent fair warning and yet the flies told me you're still here. What have you got to say for yourself?"

"Me? Ah, nothing sir. That is... I'm sorry. I didn't think... I... I thought I had more time."

"You've one day to get out."

"You promised..." Fagioli fell easily into the role of supplicant. "Sir, you promised you wouldn't close me down. Not yet... not now. You can't."

A gendarme struck Fagioli on the chin. The wine merchant crumpled atop the trapdoor. Antoine's chest tightened. He put his hands up; an act of submission that took him back to his childhood and the distorted terror of his mother's fury. The law was a dangerous beast at the best of times, maternal or otherwise. He didn't want to die. Not like this. Not in a cellar in the Court of Miracles. Who would run and tell Catherine? The barmaid? That old grandfather, who still sat on his bench as if all was right with the world? No, no, he didn't want to die like this. De La Reynie cocked his head and stepped towards him.

"And who are you?"

"Me? No one sir. No one."

"But you have a name?"

"Oh, that. Montvoisin. Antoine Montvoisin. Yes, that's me. A marchand-mercier. A master... master marchand-mercier." It was an important distinction.

"A haberdasher. Do I know you?"

"No. I don't think so. Er... that is, perhaps you've been to my shop?"

"I wouldn't..." De La Reynie gave Antoine a curious look. "Your name has a familiar ring." He frowned. "No matter." He nodded to his men and one-by-one they abandoned Fagioli's den, all save for one man, who lingered for a moment until the barmaid found the courage to wink at him, at which point he too, left.

"Who was he?" Antoine crossed the cellar on shaky legs. The barmaid crept behind him.

"De La Reynie and his dog Desgrez," replied Fagioli, rising unsteadily. He bent to raise the trapdoor.

Antoine peered out into the alley. Naught but a flapping canopy and the caw of a bird greeted him. The wind whistled through the slats on the shutters of the house opposite. He shuddered; someone had walked on his grave. Behind him the drunks surged up from the hellhole.

The barmaid hissed in Antoine's ear, "Take me with you. Don't leave me here."

"Ha," said the grandfather. "I wouldn't hitch your cart to that horse."

The barmaid cocked her head, hands on hips. "And why not?"

"You know who he's married to, don't you?" said the grandfather.

The barmaid scowled at Antoine. "You're married? You never said."

Antoine sensed a storm coming. "Why would I?" He loved his wife. The idea of taking another woman… well that was just double the trouble.

"Oh, he's married alright," came the grandfather. "And to the most feared woman in all of Paris."

Antoine's eyes locked with those of his accuser, the walls of the old wine closing in, reducing the space between them in an instant. Feared? What did the old man mean, feared?

"Oh yes," said the grandfather. "The whole of Paris knows who *his* wife is."

The whole of Paris? Really? What on earth… The barmaid took a step back. Fagioli raised his head to stare at him. Antoine's chest tightened and tightened. Why, in times of strife, was it always so hard to breathe? The whiskery grandfather smiled, his twinkle still bright.

"You're married to the Angel-Maker, La Voisin. Isn't that right Monsieur?"

The Angel-Maker? La Voisin? Did they mean Catherine?

Chapter Seven

In a narrow thoroughfare close to the river, where the all-pervading acrid stench of the tanneries poisoned the air and seeped into the very fabric of the houses, lived a strange man by the name of Lesage. The environs suited him very well because he fancied himself as something of an alchemist, and where better to obtain the stuff of experiment than a tannery, with its ease of access to all manner of diabolical ingredients?

The nature of business on this forgettable street was so repulsive that few chose to walk its length. Thus, the scuffed blue door, with the sign of a pentacle scratched on its surface went, more or less, unnoticed. Behind this door lay Lesage's laboratory, where he laboured with ambit, cucurbit and retort to manufacture magical substances he claimed would set the world to rights. For the most part he produced naught but venomous clouds and deadly powders. Up one flight of steep stairs lay his sleeping chamber and up a second to the eaves, was a black-walled room, where no sunlight ever reached. Set against the far wall of this attic space, Lesage had gathered the accoutrement of religious practice. On an oaken altar lay a cloth of thick dark velvet. Atop this rested those items usually found in a church: a chalice, a paten, a ciborium, a monstrance, luna and theca, an ablution cup, a pyx, a holy water container and an incense boat, a bobache and a missal stand. At the rear of the altar stood the tabernacle and either side, the purest beeswax candles. Finally came a Crucifix, which, for the most part, remained hidden beneath a silk cloth.

Lesage pretended to the life of a religious man, although he had never been ordained and relied entirely on those of the clergy he could persuade with ready cash to do his evil bidding. The clerics of the Sun King's Paris were easily swayed from the path of righteousness, for the whole of Parisian society was obsessed with prayers and spells, potions and powders with which to torment their lovers and transform rivals.

On this evening, Lesage expected five guests, one of whom was the Angel-Maker, Catherine Montvoisin. The two masked women accompanying her were ladies of the court. The shorter of the two, Madame de Montespan, was a lady-in-waiting to Queen Marie Therese, and the other, Madame's dear friend and confidante, Madame Des Œillets. The remaining two visitors arrived only minutes later. These were the officiating priests engaged for the ceremony. While Lesage lit the candles, the priests disappeared into an adjoining room to prepare for the ceremony.

Hazel staff in hand, Lesage beckoned Catherine forward and whispered in her ear, "Do you have it?"

She pulled out a heavy purse. Lesage grabbed it from her.

"She must state her desire before the Lords of the firmament. She knows that, doesn't she?" He'd never met Madame de Montespan, but her beauty and wit had preceded her. She lived with her two small children and her husband, the Marquis de Montespan, in a house close to the Louvre. It was said she had several lovers and despised both the Queen and the King's present mistress, La Vallière. Lesage had no doubt she wished to be rid of her rivals in love, or she wouldn't have asked for a black mass.

"She's ready," said Catherine.

"And what of your husband?" He pursed his lips, as if to kiss her, but thought better of it. Instead, he dug his nails into his palms and wished for a knotted rope with which to flay himself.

"He has the constitution of an ox."

"Ridiculous. You poison husbands every day. Put it in his wine. It's the venom of serpents, the deadly poison of cobras. It can't fail."

Catherine gave him such a curious look, he would have taken her to task about it, but his attention was drawn away by the priests entering. They stationed themselves either side of the altar. Even in the low light, one of them would have been instantly recognisable to Antoine, had he been there, for this man was none other than the raven from Notre Dame de Bonne Nouvelle, the Abbé Davot. The other priest was from Saint-Severin: the Abbé Mariette.

Lesage waved Catherine away. This was a ceremony of high superstition and much trickery. All had been planned, meticulously. Nothing could go wrong. Lesage muttered a few prayers and tapped his hazel staff on the floor.

"We are here to pledge ourselves to a Higher Power. In return for our obedience, He will grant our desires. Bare yourself before Him."

Madame de Montespan unlaced her bodice and stepped out of her petticoats beneath which she wore a gossamer-fine chemise. Lesage let out a momentary gasp, but covered it well. She was fair of face, with lively eyes and clear skin. Caught in the candle's glow, Madame seemed wondrously young. Madame des Œillets helped her friend undress until she stood shivering in a gossamer-fine chemise. Lesage lit a single black candle, and indicated for the near naked woman to drape herself across the altar. Some of the accoutrements of his charade got in her way. Davot moved them aside.

It was taking too long. Too long by far. Lesage could hear Catherine and the other woman whispering. He glared at them. Yes, there they were, huddled together at the back. He strained to hear their discussion, while all the time making signs of the demons over the prostrate woman. He heard, "She would rather her enemies die than live to perpetrate further indignities". Lesage's attention wavered. Libidinous intrigue or…

"What is it you desire?" He muttered. To Madame de Montespan.

"The King's love," she replied.

Lesage stroked her arm with a fingertip. A proverb came to mind: the lips of an immoral woman are as sweet as honey, and her mouth is smoother than oil, but in the end she is as bitter as poison, as dangerous as a double-edged sword.

"The King's love? Do you not wish for something more? His death perhaps?" He had to admit, the King's death would be quite something.

"His love is all I desire," Madame De Montespan said.

Lesage twitched in annoyance. Damn it, but the time was right for a royal murder.

Chapter Eight

Antoine avoided going home for as long as he could. He wandered the filthy streets and worried about the parlous state of his marriage, and about how he still missed his mother, despite her moods, her anger, the beatings, and her eyes. Yes her eyes. Like Catherine's. Just like Catherine's. No light in them. No smile. No soft gaze. No love.

The bustle of the daytime city gave way to that of the evening. Out came the nightwalkers, cavorting prostitutes, dashing young men, inebriated cutpurses, and ancient crones. Antoine ambled along feeling right at home. He was a drunken good-for-nothing. Catherine had told him so often enough, and his mother before her, though perhaps of his father and not him. No matter, it was as if the women were one and the same and he, his father. Light flooded the footpath in front of him, and a peal of laughter rang out. A door slammed the brightness out. Murder and mayhem, right under his nose and he'd not noticed. Or perhaps he had, but made a choice not to register it. He'd been so unhappy since the flood, it had been hard to notice anything much. Now though, he had set course on a voyage of rediscovery. He was a marchand-mercier and... he stopped in his tracks. How could he sell the house and raise the money he needed if he had a cemetery in his garden? How?

He started up again, side-stepping a pile of dung. Ah, but the flood had changed everything. If only he still had the old shop with its neat frontage, and small windows, solid oak door all business-like. The shop had been everything; pain and joy. Mostly pain, and now he couldn't even bring himself to think about walking over a bridge, let alone living on one again.

He lingered beneath an archway leading to a bakery yard, where the smell of fermenting yeast took him back to his childhood. His mother once sent him for a hot loaf, telling him to 'come straight home.' It had smelled so good he'd eaten most of it on the way back. She'd hit him so hard the half-masticated lump had flown right out of his mouth and stuck on the wall. He stroked his cheek, feeling the sting of her hand all these years later. Love of a kind, but not real love. Not the kind that touched you deep in your soul. He hit the wall with the palm of his hand. What did he know of love, he who had grown in sorrow, recognising only hatred as the nurturing emotion? Rumour had it on the day of his birth he'd been put in a basket and shoved to the back of a shelf. An old lady told him so, years later. She'd said: "When your mother's time came, she closed up and prepared a cot in the corner." Here, the old lady had pointed to nowhere in particular and Antoine had turned to look. A fat duck had chosen that moment to cross his path. He remembered it because it gave him such a knowing look he could have sworn it was no duck at all, but an angel of the Lord.

"Yes, she cursed and screamed, pushed and panted, while we all cupped our hands to the window and tried to see what was going on. We banged on the door and shouted *are you alright? Do you need help?* I saw her face. As red as the King's heels, it was."

Antoine couldn't rid himself of the image of a duck as an angel.

"When you slipped out, she snipped the cord with her dressmaker's scissors and dropped you into a basket of the softest Fontainebleau wool, as if you were no more than an unwanted skein."

"And then what?"

"And then she opened up, that's what. It was before the bridge. When your father had that tiny place on the Île Saint-Louis, but don't you worry yourself about it, dearie."

It was at this point that the old lady had given him such a glorious smile Antoine supposed it was what real love looked like. Oh yes, the old lady had shown him her heart, right enough.

Antoine kicked the wall. A moonlit mouse, its whiskers twitching, peeked out from between a stack of empty flour sacks. It blinked out of sight as a cloud filled the night sky. God knew it, but he'd tried his hardest to charm a love-filled smile from his mother. For fourteen years, birth to young man, he'd tried, enduring her spite and bitter hatred, and then she'd died and grief had tormented him. For a while, Antoine had roved the bridge back and forth, back and forth, desolation his only companion. Their neighbours, people he had grown up with, shook their heads and muttered sorrowfully.

"Such a shame."

"What that boy needs is a good hot meal."

"A mother's love is hard to replace."

One day he found dry land and ventured into the city alone. He'd only ever been before with one or other parent. He hugged the pain of his mother's death so close it gave him heartburn, the fire of which could only be quenched by alcohol. He stole a jug of wine off a street vendor and drank it down in one. He scowled at the world and it scowled back at him. No one understood. They thought he was just another drunken lout. He wasn't. He just didn't know how to deal with the hand life had dealt him.

Adrift, Antoine's wanderings took him to the Jardin des Tuileries, over which the Royal Palace stood watch. Here, he gazed at the parterre and neatly kept grass, nursed his hangover and drunk in the aroma of the lavender.

"Why did you have to die Maman? Why?" Tears came in floods. He'd have himself a garden one day: a beautiful flower-filled garden. He'd dedicate it to his mother and nothing and no one would sully it, and yet there it was: a graveyard. Molehills be damned. She'd buried babies beneath his green sward. Babies!

"Catherine, Catherine, Catherine," he muttered, sliding down the wall and sitting in a crumpled heap. He trailed a finger between the cobbles, dredging up thick black dirt he couldn't see properly for his tears and the evasive moon. He stared into the blur and then flicked it in the general direction of the mouse, who'd long since sniffed out richer pickings elsewhere.

Damned mother.

Damned wife.

Damned shop.

Damned bridge.

Damned flood.

He spat into the yeasty air, let out a dry sob, found his feet, weighted himself against the wall for a moment, and then took off in the direction of the Rue Beauregard and home. The tower on the Church of Notre Dame de Bonne Nouvelle appeared over the tops of the houses. He stumbled across a road, the stars glimmering like new cut diamonds in the black sky, the air redolent with the acrid aroma of chimney smoke and dung. He rounded the corner and spotted the house: a rambling old place with lime-washed walls and an air of respectability that belied its location. The long street angled south-west to north east. The church loomed large at one end and at the other the city petered out, hit the ramparts and passed into countryside.

A good house with a good garden. He should be pleased to own such a house... and he did own it and that being the case, he *could* sell it, cemetery or no cemetery. He crossed the street and slipped inside the gate, noting the creaking hinge. He made a mental note to oil it, and skirted the lumpy grass to listen outside the kitchen door.

Nothing.

Perhaps Catherine was abed. If so, then he wouldn't wake her. He'd leave it until the morning to tell her he'd made up his mind to sell the house. She'd just have to get used to it. He glanced up at the twinkling firmament. He missed his old life and that was the truth of it. He missed it with a passion. Of course, he might not be able to find a buyer and what then? He wasn't sure. Perhaps best not to think of failure. He let himself in and started up the stairs.

Giggles.

Joviality? At this hour? He waved it away and took another step. More giggles. He almost fell back down the stairs. Who was it? Catherine? Had she dared to bring a lover into the house and were they, even now, in the process of… It was an old fear, fuelled by insecurity. The offending fun originated in the fancy receiving chamber. He threw open the door. The sound of furtive fumbling and a shushing greeted his entry.

"Catherine?"

Someone leapt to their feet. The darkness hid their identity.

"Papa. I thought you were…"

"Marguerite? What are you doing?"

In the past, Antoine would have turned tail and left his daughter to it, but not now, oh no. Now he stood his ground. The women of this house had a lesson to learn.

"Tell him to come out."

"Papa," pleaded Marguerite.

"Young man, make yourself known." Antoine spoke into a void of withheld breath. The man was there, just a few feet from him. Marguerite's beau cleared his throat.

"Right now," repeated Antoine. There came a shifting of feet and a disturbance in the air.

"Monsieur, I can explain. I was going to come and speak to you. Only…" A swarthy young man loomed out of the gloom. A stranger? Marguerite had taken up with a stranger? It couldn't be; there was something familiar about him. Antoine couldn't put his finger on it. The way he stood? The incline of his head?

"Papa. It's Romani. We're going to be married."

Romani, of course. He was always hanging around. He'd been in the Guard or something, not that this was any kind of recommendation.

"Married? Does your mother know?"

"Not exactly."

"What does that mean?"

"She knows we're courting. She doesn't know we're to wed."

"Hmm. Well Romani, you better get going before my wife wakes up. She's an Angel-Maker, you know. Yes. The whole city knows." Antoine amazed himself with his sarcasm.

Marguerite gasped.

"I'll go. I'll go," said Romani. "But I'll be back." He gave Antoine a look that said 'if I catch you in a dark alley, you'll be sorry' and slipped from the room.

Now what to make of that?

Marguerite stood hands on hips. "We weren't doing anything wrong. Why did you say that about Maman?"

"Because it's true."

"Are you drunk again?"

"Again?"

"Papa, you're always drunk."

Antoine sensed her frustration. This too amazed him. Usually, he didn't sense anything much. Had he believed more strongly in God, he would have looked to the heavens at this point.

"Come sit with me," he said.

"Why?"

"Because we don't talk anymore and I miss my darling baby."

"I'm nineteen years old. I'm not a baby anymore."

Nineteen? How long had she been a woman?

"You'll always be my baby. My smiling baby." Yes, Marguerite's eyes were filled with love and always had been, but the thought that she had now turned those eyes on Romani? It was as hard to reconcile as…

...as the babies in the garden. Perhaps not that hard, but what was a man to do? He'd always thought she favoured him; thought he could teach her the mysteries of cloth; thought she would one day work in his shop.

His shop – some hope.

What was it his father used to say? "Odysseus made Penelope weave her father-in-law's shroud by day and unpick it by night. That way her suitors were kept at bay." Antoine didn't know who Odysseus was, or Penelope, for that matter. They weren't customers. They weren't family. Oh but, his father was fond of tall tales, particularly those that braided life's mysteries with philosophical insight. This had been one of those occasions.

"Yes, well. I will away to bed," said Marguerite.

"How long have you known?" Antoine's mind had flitted back to Catherine. He should have kept her busy; not let her gad about telling fortunes. Fortunes... pah!

"About what?"

"Your mother's sorcery."

"Papa!"

"Well? How long?"

"Forever."

"Forever?"

Marguerite hugged her shawl close.

"Can I go now?"

"Yes, go. Go." Antoine waved her away.

With the door shut, the house fell as quiet as the grave. Broken-hearted, Antoine sat and picked at his troubles. It wasn't enough that Catherine had taken a lover - and who was *he*, by the way - no, and it wasn't enough that she'd turned the garden into a cemetery. No, she had to be the most feared Angel-Maker in all Paris.

THE
MOST
FEARED

Antoine sniffed. A tear rolled down his cheek. He'd sleep-walked through the last few years of his marriage. What he'd give to see Catherine smile. A flood of tears came and he did nothing to stop it.

***

"*Ruptoire.*" Lesage dropped the glass phial into Catherine's outstretched palm. "A few drops; that's all it will take."

It was late and Catherine had delayed returning home so she could obtain the poison she thought would put an end to Antoine's life. She placed the phial in her silk draw-stringed purse and threw her cloak over her shoulders. The others had gone. Even the Abbé Davot.

"You're not having second thoughts are you?"

"No. I'll do it tonight."

"It will be a painful death, but…" Here Lesage gave a shrug. "You said it yourself, he's served your purpose. He's provided you with a fine home and a pretty little daughter, but now? Now, you serve the royal house. You can't be encumbered by fools."

Catherine sighed. "It's not the same as giving it to people you don't know."

"Do you want me to do it?"

"No. It's just… I shouldn't have to kill him for my freedom. It's not as if he beats me. It's not as if he does anything much." Once upon a time she'd pretended to love him. It wasn't like Antoine was a wholly bad man. He was just…

"Leave him then."

"And where will I live? Here?" She'd grown accustomed to a certain level of comfort. Lesage lived like a monk, although his libido told another story. For a while Antoine had been a good provider. He could be again… but no, it was too late for that. He'd beggar them both before he got the shop back. It was a pipe dream. Nothing more. Nothing less.

"It's your choice."

Lesage offered a cheek. Catherine pecked at it and then the other. "A bientôt," he said. "Remember, you don't need much. Two or three drops will do it."

Chapter Nine

Not far from the Rue Beauregard, in a narrow house squeezed between medieval tenements, lived a certain Madame Marie Bosse. The door to her lair was similar in size and colour to all the others in the street, but the step had been eroded by the footfall of many visitors and the cuplike place beneath the knocker had been worn to a sheen. Once inside, the first dark-patinated chamber opened out onto an internal courtyard garden, cloistered on three sides and filled with sweet-scented roses and herbs of every variety. This unexpected floral boon delighted visitors and eased their anxieties. No one could be that fearsome a woman when they possessed such marvellous scents and such brilliant blossoms. La Bosse though, was by nature a jealous creature given to intrigue and gossip, the like of which often caused her much anger. Today was no exception. It was common knowledge that Madame De Montespan had designs on the King. She travelled in his entourage; she faked delight at everything and fawned attention on the Queen, all the while eyeing His Majesty, coyly, an impish grin on her all-too-pretty face. La Bosse sneered. De Montespan should have come to her. It was *she* who held the answer to a woman's prayers; *she* who knew how to harness the secrets of the herb garden and spellbook; she who conjured the best poisonous concoctions, all the better to serve the needs of the lovelorn: Sorcerer's Violet, Butterbur, and Artemesia, Hawkweed, Nightshade and Centaury.

That fat thing La Voisin knew nothing by comparison. What was she, but a haberdasher's wife, and oh yes, La Bosse knew of Antoine: pathetic creature, fawning, running hither and thither like a mouse. marchand-mercier. Think of it.

She crossed the courtyard brushing the blooms with an open hand, the velvet red trim on the hem of her gown curdling around her ankles, petals dropping in her wake. There were too many 'fortune tellers'. Why hereabouts she could count fifteen within a three-street radius. Poor creatures for the most part, offering charms meant to turn a lover's head, or guard against the pox. Then there were those who peddled poisonous remedies, all the better to rid silly women of the undesired product of an illicit night's love. Hah. None were as efficacious as those she mixed, and not one of these 'fortune tellers' as cultured or as knowledgeable as she. Not a single one.

But wait. Someone lurked in the cloister.

"You came straight here? What news of Madame de Montespan?"

A shuffle of feet. A cough. "La Voisin arranged a black mass."

"What?" La Bosse tore the bloom from the stem. La Voisin had a growing clientele and self-esteem to match, but she could not be allowed to rule the roost. "She must be stopped."

The shadow in the cloister shifted. The wind sighed and a man stepped out into the light. The whiskery grandfather inclined his head.

"What's done is done," he said.

"Stop being so cryptic, old man. La Voisin grows fat on the proceeds of the court. It should be me. Me, you hear?"

The grandfather shrugged. "She eats well. It's true."

La Bosse sniffed. "She takes my business."

"Wealth obtained by fraud dwindles, but the one who gathers by labour increases it."

"Then labour old man. Labour." La Bosse dropped torn bloom onto the humus-rich soil.

***

Catherine crept into her house like a thief. Ear to the kitchen door she strained to hear anything that might signal Antoine had deposited himself at the table to sit the night out with a jug of vinegary wine. She heard nothing. He could be abed already, but then he might just as well have fallen asleep at the table. If that was the case, she must creep in without waking him. As she listened, a chair scraped on the stone floor and something, or someone, bumped the table. He was there alright. She pushed open the door. The moon shone brightly through the window, illuminating the table. Antoine sat nursing his jug of wine, and behind him on the wall lay his shadow. Catherine grabbed the jug out from under Antoine's nose.

"Oi, I've not done with that."

Catherine swilled the remaining dribbles of wine around in the bottom of the jug.

"Needs topping up," she said, and put the jug under the tap on the stoneware crock sitting on a trestle near the door. With her back turned, she produced the phial of *Ruptoire* and poured the contents in. Next, she turned the tap on. The wine spurted. The crock was almost empty. The dregs were full of sediment. No matter, it would serve to disguise the poison. Jug three-quarters full, she shoved it at her husband. Antoine gave her an alcoholic grunt. Catherine walked round him and out.

The stairs creaked. She waited and listened. This time he wouldn't survive; he'd be dead by day break.

Chapter Ten

Antoine got up before the dawn chorus and, with his nightshirt pooled around his ankles and his knees near touching his ears, emptied his bowels into the pot. The result came with a venomous aroma. He'd had the most uncomfortable night's sleep he could ever remember. He put it down to the disturbance with the moles and finding out his wife was an Angel Maker. Never for a minute did he think he'd been poisoned.

He shook his aching head. His dry mouth tasted like he'd been sucking on an old sock. The empty wine jug lay on the floor by the bed. He picked it up. Not a drop left. He really must give up the demon drink. It did him no good and it stopped him from thinking straight. He expelled the last of his poisonous load and grunted as he struggled to stand. He glanced at the glutinous mess and toed the pot back under the bed. The maid would empty it. He found his breeches, and danced on first one leg and then the other as he put them on. He needed fresh air. He had to find somewhere to clear his head. Not the garden. Not there, where every plant reminded him of what lay beneath. No, he'd go for a walk. He'd go out to the hills up at Montmartre. Find a nice tree. Sit there until his mind had cleared, and his belly… Oh God, his belly.

***

Catherine lay in her bed, fists clenched, teeth gritted, eyes narrowed to an angry squint, while a foetid smell drifted through the house. Listening to Antoine getting dressed she wondered if he was immortal, but no, that was impossible. No man was immortal. Bastard man, all the same. Her mind looped a ribbon of happier memories and fluttered it up and down, back and forth: her wedding day; all pink and silk, pastel coloured satin slippers and flowers; the birth of her dearest baby Balthazar and the smell of his soft down skin; the moment Marguerite had walked baby steps from the shop door to the tray of buckles on the low shelf by the back window; the curling warm breeze from the river and a fleet of barges up from the coast. They'd been happy days. The shop had been cramped, but it had been cosy. Balthazar had died of course. It hadn't been her fault. She'd only left him for a minute, just a minute. In that time he'd stopped breathing; precious joy gone in an instant. She'd clung onto him tight and prayed and prayed for the good Lord to give him life, but her prayers had been in vain.

Marguerite had come a year later, but baby Balthazar had been special – sacred even and there he was, taken from her; no life to live out like a thread into the future leading who knew where. Antoine had blamed her, but then men blamed women for everything. What could he know of a woman's pains? Nothing, that's what. Nothing. She turned over. The sheet beneath her rucked up. Perhaps she hadn't used enough poison, or Lesage had made a mistake and not given her the right thing. She should have used wolfsbane. She heard the door slam. Antoine had gone out. Good riddance, she thought and pulled the covers close around her neck and closed her eyes.

Chapter Eleven

The city gates stood wide open. Antoine nodded to one of the guards, mumbled 'bonjour' to a merchant with a cart full of vegetables and side-stepped an inebriated wench, who staggered in the filth-filled ruts. It wasn't such a bad morning, but Antoine wasn't paying it much attention; his mind was a jumble of thoughts and his belly ached so badly he thought he might have to detour into the bushes to relieve himself again. He didn't though. He kept on walking, his arse pinching and puckering, until he reached a field close to Montmartre, where, behind a bush, he finally gave way to his intemperate bowels. Pulling his breeches back up, he gazed round furtively, worried in case he'd been watched. The ground rose and gave him a fine view of the city. There wasn't a single person in sight. He took himself across the grass to sit under an oak tree.

What in God's name was he going to do? There were dead babies in his garden – under his grass. He'd expected moles… would have welcomed them even. No, that wasn't right. He'd wanted to kill them. He couldn't deny it. All the same… dead babies. His wife was a murderous old witch. The most feared, murderous old witch. He couldn't get his head round it. His bowels groaned. He felt sick. Life wasn't fair. All he wanted was to fill a little shop with the most glorious fabrics. Oh, and to see his wife's love-filled and wonderful smile. He'd give anything for that, but how to win her over? If she loved him enough then she'd not care where they lived; she'd go with him to the ends of the earth. Other women would.

Other women.

Catherine wasn't other women. Catherine was an Angel-Maker and how exactly do you court one of those? Flowers made no impact. Tasty sweetmeats, likewise. Gold trinkets brought a glimmer to her eyes, but he had no money and couldn't afford jewellery. If only he had the shop. If only. Perhaps if he'd been a better husband; a better man; a better son, things would have been different. Perhaps then both mother and wife would have smiled and loved him for who he was. Or perhaps it wouldn't have made any difference. You're not meant to compare your mother with your wife. You're not meant to think of them as interchangeable, but it seemed like they were. That wasn't right. Not at all. Antoine lost track of the time and the day passed in a mournful blur. He fell asleep with an acorn sticking in the side of his face and when he woke the next morning he heard the cheery whistle of a passing cowman. He hadn't meant to stay all night. He begged some milk, gulped it down, and nestled back against his tree to watch the noxious Parisian haze and the march of properties up the hill. Soon they would reach Monmartre and then these green fields would be gone.

Another day passed and another night, the wished for smile no more realistic than a dream. Often, he woke from a fitful sleep with a crick in his neck, or sunburn on one side of his face, or damp breeches from the wet grass. He let the days turn into a week and thought nothing of it. The cowman left him a jug of milk each morning and wedge of claggy bread. Antoine drank his milk stoically, watching distant chimney smoke rise and disappear into the sometimes blue sky. He watched clouds gather and rain fall. He watched the blades of grass at his feet quiver in the soft summer breezes, and he meditated on the slow chew of the cows, whose pasture he shared. He sheltered beneath the oak's outstretched branches and had absolutely no desire to go home and face his wife's wrath. How was it possible to love someone so much and yet find their actions so foul, so horrific, you couldn't bring yourself to face them? He didn't know.

One morning his complaining bladder woke him earlier than usual. As he relieved himself in a nearby hedge he noticed someone making their way up the rutted lane. It wasn't the cowman. He'd already passed. The grey light and slight mist prevented further identification, so Antoine waited patiently for the traveller to come closer. In all probability, it was the farmer, or the farmer's wife, come to tell him to move on.

"You've been here long enough," they'd say. "Haven't you got a home to go to?"

Eventually, the blurred traveller became the whiskery grandfather. Out of place, Antoine couldn't quite put his finger on why he knew this person. He had a vague recollection of encountering him somewhere, but where? The grandfather pointed to the oak tree. When no reply came, the old man stamped across the field and sat down under the oak's branches in the exact same spot where Antoine usually sat. Here, the old man gazed out over the view, taking in great gulps of air, his whiskers quivering with each breath.

Antoine tied up his breeches and approached cautiously. "What d'you want?"

"You're of the earth, I think," said the grandfather. "Melancholic. Full of black bile."

Antoine checked over his shoulder. Did he mean...? He pointed to his own chest.

"You're wondering where you've met me before."

Antoine said nothing. Sometimes it was better to let others do all the talking.

"The afternoon before the siege in the Court of Miracles, I was in Fagioli's wine cellar."

Antoine shook his head. The grandfather's identity still eluded him.

"Your wife; the Angel-Maker?"

Ah. "You! What are you doing here?"

The grandfather twinkled a smile. "What are *you* doing here?"

Antoine shrugged. He didn't have an answer that made any sense. Not yet, anyway.

"Women eh?" said the grandfather.

Antoine nodded and stared at the brown smudge that was Paris.

"She's not the only Angel-Maker, you know. They're everywhere these days," said the grandfather.

Antoine sat down next to the old man.

"But why?"

"Too many people make bad marriages, that's why."

Antoine started. Not him. He'd made a good marriage. A very good marriage. Everyone had said so. So go home, urged the demon on his shoulder. "Not now. Not me," he muttered.

"No, not you. Your wife's clients. They marry impotent fools, or abusers, or time wasters... and then, there are the old men." Here the grandfather gave a soft chuckle. "They even marry counts, dukes and princes, but however it is, they want rid of them so they can take up with the love of their life. Or…. Or they're unwed and in the family way. Ah, there are thousands of reasons why they turn to women like your wife."

Antoine winced, and his problems rushed at him in a great panoply of twisted thought: the shop, the dead babies, mother and wife, the smile that didn't exist. She loved him. She had to. He loved her. That counted for something didn't it?

He said, "I don't understand."

"There are remedies for everything."

"Poisons, you mean?"

"I prefer to call them potions. Love potions. Charms. Powders."

"How d'you know all this?"

"Ah, that would be telling, wouldn't it?"

Antoine sighed. "Are you one of *them*? An Angel Maker?"

"*Who? Me*? No. Not me."

"What then? Why are you here? It's a long way from the city for an old man."

While they'd been talking, the sun had burned off the mist and the distant smudge had become rooftops and spires.

"Go home," the grandfather said. "Go home and make yourself useful. Watch. Listen. Be cautious. Keep your wits about you." He looked deep into Antoine's eyes until the latter wriggled with discomfort. "You've a testing time to come."

Antoine flicked an ant off his knee. "More so than what's already happened?"

"What's happened? Nothing's happened. You found something out you weren't prepared for. Now you are. That's all. Believe no evil, 'til the evil's done."

"Riddles," muttered Antoine, holding his head in his hands. The grass between his legs had worn away to dirt.

The grandfather's knees cracked as he rose to his feet and walked away.

"Go home. Trust me. Your time is coming."

The dirt moved. The ant had friends. Antoine stood up. A damned nest, and beneath his tree. When he gazed out over the pasture, the grandfather was nowhere to be seen.

***

Catherine's bedchamber door stood ajar, the light soft, the air full of the smell of old wood and beeswax. Antoine watched his wife from the relative safety of the adjoining chamber. Auburn curls crept out from under her silk cap. He wanted to kiss the nape of her neck and breathe in her scent, but he was scared to interrupt her privacy. She'd shout at him. She'd send him away. At least this way he could pretend to the intimacy. She was still a fine-looking woman, if plump – yes, plump. He didn't mind that. Too many women laced themselves too tightly. He noticed the length of her fingers as she clutched at her gown. They were short and fat, like stubby sausages. His belly groaned at the thought of food and Catherine turned her cold eyes on him. For the briefest of moments he thought he detected a smile, but no, it was just a trick of the light.

"What are you doing skulking around?" She threw the gown aside.

No, 'where have you been' or 'welcome home'.

"Nothing," he mumbled. Longing welled up; an irrevocable yearning; a craving for something he'd never had, but which he knew existed, if only he could just... why couldn't she smile and mean it?

"Take this message to Lesage." Catherine proffered a folded letter.

It had been the same with his mother; the very same. He'd tried so hard to win her love, but nothing had worked. What did he have to do? Who did he have to be? Perhaps he was unutterably flawed; damaged in such a way it was impossible for anyone to want him. He'd loved his mother and she'd hated him. He loved Catherine and it was the same story. The two entwined as one. If only he had a little shop, then everything would be alright again. Catherine had loved him when he'd been making money. There'd been smiles a plenty then, oh yes. Ah, but it wasn't him though was it? It was money that made her smile. Money and nothing else.

"Why?" was the only thing he managed.

Catherine waved the letter. "Why? It's none of your business why. Take it. Take it. You know where he lives."

"Yes." Antoine had been there before. Not inside; he always waited on the street. It had never bothered him. He'd brought parcels back and he'd never opened them. He should have, but he wanted her to think he was trustworthy. Mon Dieu, but he *was* trustworthy.

So why did they, Catherine and Lesage both, treat him like a bumbling idiot? The trouble was he'd done nothing to disabuse them of that notion; nothing, save try to be kind and useful... and there it was again: they hated, he loved. It was like a passionate dance, or a bull fight. He'd heard the Spanish jousted against the beast. Perhaps that

was why he'd come home; to joust with the beast. Lesage
was a snake though, not a bull; a venomous serpent of a
man, and Catherine... Antoine grunted: a knot of anger in
his caw. He'd have his shop. He'd show her. He'd sell the
house. But wait, what about the dead babies under his
grass?

"They say you're an Angel-Maker," he spluttered,
hoping she'd deny it; hoping it was all lies and that the last
few weeks had been a dream. They hadn't. He knew they
hadn't, but he could hope.

"Do they now?" Catherine continued to wave the letter
at him. "And who are *they*?"

"Is it true?"

"What if it is?"

"How do you do it? With poison?" Antoine's insides
curled. Bile rose in his throat. It took a special kind of evil
to kill people deliberately. He'd never thought of Catherine
as evil, but she must be.

"Sometimes."

How could she be so offhand? Death was a serious
matter. For certain, he didn't wish death on anyone. Not
anyone. Not even his worst enemies, not that he had any
enemies save Catherine and then... she wasn't *his* enemy,
though it seemed *he* was hers, just like he'd been with his
mother.

His mother. Round and round his thoughts went.

"Are there others?" Little Balthazar's baby face came to
him; his own dear child, dead now many years. "Who do
you poison beside the babies?"

Catherine threw the letter onto the bed and tucked her
curls back under her cap.

"Unwanted husbands," she snapped.

Antoine flinched. It wasn't just the hate; it was not being wanted too. It was feeling lonely and lost; like living wasn't worth the effort. Like the rest of the world carried on around you, but there wasn't any point in any of it. His marriage had been a trap learned at his mother's knee, although he couldn't remember actually ever sitting on his mother's knee.

And Catherine wants me dead. He blinked, surprised at his own insight.

"I've got six mouths to feed. I have to make money somehow. You certainly don't," she said.

"Six?" Antoine counted the household off on mental fingers. Him and Catherine, Marguerite their daughter, Margot the Maid – that made four. Oh yes, Catherine's mother, who lived in rooms three streets away. He hardly ever saw her. It was like she was a ghost. Who else? Who? No one. Oh, a hundred dead babies. Maybe more. Maybe a thousand. Two thousand. Five thousand.

"Five," he mumbled.

"What did you say?" Catherine gave him a withering look and started towards her. He hung back. She reached the adjoining door.

"There's only five of us," he repeated. Had she included his daughter's beau, that insect Romani? Then it would be six.

Catherine shook her head. The curls escaped.

"You've been gone for weeks and you dare to question me? Take the letter to Lesage."

"Is he your lover?" Antoine bit his lip. Now how had he found the courage to say that?

"Him?" The word was edged with deceit. Catherine snatched up the letter from her bed and threw it at

Antoine. He made no attempt to catch it. It fluttered to the floor like a butterfly with broken wings. He stared at it for a moment, trying to block out the torment; trying to keep his emotions in check; an endless well of pain.

"Please," he said. "It's killing me."

"I wish," Catherine mumbled as she walked the full length of her chamber.

"Please," Antoine said, louder now. "Why are you doing this?"

Silence. He felt his blood thin, and his skin shrink.

"Catherine, I beg you." He fell to his knees. Vaguely, he heard her petticoats crackle like new ice, and imagined her exhaled breath as frozen plumes. The door slammed. The spell broke.

He found the letter, unfolded it, and held it fast against his chest until he could bear to read it. It was a request for *Venin de Crapaud*: toad poison. He turned the paper over and sniffed it.

Venin de Crapaud.

She meant to kill him – to take his life – a life he'd not thought worth anything to anyone. Well, he'd refuse to die. He'd open his shop and she'd smile. She would. She'd love him. He'd make her love him. He flattened the paper, folded it neatly, and pocketed it. 'Take it to Lesage' she'd said. 'Take it to Lesage.' Maybe that snake *was* her lover. He wiped his face on the back of his sleeve. The sweat left a greasy mark. He'd heard rumours Catherine had a string of men at her beck and call. He'd have to watch her more closely. He was bound to his ice maiden, as he had been to his mother. He'd melt the rime. He would.

Chapter Twelve

North of Paris, close to the town of Arras, the Sun King's Queen, Maria Theresa, picked at her food and wished she was back in her royal apartment in the Louvre, or perhaps the Tuileries. Anywhere would be better than this tent in a field in the Spanish-held wilderness. On the previous evening she and her entourage had encamped while the King busied himself laying siege to Lille. Before he rode away he'd told her, "The Spaniards are so tiresome. Why can't they stay in Spain," conveniently forgetting, or perhaps purposefully remembering, that his wife had once been heir to the Spanish throne. She'd reminded him on numerous occasions that she'd renounced her claim, but it hadn't made any difference, and so here they were, at war with the country of her birth.

Arras was meant to be safe, but it was cold, wet and boring. With time on her hands, the Queen's mind soon turned to gossip. The evening before she'd received an unsigned letter, and, though she'd tried not to think about it, she'd worried herself silly all night long, tossing and turning on her cot, while an owl kept watch in the spinney nearby, and a rat ran along the tent edge. Even that building site at Versailles would be better than this.

The next morning the letter was where she'd left it on the portable table, but it now sported rat-nibbled corners and suspicious black droppings over the word 'mistress'. The Queen shook the letter clean and called her lady-in-waiting, Madame de Montespan, to her side. She had it in mind to question the beauty, but it was it just so difficult to address these matters. She didn't want to appear ungracious.

The Queen breathed in the miasma of early morning fog drifting through the open tent door, and the stench of the commode, and said, somewhat imperiously: "Yesterday, I learned certain information, which I cannot credit." Here she paused for a moment, to give weight to her words. Madame de Montespan remained blank-faced.

"I am advised that the King is in love with you." This was the part that gave the Queen the most cause for concern. She searched her companion's face for an indication of guilt. Finding none, she continued. "He no longer cares for La Vallière. I'm told that the Duchesse de Montausier finds a ready surfeit of young women in my household to throw at him."

Still, Madame de Montespan held her poise. Was there nothing that would rile this impertinent hussy?

"He was with you in your apartments nearly the whole time we were at Compiègne. Is it true?"

The Queen's silk-shoed foot ground the rat droppings into the Turkey rug, spread directly on the soft Arras earth. If the lady before her had erred then she would rather hear it from her own lips. Insidious gossip was so divisive.

Madame de Montespan gave a slight shake of her head. The Queen couldn't make out whether this was a denial or disappointment.

"I've sent the letter to the King," she said, forgetting she had it in her hand.

"How... how is it possible for anyone to imagine that I could do such a thing?" blurted out Madame de Montespan.

The Queen saw tears in the accused's eyes and wondered if, perhaps, she'd been too hard on her.

Madame De Montespan went on, "You have received me so warmly. How could you think me guilty of such a base intrigue? Who is it that thinks to dupe you with such lies?"

"I am the dupe of no one," replied the Queen. It came out all wrong; as if she was the guilty party. "You have always been a dear friend." She had been so sure. For certain, she now considered she'd acted in haste. She crumpled the letter.

"And you mine."

How embarrassing. The Queen wished she hadn't mentioned the matter at all. What a humiliating discussion. Who was it that had spread these rumours? She'd have it out with them on her return to Paris.

"Rest assured, we will say no more of it," she said, and would have caressed her companion's hand, save that protocol forbade such an expression of affection.

Madame de Montespan curtsied and backed out. The Queen watched her go. Did she detect a wry smile on Madame's lips? She couldn't tell.

Chapter Thirteen

Antoine stood in an alley over the street from the scuffed blue door with its magical symbol. He made no play of trying to hide, though he didn't want to be challenged on his lurking. Seemingly impervious to the stench of the tanneries, he watched and waited and watched some more.

Unbeknownst to him, he too was being observed, but this spy was keener of intellect, and better able to disguise his purpose. Indeed, not a single person knew of this spy's design, for the bundle of rags on this rank street signalled naught but a worthless beggar, and no one gave him a second look.

When the sun reached its zenith Antoine slunk up to the door and knocked dead centre on the pentacle. Catherine had sent him here for *Venin de Crapaud*: toad poison; the very thing she'd use to kill him. How ironic. He knocked again and this time came sounds like the great uncoiling of a snake: a slithering and a shuddering. The door opened and a gastric warmth rushed out.

"Yes?" said Lesage, his eyes half-open, as if he'd been roused from a deep sleep.

Antoine fished the crumpled letter out of his pocket. "This," he said and thrust it forward.

Lesage shot out a hand and plucked the letter from between Antoine's fingers. Then he turned and slid back into the darkness, leaving the door open. Ordinarily, Antoine would have waited quietly outside, but not this time. Newfound purpose had imbued him with courage, at least, for the moment. He stepped over the threshold and found Lesage bent over his apparatus, pouring a green liquid into a phial, which he sealed with a cork.

"Don't touch anything," snapped Lesage, pushing past Antoine, to reach inside a cupboard.

A cloud of sulphurous fumes made Antoine gag. He covered his nose and mouth.

"Will it take long?"

Lesage didn't reply. A human skeleton stared at Antoine from its stand on the far side of the laboratory. A dead crow lay belly up on the table, its legs like stiff sentinels. A bowl of what looked like the entrails of a cow festered in a corner, a flayed dog's head on a stick standing guard over the entire proceedings. Antoine swore its bulging right eye followed him around the room. Curiosity quashed any remaining fear. This was interesting. This was something new. Terrible, but new.

"What do you want with all this?"

"Serious requests demand serious solutions." Lesage opened a drawer, took out a piece of parchment and a spoon. He laid the parchment out flat on the table and shovelled white powder from a jar onto it. When he'd done, he stoppered the jar. Then he twisted the paper into a screw so that the powder was safe inside..

Handing the twist to Antoine he said, "There. She'll know what to do with it."

"What *will* she do with it?"

Lesage turned on him. "It's none of your business."

"I think if she intends on using it to kill me, then it very much *is* my business."

Lesage started, "Go home little man. You don't know what you're talking about."

The demon on Antoine's shoulder prodded at his conscience. "It's not right is it? What she does? It's not right. It's murder. They execute murderers." Oh, but he hadn't meant to say that. It had just come out. Now he was for it.

"Only if they can prove it. Besides, theft is a greater crime than murder. Don't you know that?"

"I've got a garden full of dead babies." No, don't say that! Keep your mouth shut.

Lesage snorted. "They never breathed. Were never baptised. That means they were never born. Go home."

"Never born? But they're there in my garden." A writhing spire of nauseous anger caught in Antoine's chest. "I'm next aren't I? She kills husbands. She's going to kill me. I know she is."

"Who told you that?"

"She did." She hadn't - not in so many words, but it was obvious. He was next on her list.

Lesage blinked, licked his lips, and softened his gaze, and with it his voice. "All she does is aid women whose men have become a burden. Love charms; pills for potency; nothing more than that. She wouldn't kill you. She loves you. Are you prepared to see her burn at the stake?" He smiled and it sent chills down Antoine's spine. Not a smile of love. Not one of sympathy or care. This was a smile of deceit, plain and simple.

Antoine took a step back.

"Well... she... she..." Dead babies. Dead husbands and he, her next victim. He clutched the screw of paper so tight his knuckles showed bone white..

"I told her you were up to no good." Lesage's tongue flashed out as he took a menacing step forward. Antoine bumped a cabinet.

Lesage hissed, "Always meddling where you aren't wanted."

Escape! Run!

"Me? Meddling? Me?" No, that wasn't right. He made himself useful and when he wasn't he... he.... gardened. Yes, he gardened, and soon he would open a new shop. The tannery next door belched out a cloud of sulphurous smoke. The noise made Antoine jump.

Lesage snarled, "You've got what you came for. Go away."

Venin de Crapaud, thought Antoine. Death never takes the wise man by surprise; he is always ready to go. He backed out of the snake's lair as fast as he could.

Outside, the sky had turned yellow; the air thick with the tannery's contagious fumes. Antoine emptied the screw of paper into the gutter and instantly regretted it. Catherine expected him to bring it back safe and sound. He couldn't go home empty-handed. He couldn't. He bent down, his hand poised to scoop the white powder up. Should he? Could he? He twitched. His hat fell off. He snatched it up. Best not touch the nasty poison. Best just go home. He'd find some excuse for his failure. Catherine already thought he was an idiot. Very well then, an idiot he'd be. He slapped his hat back on his head and set off.

Hard against the opposite wall, the bundle of rags began to uncurl. A finger, moistened by a pink tongue, came out to test the air. The spy threw back his hood and the whiskery grandfather revealed himself.

***

Catherine grew more and more impatient with every passing hour. The man was impossible. He cared only for drink and gambling and... and... Oh, but she couldn't remember a time when he'd gone out gambling. No, that was *her* favourite pastime, and she'd had little opportunity for it recently. That was Antoine's fault too. Eventually, she gave up waiting and went to bed. Here, she tossed and turned, cursing her misfortune and calling down all manner of ills on her errant husband. At a little past the darkest hour she heard Antoine return home. She waited for him to come upstairs, anger increasing with every second. Eventually, she went downstairs to look for him. The kitchen window stood ajar and the cold night air and bothersome insects had crept inside. Antoine sat at the table, chin to chest, eyes closed.

Where have you been? Well? Have you got it?"

Antoine woke with a start. "What?"

"What I sent you for."

"What you sent me for?"

"To Lesage. I sent you on an errand."

"Oh... no. He didn't have any."

"He didn't have any?"

"Toad poison wasn't it? He didn't have any."

Catherine wondered how easy it would be to take the iron skillet from its hook on the beam above, raise it high with both hands and smash it down on this idiot's head. There'd be blood everywhere, but at least he'd be dead.

Dead, so dead.

She'd have to feign distress. She'd have to weep. She'd have to make up a story about an intruder. The new-fangled gendarmerie would be called in. There'd be an investigation. There'd be no way to hush it all up. Quicker was not always cleaner. No, no, no. It would have to be poison. It was far easier to explain away. She'd say he'd been struck by apoplexy, and once he'd been buried, well then the house would be hers - all of it, from the cellar beneath her feet to the dusty attic. Without the *Venin de Crapaud* though, she'd have to use something else. Now, what did she have to hand? The mixture of belladonna and opium, bruised datura and stramonium? She'd made it months ago. Surely it would have matured by now? All she needed to do was waft it beneath his nose. Then again, it might not work. She might get a whiff of it too. Still, if she could remember where she'd put it.

"Inheritance is not to be sniffed at," she said.

Antoine twisted in his chair. "Inheritance?"

"This house."

"Yes?"

"If you died, it would come to me."

"I suppose, but what would you do with it? It's too big for one person."

"Marguerite would be here."

"But she'll get married one day, won't she? And when that happens, well then it'll be her husband that'll inherit. Perhaps he won't make provision for you, my dear. Especially not if he's that rogue I caught her with. Best Marguerite remains a spinster."

He sounded petulant; like a child. She'd strangle him if she had the strength. She'd suffocate him with a goose-feather pillow. She rested her hand on his shoulder.

"You wouldn't try to kill me would you?" he said.

"Whatever gave you that idea?"

"Because I want to sell the house and you don't want me to. I need the money for a lease on a shop, and there's the stock too. It doesn't come cheap and, like you always tell me, I don't have money of my own anymore." He picked at a knot in the table top.

Catherine gritted her teeth. Stop! Stop it! His fingers were dirty. His nails bitten to the quick. What had happened to him since she'd met him? What had happened to them both?

He muttered, "If you did try to poison me, would there would be a remedy?"

A peacock feather and the lungs of an ass would expel all poisons, but she wasn't about to tell him and besides, he'd not find either in a hurry.

"You can't sell the house. I'll have nowhere to see my clients. I've told you this time and again."

"You have. True enough. I suppose you could always turn your income over to me." He smiled up at her.

How dare he? "I'll do no such thing." She'd worked hard for her money. This talk of a shop; it was nonsense. He'd been out of the trade for years. Look at him. He could no more start up again in business than she could raise the dead, and she'd tried. Oh yes, she'd tried.

"You do realise I'm unusual among husbands? I let you keep your money."

"You do realise I am unusual amongst wives, in that I am called upon to direct fate."

"Touché."

Antoine seemed unusually calm this evening. One might almost say, he was reconciled to whatever fate awaited him. Had he consulted with one of her rivals? La Bosse perhaps, but no, that was impossible. He couldn't. He wouldn't. He didn't know her or where she lived. At least, Catherine didn't think he did.

"How much is the house worth?"

"Monsieur Sanson paid two hundred livres for his," Antoine replied.

"But he's only got one chimney and two windows. It's on the worst street, near the Court of Miracles. We've…" Catherine glanced at the ceiling, counting… counting. "We've seven windows and six hearths. I won't let you sell it. I won't."

Antoine let out a long sigh and said, "I do love you. I do. I wouldn't let anything happen to you. You're my true love. My sweetheart. I want the shop so I can prove it to you. Everything will be back the way it was before once I have a shop again. You'll see."

A lump lodged in Catherine's throat. He'd told her over and over that he loved her. He fawned over her, desperate to win her affections, forlornly offering himself up for errands, ever eager to please. He wanted to share her bed again, but she couldn't bring herself to lie next to him. She recoiled at every touch, her mother's voice ringing loud in her ears, 'get rid of him. Get rid.'

Over and over and over.

"I love you," he said, and it just made her feel even madder. That belladonna mixture must be somewhere. She walked away, every footstep loud, the boards cold-brown and creaking, her petticoats like the heavy drapes around a death bed. Upstairs, in her bed chamber, she closed the door and rested her back against its wood. This house was hers, not Antoine's. Yes, he'd bought it, but no, not for himself, but for her.

FOR HER.

And here, she'd made two attempts on his life already and both times he'd defeated her by surviving. The house was worth ten times what that dullard Sanson had paid. That was… she calculated… two thousand livres at least. A shop wouldn't cost that much, surely? Damn the man but he was impossible to live with, and where had she put the belladonna? It would be in a lead-lined box. She must have locked it away somewhere safe, but where?

An owl hooted from the church tower.

Ah, the linen chest. That was where it was.

A door creaked, then floorboards, and the stairs. Another door. More footsteps followed by a great hrumpf. Antoine had flopped on his bed and would soon be fast asleep. The time had come to be rid of her burdensome husband. From between her cleavage she pulled out a key on a chain. Looping the chain over her head she weighed the key in her hand as she crossed to the chest beneath her window. Fitting the key in the lock, she turned it and opened the lid. Beneath blankets and linen, right at the bottom, she found the lead-lined box. It was heavy and bound around with thick cord to prevent it from opening accidentally. She closed down the chest lid and placed the box on top, then tied a kerchief around her nose and mouth. It wouldn't do to breathe in the fumes. She took the box and walked softly along the passage to Antoine's bedchamber.

It was simple. Open the box under his nose. Let him get a good whiff, and the job was done. The moon's wan light ghosted Antoine's face. He snorted, grunted, rubbed his nose, and turned over. His mouth fell open. Catherine held the box close to his face, let slip the cord and opened the lid. Instantly, Antoine coughed, spluttering up snot and snorting it back down again. He gasped for breath, his hands clawing at the covers. He convulsed, his stomach rigid. His eyes flew open. Catherine slammed the box shut, and stepped back in horror.

Goodness what would it matter if he saw her? He's soon be dead. She retraced her steps, closed the door tightly and listened to Antoine's tortured coughs. It wasn't a pleasant way to die. Not at all. After a while all went silent. Catherine resisted the temptation to sneak a look. The deed was done. Come morning, she'd send for the undertaker.

Chapter Fourteen

The following day shrugged off an early mist and presented itself bright and warm. Antoine stood in the kitchen door, staring out at the garden and the straggle of elder along the eastern wall; three trees gone wild. He'd had a restless night, beset with all kinds of nightmares. At one point he'd woken spluttering, desperate for a drink. He'd grabbed for his jug of wine and downed most of it in huge gulps before falling back asleep, only to dream of Catherine's face hanging over him like some terrifying grim reaper. He rubbed his breast bone; the pain was much worse today. He ought to give up the drink for good. He ought to concentrate on his plan and go and scout out a likely shop. He should go to the notary and discuss how to sell the house, but he couldn't find the energy. He heard Catherine behind him. Her footsteps sounded angry, if that was even possible. She was making those little noises she made when she had a bone to pick with him. He half turned. She'd been at the street door.

"Who was that?"

"The undertaker," she replied.

Oh, she was angry right enough. He could hear it in her voice.

"There are people coming," she announced.

"We do? How many?"

"Fifty."

"Fifty? What's that got to do with the undertaker?"

"Nothing… and musicians. When they arrive tell them to go behind the lavender."

"Musicians?"

"You heard me."

"The roses need tying back."

"Then get to it."

Antoine ventured across the grass. There was nothing wrong with the roses. It was the elder that needed tidying up, but cut it and the devil would dine at your table. Elder was a warped wood, full of bitterness and hatred. Catherine used it sometimes in her concoctions. He'd seen her strip the bark and collect the flowers. She was angry with him because… because… there was something. It niggled at him. He spat out across the dark earth. He tasted something sour on his tongue. It was in his throat and his belly too. His sputum was flecked with blood. He was still alive and Catherine was as angry as a gnat intent on a bloody breakfast. He'd have to be careful. She'd try again. It wasn't safe for him here. He ought to leave. Ought to, but how could he? It was his house. *His* house. Don't think about the poison. Don't think about that. Don't think about being dead, or the babies. None of that. Ah, let the roses fall where they may. The elder too. He'd not tie anything back today. So she had fifty people coming. So what? He tramped the rough path to the bottom of the garden and hid in the shrubbery. A fat beetle struggled over the soil. Antoine mulled over his plan for the shop. Shelving so high, cutting table this long, and little stock room. Nothing outrageous. It would be strictly functional. He should set up a meeting with the corporation. Bertrand… Bertrand… who was it held the secretary's role? He couldn't remember. It would come to him.

"Papa? Can you go and fetch the pastries?" Marguerite called, hovering at the end of the path.

"I suppose," grunted Antoine. Errands. Always errands. Endless they were. Endless.

"It's better than sulking in a bush," said Marguerite as he emerged.

"I'm not sulking. I'm planning." How long had he been there? People littered the grass. The musicians were trying to erect their music stands in the lavender. A stand fell over and as the musician bent to retrieve it, a sprig of lavender went straight up his nose. This made the man jump back in surprise and knock all the other stands flying. Marguerite smiled and offered her father a purse. Antoine spotting Romani, skulking beyond the difficult lavender.

"The patisserie," said Marguerite. "Two trays. Go straight there and come straight back. What are you planning?"

"None of your business." Mon Dieu, but even his own daughter spoke to him as if he was a little child.

Marguerite gave him a pointed look. "Papa? Don't spend it on anything but the pastries."

"No." He pushed past her. Damned women.

"Monsieur," said Romani. "I must speak with you."

"So? Speak." This fool would want to ask for Marguerite's hand in marriage. Antoine could see it in his eyes. Well, she had no dowry. There was nothing to give her. Nothing, save the house. She couldn't have that. Not yet. He wasn't ready to die.

"So? What is it?"

"You know I was with the guard?" Romani looked flush-faced and full of expectation.

"No, I didn't."

"I have an allowance. I'll make a good husband."

Antoine stopped, one hand on the gate and barked out a laugh. "I knew it. You're asking me if you can marry my daughter."

"She's going to anyway, whether you agree or not."

"Why bother asking me then. Do you want me dead as well?"

"What?"

"Isn't that the plan? Marry the daughter, kill off the old man and live happily ever after in this house? The house I bought with money I earned?"

Romani screwed up his face – his fists too. "You're mad."

"So I've been told." Antoine pushed the gate open and left. Idiot of a man. Waylaying him en route to the pastries. Idiot. Out in the suddenly busy street, it seemed like everyone was going to the party. Gradually, the crowd cleared, leaving just one man: the grandfather.

"You," said Antoine.

"Me."

"Are you going to the party as well?"

The grandfather shook his head. "How've you been?"

"Up and down," replied Antoine.

"But you keep yourself busy?"

"I have to. If I stop work, I worry. If I worry, I drink. I don't want to drink, especially not now, so I work." He shot a glance at the house and then back again.

"I see," said the grandfather. "May I walk with you?"

"Of course." Antoine crossed the street, turned left and then left again, the grandfather half-hopping, half-running to keep up. At the bakery, the assistant indicated a tray of pastries and Antoine shouldered it and retraced his steps. At no time did the grandfather offer to help carry the load, nor did he say anything more, until they reached the gate, whereupon Antoine took the tray down of his shoulder and leant an elbow to the latch.

"This is the day," said the grandfather.

"What day is that?"

"*The* day. Keep your wits about you."

Antoine nodded, not really understanding what the grandfather meant, unless… unless he knew about Catherine's attempts to kill him, but no, impossible; no one knew about that. He half-turned, balancing the tray carefully, and nudged the gate open.

"Out of my way, imbecile," said a striking woman. She pushed Antoine aside. The tray slipped from his hands and landed upside down in the dirt.

"Madame," shouted Antoine, but the woman had gone, the grandfather too. He bent down to pick the pastries up, but they were ruined. Damned women. Damned, damned, damned women.

"Papa?"

Antoine jumped. Guilty - guilty as charged. Marguerite slid through the gate.

"Don't do that."

"Do what?"

"Creep up on me."

"What happened to the pastries?"

"That woman… that…."

"Mademoiselle Du Parc?"

"Is that her name? She's got no manners."

"She's an actress," said Marguerite. She lowered her voice, conspiratorially. "I hear tell she's in the family way."

"Who is? Her?"

"You know who she is. All Paris talks of her. She was with Molière's troop."

"Molière? Who's he?"

"Papa, I can't believe you're so dumb."

"Dumb. That's me. What's she doing here?" He followed his daughter along the path, marvelling at how his grass now positively heaved beneath the tread of the Parisian elite. An image sprang to mind of the nasty little moles pushing aside soil and tiny corpses alike, in their attempts to flee the clodhoppers above their blind heads.

"She's come to consult Maman," said Marguerite.

"What?" he said, shaking off his vision.

"The Mademoiselle wants a solution to her problem. They say Racine wrote a play for her and she ran away to be with him."

Antoine dragged his attention back to his daughter.

"What are you saying?"

"Papa. She wants to get rid of the baby."

"Why are you telling me this? You and your mother are as bad as one another." Did his daughter poison people too? Was that it? He took a step back.

"Papa! You know I love you."

"And I, you, but really, I don't see why you've come to me with this information." He half wished he'd never seen the dead baby, or learned of the existence of all the others. It would be so much easier to live in ignorance.

"I thought you'd be pleased. I thought you wanted to understand Maman's work. Mine too."

"Yours? You're mixed up in this mess. I might have known. How can I be pleased about these poor babies?"

"Hush. Keep your voice down."

"But they've not known any kind of existence. Are they even baptised?" Yes, there it was: the irksome, loathsome horror of it all. He saw it on his daughter's face and it lodged beneath his breastbone; a dull sensation of something gone very badly awry with their lives.

Heads turned. "Be gone," he said, waving his hand at them.

"Papa. I thought..." started Marguerite. She had tears in her eyes.

He'd gone too far. He lowered his voice. "The trouble is, no one thinks in this house. No one. You know she's tried to kill me? Your mother. Your wonderful mother. Me? Your Papa. Well, I'll have it out with her right now. Just you watch me." Perhaps today was *the* day.

"No, Papa. No. You can't." Marguerite clung onto his arm.

Antoine wasn't sure he knew his daughter anymore. She was part of it and that meant she knew her mother's deepest secrets. So, what was he going to do about it? About them? Tell them he wouldn't sell the house if they would only stop their infernal devilry? If he did, he'd never afford the new shop.

Antoine shook his daughter away. He loved them both, perhaps more than either realised. He saw the hurt in Marguerite's eyes and pain knifed through bone and sinew and lodged in his chest.

"I've been patient. I've done everything I could to keep the peace, but this has to end." He made off down the path, all eyes on him. He couldn't bear it any longer.

Where was she? Where? Aha! There she was beneath the apple tree, surrounded by all those so-called ladies of quality. Oh yes, no doubt she doled advice and platitudes in equal measure. And look, there was that Du Parc woman. She'd inveigled her way into the inner circle and now stood in rapt attention. She didn't look pregnant, but then it was hard to tell beneath the many silk petticoats and pretty bows. Antoine thrust aside the hangers-on, and wriggled his way through to the front.

"Out. Now. Out," he shouted at Mademoiselle Du Parc. "You upset my pastries. You come here with your demand to get rid of your unborn child and who knows what else."

The surrounding ladies gasped in horror. The woman in question put a hand to her belly.

"You have no right to say these things."

Catherine gave Antoine a withering look and laid a reassuring hand on the lady's arm.

"Sadly, my husband suffers from mental distress. Take no notice of him."

"Mental distress!" shouted Antoine. "I should think so with what I have to put up with."

Catherine pulled Mademoiselle Du Parc away.

"Come, sit in my chamber."

"I haven't finished with you," said Antoine.

Catherine laughed derisively and said, "Which is it? Go, or stay?" She turned to the amazed guests. "You see how he ties himself in knots? Really, I keep him here out of the kindness of my heart." She led Mademoiselle Du Parc into the house.

Antoine grabbed a glass of wine from the hands of a nearby guest, downed it in one and rammed it back at her.

The wine fizzed up a storm in his belly. What was it the grandfather had said? Today was the day. Yes, that was it; today *was* the day. He wiped his mouth on the back of his sleeve. The pain in his chest abated. He snatched another glass from a tray and swallowed the contents down as fast as he had the first. He passed a bevy of kitchen staff, taken on for the party, passed the maid, and an elderly woman who looked lost or drunk or both, and so to the door of the fancy receiving room. Here, he would have burst in, but he stopped himself just in time and instead, put his ear to the wood. Mumbled words. None clear. Possibly from the Du Parc woman. Sweat dripped down the nape of his neck. Dead babies in the garden, his wife had tried to kill him and now this.

Footsteps. Catherine's voice rang out. "You're too far gone. You need more than a potion. Take yourself to La Lepère. I won't lie to you, it'll be painful. You should've come to me sooner."

The woman cried something out, but Antoine didn't hear her.

Catherine said, "By morning, all will be well."

The door opened. Antoine jumped back and tried to blend in with the wood panelling. Thankfully, it was quite dark inside the house. If she'd seen him, she gave no indication. She swept by, Mademoiselle Du Parc at her back. At the street door, Catherine wished the woman God speed and sent her on her way.

"You can come out now old man," she said.

Antoine felt very sheepish. "Where have you sent her?"

Catherine gave him a withering look. "What does it matter?" She pushed past him.

95

"What have you done?" he said, following her into the kitchen, narrowly avoided a serving maid carrying a large plate of sweetmeats. He skirted the table laden with confections, and shoved past assorted guests bleeding from garden to house and back out again. He lost sight of Catherine and wished he was anywhere but standing in his own garden. The situation was impossible. "It will be painful, but by morning all will be well" is what she'd said.

Painful, but all would be well.

The woman wanted rid of her unborn child and Catherine had sent her to some harpy with a crooked piece of wire and a bucket. He couldn't be sure about the exact details. Whatever, he had to stop it. The baby was precious. It was as simple as that. He forced his way back through the kitchen and down the passageway to the street door.

Mademoiselle Du Parc had disappeared. Antoine checked both ways. Not north. That would lead out of the city. South then. He'd never find them. He ran to the top of the Rue Beauregard, and turned right onto Rue St. Denis. He trotted through a throng of people spilling from a tavern, dodged a carriage and craned his neck to try and spot his quarry up ahead. Was she on foot? It was unlikely. She'd take a carriage or a sedan chair. He hoped not the former; if so, he'd never catch up.

At the northern end of the Rue St. Denis stood the Saint Denis Basilique: the royal necropolis. At the city end it reached as far as the Seine and the bridge called the Pont au Change. He watched the chairs travelling south. He had to check the occupants of each. It was a tall order, but he had to try. Perhaps if he found the woman in question he wouldn't have to go as far as this mysterious La Lepère.

He hoped he could persuade Mademoiselle Du Parc that keeping the child was a far better option than doing away with it.

He ran past two empty chairs. Another turned off and he spotted a man's gloved hand on the sill. Not the Mademoiselle. That left three further carriages up ahead and any number that had already turned off. Antoine balled his fist and stuck it to his breast bone, rubbing and rubbing. The pain in his chest had returned with a vengeance. One of the chairs stopped and a finely dressed woman stepped out. Not her. Very well, there were two more chairs up ahead. Ignoring the nagging pain, he picked up the pace and caught the trailing chair at the next crossroad. He touched the rear chairman's shoulder briefly. The man flashed a look behind, and stumbled, almost dropping his burden. Somehow he managed to stagger on with little change to his pace. The occupant though, was jostled from side to side and gave out a great shout.

Not the lady in question. Another struck off the list.

Mademoiselle Du Parc must be in the remaining chair, unless… no, she had to be, but even as Antoine made a beeline for his quarry, it was joined by two other chairs from adjoining streets. He mustn't lose his quarry. As long as it stayed this course it might end up crossing the river and that would put paid to this ridiculous jaunt because he would not step foot on a bridge. Not for anything. With his eyes fixed steadfastly on the chair in question he prayed it would come to a halt sooner rather than later.

They passed a house where for no more than a few sous Antoine could have bought himself an afternoon's pleasure with a woman of ill repute (not a thought did he give to this; they were malodorous creatures and you never knew what disease you might catch from them), side-stepped a hay cart and narrowly avoided being mown down by a platoon of marching militia. Out of breath, the pain in his chest leaching now into his stomach, he wondered if he should just give up and go home. What was he doing for God's sake? He didn't know this woman. All she'd done was upset his pastries. So she was pregnant. So were a thousand other women. Babies died every day. What was one more death? Why should he care? He had other things to worry about.

They passed the boucherie, where the air wafted rank, and the fleuriste, where the scent of the blooms offered his nose respite. He couldn't very well creep back, tail between his legs and act as if nothing had happened. At least, not in front of the guests. He'd have to wait until everyone was drunk and well past caring.

On and on the chair-men walked, with Antoine following after; wishing, hoping, praying that it contained Mademoiselle Du Parc because if it didn't… if it didn't then truly he was a fool.

And there it was: the blessed river with its cursed bridge. The bridge was the thing. If they crossed it then the game was up. Antoine's heart leapt over and over, the irksome pain grabbing at him with every breath.

Turn back. Turn back.

No good will come of it. No good.

He teetered on the brink. There seemed no point in continuing; not now they were at the river, but look, Catherine is an Angel-Maker and has sent this woman to who knows where? Someone called La Lepère, and what would she do, exactly, to procure the solution to

Mademoiselle's ills? It would be painful. Catherine had said so herself. Painful. Bloody. No, no. Could he let even one solitary woman go through such misery? Well, could he? And there would be others. Ah yes, an inevitability, given Catherine's line of business, but if he could raise the capital... sell the house... no, not sell the house... no matter which, if he could open the shop and prove he was a worthy husband, then...

A man came at Antoine from the direction of the bridge stopping his thoughts dead. Dressed in russet, this man had a button nose and pin-prick eyes set in a pinched face. He wore a large-brimmed hat, and carried no sword, but just a simple swagger stick and a sheaf of number-scrawled paper.

...then Catherine might stop all this nonsense. She might even fall in love with him again. Had she ever loved him? The thought hung in the air as the button-nosed man closed on him. Oh, but of course, the Pont au Change was occupied by moneylenders.

"Monsieur?"

The man stopped in his tracks.

"Can I help you?"

"I..."

"Yes?"

"You have premises on the bridge?" The sedan chair was getting away. He mustn't lose it. He mustn't. He'd never tell it apart from all the others.

"I do. Monsieur Tournier at your service." The man bent in, as if to share a secret. "Financier to His Majesty."

It seemed like the grandest of lies. Antoine remembered his own: 'marchand-mercier to His Majesty, the Sun King'. It was a common ploy. He snatched a look down the street. Soon, the chair would disappear completely.

Monsieur Tournier sighed. "I can tell, you are not a man who is impressed by credentials. No, no, not credentials." He shrugged. "Ask anyone on the bridge. They will tell you where to find me." He doffed his hat and walked away, leaving Antoine to stare after him.

The bridge. Mon Dieu, the bridge... and now the sedan had gone. Completely. Gone. Go home. Not yet. Not yet. Antoine ran towards the Hôtel de Ville, dodging this way and that. There were too many people. He tripped on a cobblestone, slipped in something unpleasant, and came face-to-face with a sour old woman. He tried to sidestep her. She matched his dance. Eventually he pushed her aside, gently mind, gently, and ran as fast as he could, catching up with the sedan chair at the next corner. Well, he thought it the same chair. It was hard to tell, and where on earth were they going? The giant fortress of the Bastille loomed up ahead. The chair-men carried their burden through the new archway, past saplings planted to replace the city wall, and out along the road which was crowded with the premises of cabinet makers, carvers, gilders and polishers surrounding the Royal Mirror factory.

Someway along the road, the chair came to a halt. Antoine, exhausted from the chase, hung back in a doorway. Perhaps he'd followed the wrong one. How foolish he felt. How stupid, but no, Mademoiselle Du Parc struggled out and glanced round nervously. Antoine screwed up his eyes to get a better look. She approached one of the houses on the northern side of the road and knocked on the door. Damn it, but he couldn't see who opened up to her. Madame disappeared inside and the door closed. Antoine peered hard at it. He should have taken the opportunity right there and then to stop her. He should have run across the road and… He was about to step out of his hiding place when a small wooden window opened in the door behind him. The noise made him jump. A face appeared with broken teeth and wrinkled skin.

"We've no money for beggars. There's soup on Thursdays."

"I didn't knock. I was…" Nuns made him feel uncomfortable.

"Well someone did."

"Not me."

"But you want something." The nun's eyes narrowed. Antoine felt like a naughty child.

"Information?"

A curse-filled nun used to walk past his father's shop on the bridge every day, terrifying him with her threats of hellfire and brimstone.

"What sort of information?"

Antoine didn't reply. His father had called the nun Mother Trout because she smelled like a fish.

The nun sighed. "Go to the Church at the end there." A hand came out of the small window and pointed.

"I don't need a Priest."

"That's alright then because there isn't one."

"Do you know the woman who lives over the road?"

The nun craned her neck to see, grunted and slid the window shut. The bolts were thrown, the door creaked open and the tiny little nun kicked aside the footstool she'd been standing on.

"What business do you have with her?" She came up to Antoine's chest. He looked down at her, wondering why he'd been so afraid. She was nothing but a crooked old lady.

"Is she called La Lepère?"

"You stay away from her. You hear me? She's an evil woman. Evil."

"Yes, only is she…?" Antoine didn't know how best to say it.

"What? Doing God's work?" The nun folded her arms and tapped her foot. "Is that what you want to know?"

"Erm… I suppose."

"God had nothing to do with what she does. Has that answered your question?" She arched an eyebrow; a curious curl of sarcasm.

"Not really."

The nun huffed. Antoine twitched.

The nun bent in closer. "What is it you want then?"

"It? What…? How…?" He threw a glance at La Lepère's door.

"You don't know?"

"Not really." He'd heard rumours. Imagined the worst, but the actual means by which… He shuddered.

"Monsieur, the woman you seek is a midwife, and that's putting it politely."

"A midwife?" A mediator between the unborn and the living. "She delivers babies?"

"If you can call it that. An abomination. That's what it is. Every babe, knitted in its mother's womb. Where is the compassion in killing it? If your wife has gone through that door, then you best get after her, and be quick about it."

"Not my wife no, but…"

The nun narrowed her eyes. "Your daughter? Mistress? Ah, it doesn't matter. The Lord does not look kindly on those who take a life as she does. Have you forgotten the Ten Commandments? Thou shalt not kill." With that, the nun went inside and closed the door.

She was right; children were a blessing, and the sin of murder the first commandment. Antoine eyed La Lepère's house and took a few steps across the road. As he did so a young woman rushed out. He stopped in his tracks. Well, *she* wasn't Mademoiselle Du Parc. The woman hugged her shawl tight and hurried past. Antoine noticed the fine silk of her petticoats and imagined it on a bolt on a shelf in his shop. The finest sea silk; a rare commodity from the distant shores of Sardinia.

"Excuse me," he called out. "Mademoiselle? Excuse me. Mademoiselle! I mean you no harm."

The young woman stopped mid-street, tears streaming down her face.

"Here now, let's find somewhere for you to sit down."

"No. I can't," she said and started walking.

"At least…" Yes, yes, he understood. He was a stranger. She was scared. "I mean you no harm. It's just… you look so distressed. At least rest a while until you are recovered." He indicated a nearby tavern.

"No, thank you." She started down the road, but then obviously thought better of it because changed direction and walked directly into the tavern.

Antoine ordered a jug of wine and two glasses. Positioning himself across the table from the poor women, he watched her with some trepidation. He didn't want her to think he had malign designs on her. For the longest time, he remained silent. She seemed about the same age as his Marguerite. She had dark, well-dressed hair and her hands were white and soft. Her clothing was finely embroidered, but the bodice was incorrectly pinned, as if she had dressed in some haste. A fine lace-fringed chemise peeped forth at her décolletage. She bit her lip and raised her eyes. Antoine softened his gaze.

"Reckon you've had a bit of bother. They won't mind if you stay here until you feel better. I'll be on my way in a bit. I won't bother you."

"I have to get home." Her voice was weak. She tried to stand up. Antoine noticed blood on her petticoat. His eyes travelled back to her face.

"Are you hurt?"

Her bottom lip trembled.

"It's nothing."

"The midwife?"

The young woman nodded.

"Did you leave the baby with her?" He was too abrupt. He should he have asked something less intrusive.

"Not exactly." She dipped her head in shame.

Antoine dared to take one of her hands in his own. She didn't pull away. Part of him didn't want the gory details and part of him did.

"I need to ask you something. Was there someone else there? A Mademoiselle Du Parc by any chance?"

The young woman frowned. "Why do you ask?"

"I can't say. It's…" What? Delicate? Difficult? Wrong? "I just need to know."

"There was, but I don't know her name."

"Was she there for the same reason as you?"

The young woman withdrew her hand.

"Why'd you ask? Who are you?"

"I'm on an errand for my wife." A lie. A total lie. Man is ice to truth and fire to falsehood. Antoine bit his tongue.

"Your wife?"

"Madame Montvoisin." He waited for the gasp of fear.

"Your wife is La Voisin? Oh, I must leave now. Thank you for the…" She glanced down at the glass. She hadn't touched a drop of wine. She held pulled her shawl tight and hurried out.

"You're welcome," said Antoine, to the empty space. He sat for a moment, his thoughts all a-tumble. La Lepere had a regular trade in misery. Catherine fed her sad-eyed victims; those she couldn't deal with herself. Whatever that meant. He gulped down his glass of wine, and then the young woman's. Happier now he'd well and truly relinquished his sobriety, he belched loud and long. He had a problem. A big problem. Mention of his wife's name had been enough to strike fear in an innocent girl's heart, and good Lord, but he'd felt a tingle of pride. That wasn't good. That wasn't good at all.

Chapter Fifteen

Mademoiselle Du Parc sat on the edge of her seat in La Lepère's consulting chamber and worried about whether she'd made the right decision in asking for help. Her hand rested on her belly, her brow damp. She'd been with child for four months. She would have done something sooner, only her days were filled with rehearsals and performances. The writer, Jean Racine, had created a wonderful new play and had promised her even greater fame and fortune than she'd had with Molière. Rehearsals had gone well and the play had received astoundingly good reviews. Mademoiselle had revelled in the glory and Racine had taken her to his bed, the result of which now grew in her belly.

She wiped her brow with the end of her sleeve. Goodness, but she felt hot. Where was that old woman? As if on cue, La Lepère nudged the door open. She carried a bowl of scalding hot water. The skin on her face was almost translucent. Her hair was as white as snow, her eyes as pale as those of the blind. She set the bowl down on a table and disappeared into the adjoining room. When she returned she carried a large metal syringe with a long thin tube and a knob at the end.

"Now my dear, I'm going to need you to come rest on this cot a while."

Mademoiselle Du Parc took a step back. A year ago she'd taken the herb savin, given to her by La Voisin to resolve a similar situation. She'd suffered excruciating pain and produced a lump of flesh that bore no resemblance to a baby. Now however, the situation was wholly different; she'd delayed; this baby would be larger, perhaps even fully formed. Savin was not a good enough purgative. La Voisin had sent her to La Lepère with a promise that all would be well. She hoped beyond hope that that was the case because if not she feared her life on the stage would be over.

"It's quite natural to be afraid, but really, there's nothing to it," said La Lepère. She took the long tube off the end of the syringe and drew hot water from the bowl up into the body of the instrument. Mademoiselle Du Parc shot a wild look at the door, then back at the midwife. La Lepère rolled up her sleeves.

"Has the child quickened?"

"Two weeks ago." Mademoiselle Du Parc burst into tears. The baby's movements had been like butterfly wings beating softly against the inside of her belly. At first she'd been afraid; it was like a demon had taken up residence, but, as the days passed, she grew used to the sensation. It was no demon. It was made of her own flesh and blood. She couldn't go through with it. It was a sin. There'd be no place in heaven for her and what would the poor baby's soul do? Unbaptised and carrying the burden of original sin, it would spend an eternity wandering in limbo. How many others occupied the shadowlands between heaven and hell? La Lepère touched her briefly on the arm.

"We can't delay. There are other ways, to be sure, but you wouldn't like them. Long instruments that cut and… no… no… Aren't you the brightest of stars? Don't men fall at your feet? How wonderful. Do you want that to end?"

For all her worry about the baby and the pain, Mademoiselle Du Parc couldn't even begin to think what life would be like without the adulation of the crowd. If she had a child, she wouldn't be able to continue on the stage. No one would give her work. She'd have to fall back on that oldest of professions; whoring.

La Lepère pursed her lips and said, "It'll all be over in an hour and then you can go home and rest."

Mademoiselle sighed. She supposed there'd be other babies.

As if guessing her thoughts, La Lepère said, "Time enough for a family. Come now."

Mademoiselle Du Parc genuflected, muttered a short prayer, and lay down on the cot.

***

Antoine dallied longer than he'd anticipated. The late sun slanted in through the tavern window and warmed him through. His eyelids drooped. It was easy to fall asleep on a bellyful of wine.

He dreamed of a forest and fresh bubbling spring. An old woman sat on the bank weaving a wonderful cloth of many colours, which fell, pleated, into the water and metamorphosed into a hundred or more babies, which splashed and sang as they drifted. Mid-stream another old crone sat on a rock and measured out the lengths of cloth, the babies growing and becoming young men and women. Even as Antoine grunted and snored, wrestling with his visions, a third woman interrupted the cycle created by her sisters, cutting the cloth to suit herself. Both new life and old fell dead and floated away. Antoine shouted "Stop!"

and she looked up from her work. It was Catherine. Catherine was the deadly nightshade come to cut down life.

Footsteps hurried over the cobbles.

Shouts.

Be quiet! Bloody neighbours. The daughter of Nyx aren't done with their work yet.

More footsteps.

Antoine jerked awake. Mademoiselle Du Parc! Damn it. He'd forgotten all about her. He jumped up, caught the table corner with his thigh, yelped with pain, but didn't stop. He was in too much of a panic for that. A sedan passed by, the chairmen at a run. Antoine glimpsed a dimpled cheek, and a woman's gloved hand. He ran after the chair and yanked the rear man to a halt. The sedan hit the ground. A scream from inside. The front man fell over. More screams. Antoine tore the door open. The woman inside howled in his face.

Not her! So… where? A horse and rider galloped past in a cloud of dust. When it settled he made a beeline for La Lepère's house, the bellyful of wine having bestowed on him the courage he normally lacked. The wisdom of a foolish man is often late to the party.

He banged on the door.

No answer.

He peered through the window.

No one at home. At least… He banged on the door again.

"Open up!"

Nothing. He was too late. He glared after the now disappeared sedan chair, then back at the house, and then over the road at the Convent. The old nun stood in the doorway, as before, watching Antoine's antics. He started toward her. She vanished inside. The door slammed, leaving him mid-street.

Very well, if it was going to be like that, then it was time to go home and face the music. If she cut up rough, he might tell her she had to stop this nonsense. It all depended on whether he could hang on to his new-found courage. He had a habit of losing his nerve at the most inopportune moment. He hopped from one foot to the other, wondering if and why and when. Eventually, he set off home.

By the time he reached the Rue de Beauregard it was alive with the sound of raucous partying, though it was well past twilight and the air abuzz with all manner of flying insects. Wincing at the noise of the party, he entered his garden and squeezed between a woman wearing a mask and a man with an especially fat belly. Tall tapered candles lent a festive air and exuded a waxy smell not dissimilar to that of the church next door.

Too many people trampling the grass.

Silk shoed clodhoppers.

Noisome infiltrators.

A howl of laughter went up. A servant wove through the crowd with an obligatory tray of sweetmeats. Antoine grabbed a handful. He seized a glass of wine from a drunk leaning against the apple tree.

And Catherine? He scanned the swarm, but couldn't see her. How many women had ripe bellies? How many had consulted his darling wife? Not this one, surely; the one coming towards him as if he was the most handsome man in the garden and she the most desirous lady. She too wore a mask. The ladies of quality were ever anxious to remain anonymous. Certainly, she was by far the most splendidly attired guest. Antoine judged her dress to be of Pernon silk, woven in Lyon, though doubtless cut and sewn by the best Parisian dressmaker. Perhaps one who even worked for the King.

"You are *the* husband?" the woman enquired, with a raised voice.

The husband? Antoine dipped his head, cautiously. "Madame, you have me at a disadvantage." She smiled with her lips but not her eyes, just like Catherine. No love in this one, he thought. The music swelled. Oh, but how could anyone hear anything? The louder the music, the more the guests shouted. The more the guests shouted, the louder and faster the musicians played.

"Where is she?" the woman shouted.

"Who?" Antoine bellowed back.

"Your wife, of course. La Voison."

"I..." he cast about. "I don't know. Perhaps *I* can help you?" My, but an afternoon of wine had done him the world of good, despite the trouble over Mademoiselle Du Parc. He brushed the woman's petticoat with the back of his rough hand. He missed the feel of fabric against his skin. He'd fill his new shop with the finest silks, the best lace, the most sumptuous velvets, and everyone would flock to his door. He would take something from this gathering, if only potential customers. The woman looked Antoine up and down until he was overcome with embarrassment.

"Forgive me. Where did you obtain the fabric for your..." He stopped mid-sentence. The woman gazed over his head, obviously bored with the conversation.

"I can go and look for her, if you like," Antoine ventured. "Who shall I say?"

"What did you say?" The woman leaned towards him, ear cocked, but eyes elsewhere.

"Who. Shall. I. Say. Wants. Her?" He enunciated each word carefully, his voice rising over the music.

The woman gave Antoine a pointed look. "Tell no one but La Voisin. Promise me that."

Antoine nodded.

She mouthed, "The Countess of Soissons."

Antoine stifled a gasp and bowed. She had the tiniest silk-shoed feet. The Countess had been the King's mistress. It was years ago now. Years and years. What was she doing here? He backed off, still at a bow. The Countess of Soissons. Her uncle was Cardinal Mazarin, the King's Chief Minister. He bumped the kitchen door and straightened up. Marguerite came out with a plate of cold meat.

"Papa, where have you been?"

"Around. You see that woman over there?" He couldn't take his eyes off the Countess.

"Which one?" Marguerite followed his gaze.

"That one, in the Pernon silk." Antoine pointed.

"Her?"

"She's the Countess of Soissons."

"I know."

"You do? How? Has she been here before?"

"Not recently, but when I was little she would come to consult Maman. You've met her before. You must have. Have you been drinking again?"

"Me? No. What for?"

"What d'you mean what for?"

"What did she consult your mother for?"

"Ah… don't know."

"Oh, confound it child, of course you know. You and your mother are as thick as thieves."

"They do say her father was a renowned necromancer."

Antoine arched an eyebrow. "Do they now?"

"Why d'you want to know?"

"She wants to speak to your mother."

"So does everyone." Marguerite vanished back inside the kitchen.

What was it with these women? Antoine stared at the Countess. She gave a little wave. He returned it with a brief waggle of his fingers. He should question her on the morality of burying unborn babies beneath the now well-trodden grass. She might know something about killing unwanted husbands too. He smiled, aware of his insincerity; no crinkling of his eyes; no soft gaze or kindness… and made his way back to her.

"Madame." He knew very well how to charm women. It had just been a long time since he'd had to do it. "Madame, I must apologise for deserting you. Unfortunately, my wife is detained elsewhere. May I ask what it is you wish to consult her about?"

The Countess looked decidedly uncomfortable. She fluttered her fan and looked around. No one paid her any mind or rushed to her side.

"Not here." She didn't seem as sure of herself as she had at first. "Is there somewhere we may speak without this noise?"

Antoine thought about it. There was his potting shed, behind the sun house, at the far end of the garden, but he couldn't ask a Countess to huddle in a potting shed.

"Not really." He didn't want to take her inside. He didn't want to get caught in private with the King's former mistress. Particularly, not a beautiful one dressed in Pernon silk.

"Then at least let us…" She beckoned Antoine follow her to the wall, where church met garden. Intrigued, he fell in with her. It may not be 'the day', as the grandfather had put it, but it certainly was a day to remember.

"I don't know where to start," the Countess said.

"At the beginning?"

"There's no time for that."

"Then start where you may, my lady." She smelt of lemons. The evening was still young. She may yet offer that elusive smile; the one that said she knew love. The Countess touched his arm. He looked down at her delicate, gloved hand.

"His Majesty has taken another mistress."

This wasn't a surprise. The King had a lot of mistresses. The King wanted to have his butter and eat it. Not to mention a kiss from the milkmaid. The King liked butter… and probably milkmaids too.

"Louise de la Valliere is finished. That fat thing has taken her place."

"Fat thing?" He thought briefly about Catherine. Fat as fat could be and still lovely, but yes, evil. Then again, he thought, evil is as evil does. He wrestled his attention back to the Countess.

She spat out the words, "Yes fat. Madame De Montespan. Of course His Majesty will not simply get rid of La Valliere. He will keep her close, but it is *Madame* who occupies his attention."

"Ah, and you wish for…?" Here was the nub of it; the crux; the very essence of the matter. For one moment he thought she might say 'the King's death', in which case he would have to report her to the authorities. He wasn't sure which authorities. The gendarmerie? The musketeers? One or the other.

The Countess continued. "Reconciliation that's what I want. I wish for reconciliation with the King. It's time, don't you think?" She cocked her head, stretched out a hand and admired the huge diamond ring on her middle finger. Antoine followed her gaze. It was quite plain, she didn't love the King. She coveted shiny things and acted out of jealousy.

"And how does my wife figure in this reconciliation?"

"She must provide me with a potion. She knows which one."

"A potion?"

The Countess lowered her head and spoke in a conspiratorial whisper. "I need to get rid of La Valliere *and* De Montespan, and I don't mean exiled or put aside. I want them..." She mouthed the word 'dead'.

The Countess looked down her nose at him and, for a moment, Antoine didn't know what to say or where to put himself.

"Well? Will La Voisin oblige?"

"I don't know." But he knew she would. Hers was the business of death, from birth to old age. Nay, from before birth. Not for Catherine the sweetness of a life lived peacefully. No, she must dwell on the ways and means to expunge life.

"I pay well. She knows that. We have an old arrangement."

"An old arrangement? How much?" Instantly, he clapped his hand over his mouth. It was tantamount to an admission of guilt. She would think he was in collusion with his wife, and he wasn't. Not at all.

"I can't help you. My wife can't help you."

The Countess snarled, "Well, I hadn't expected... Where is she? Bring her to me."

Antoine retreated from her at speed. Neither her flawless beauty, nor her fine gown, dripping with jewels, could mask her evil intentions. Pernon silk or no Pernon silk.

"Come back here," shouted the Countess. She waved her fan like a sword.

Antoine hurried through the crowds until the Countess had become naught but a poorly glimpsed patch of brilliance by the wall. He found a bottle of wine and took himself to the far end of his garden, where the pungent compost heap kept the guests at bay and where he could lose himself and his thoughts more easily.

"Mankind once lived its life free from women," his father had once said to him. Antoine had been about five years-old and still bound to his mother's skirts, though increasingly eager to explore.

"Why?" Most of Antoine's questions were prefaced by 'why'.

"Because Prometheus only had enough clay for men, not women. The age of gold, it was. Gold. Imagine. Then again, some say God created Adam from dust, and there's always a lot of dust. Either way, women had nothing to do with it."

"Why?"

"They came later."

"Why?"

"It depends on which story you tell. The church says…
well now the church has the last word. You understand?
Don't go repeating my stories to the priest." Antoine's
father had pointed at him with his shears.

"Papa? Can I cut?"

"Cut what? This velvet?" Montvoisin senior stroked
the fabric he'd just rolled out. "No. It's too dangerous."

"Why?

"Because we don't want you to go hurting yourself do
we? Maman would get angry."

Maman was always angry. Just like Catherine.

Time looped round on itself. His father would have
said "It's the worm." Antoine would have said, "Why?"

***

Gradually, the partygoers dispersed and the candles
spluttered out. The garden looked like a battlefield: half-
eaten food mashed into the grass, upturned chairs in the
borders, flattened lavender, broken glasses and smashed
crockery, not to mention a trail of wine-sodden sheet
music leading from parterre to roses, under which lay a
sozzled violinist.

Antoine righted a chair on the path and sat on it,
staring out into the starry night sky. This much he knew:
Catherine had tried to kill him and like as not would try
again. She sent her clients to a midwife who did a roaring
trade in murder. The Countess of Soissons wanted to kill
the King's mistresses, both old and new. The grandfather
called Catherine an Angel-Maker and all knew her as La
Voisin: the neighbour.

Brilliant. Which was it? Angel-maker or neighbour?

"Papa? Are you staying out there all night?" Marguerite shouted from her bedchamber window.

"I'm coming."

He twisted on his seat and the stars fled. Marguerite had closed the window. Somehow he had to stop Catherine from killing more infants and unwanted husbands. Not only must he deter her from her evil ways, he must also find a way to regain her respect and love. Yes, that was it: love. The smile was what he wanted.

He went in, closed and shuttered the windows on the ground floor and made his weary way upstairs. There'd be time enough in the morning to clear up. A grey line in the dark told him Catherine's chamber door stood slightly ajar. He nudged it fully open, expecting to find her abed. Moonlight silvered the counterpane, but the bed was empty.

An empty bed.

An empty heart.

He turned away and almost jumped right out of his skin. Catherine stood directly behind him, holding a lit candle, the flame flickering this way and that.

"Damn it woman!" he shouted. "Don't do that."

"It's an emergency. I need your help."

Since when had she ever needed his help? She ordered him around, but she never asked for his 'help'. It was a trick. It had to be.

"What kind of an emergency?"

Catherine set the candle down and turned a sconce affixed to the wall.

"What emergency?"

The wall opened up and Catherine vanished into the dark beyond.

Antoine's jaw dropped. A hidden chamber? Here, in his own house? It wasn't possible. He'd have known about it… but then, he hadn't known about the babies.

Footsteps sounded on the floorboards.

Drawers slid open.

The hinges on a cupboard door squealed.

Incredulous, Antoine popped his head round the new door.

Pitch black. No window.

"What emergency?" he repeated. None of this had been here when he'd bought the house. He'd gone over it carefully, chamber by chamber. He stepped back to look up at the wall, trying to figure out when it must have been erected. Catherine reappeared carrying a leather bag and her cloak.

"Word came earlier, but I couldn't leave my guests." She handed Antoine the bag. "Hold this."

"What word? What's the emergency?" The wall was one thing, but if she thought he would aid and abet in a murder, she had another think coming. All the same, perhaps her request for help was a good sign. Daring to hope, he searched her face for the tell-tale smile.

Nothing.

Catherine tied the cloak around her shoulders and took the bag back.

"A client's taken ill. Her maid sent for me."

"So why do you need me?"

"Because my client's lover does not want me to attend and it's too late to ask anyone else."

Mystified, Antoine trailed Catherine down the stairs.

"If he doesn't want you then what do you expect me to do?"

"Keep him away from me."

Ah, she wanted his brawn. Nothing more.

"Who else would you have asked? That priest? Lesage? Who?"

Silence.

"Catherine? Stop. I need to talk to you."

"So talk."

"What's going on?" They reached the hallway. The door to the street stood ajar.

"You have your secrets. I have mine."

"Me? Secrets? What secrets have I got?"

"Hurry up, there's a carriage waiting."

"What secrets?" Antoine repeated, but his question fell on deaf ears.

Outside, Catherine hitched up her skirts and climbed aboard the carriage.

"Come on, come on," she said.

Not going. Not going.

Until the business with the moles he'd been perfectly happy in his ignorance. He didn't want to, but climbed aboard all the same. For certain, this had been *the day*, though he had yet to work out what it all meant. The carriage lurched as the horses set off. They skirted the Court of Miracles, turned left and headed towards the river. It wasn't the same route as earlier, with the sedan chair and Mademoiselle Du Parc; this was the way to Lesage's lair. Antoine hoped they weren't going to stop and pick him up. It would be almost impossible to talk to Catherine properly with him around.

"Stop," he shouted.

Rather than come to a halt, the carriage sped up. They passed Lesage's at breakneck speed and Antoine's momentary crisis passed. He sank back and sneaked another look at Catherine. Her profile soaked up the night. The carriage turned west at the river and rolled through the slumbering neighbourhood, a turn here, a turn there, until it reached the Pont Neuf. Why did Paris have so many bridges?

"Stop. You have to stop. I can't cross the bridge."

The carriage jolted, the horses slowing slightly.

Catherine shouted, "Continue, and hurry."

The reins cracked. The horses picked up again, throwing Antoine back into his seat. He was going to die. If not by poison, then certainly by fright.

"What's the matter with you?" said Catherine.

"You know I can't cross it." Antoine buried his head in his sleeve. He hadn't stepped foot on a bridge since his shop had been swept away. He wasn't going to start now. Bridges were wholly unreliable things. The carriage rattled over the first stone span, the horses' hooves echoing, 'his mother, his mother, his mother' with every turn of the axle.

"There are no houses on this bridge; no shops. Nothing to disappear in a deluge. It's stone. Solid as the day it was built."

Antoine heard the derision in her voice. "It's still a bridge." A bridge. A bloody great bridge, twice the length of the Pont Marie. Bridges were the work of the devil. He peeped out from behind his sleeve. Were they there yet? How much longer?

The carriage carried on rolling and Antoine carried on being anxious until they were off the other side and skirting the river bank. A couple more turns and they entered a narrow thoroughfare and came to a halt.

He'd survived! The trouble was, they were the other side of the river now with no way home, save by going back across the bridge, unless he could find a ferryman. Yes, that's what he'd do. Not that boats were much safer than bridges, and not at this time of night anyway. Damn it, but he'd have to wait until the morning. Well, he could do that. No need to hurry. He'd have a drink. Yes, that's what he'd do.

"Where are we?"

"Pres aux Clerc. Follow me." Catherine caught her heel in her petticoat. Antoine waited for her to free it, before climbing down after her. She approached a recessed door in a black wall and knocked three times. The door opened. A diminutive woman gasped out the words, "Madame. Thank God you're here."

"Where is she, Manon?"

The musty air inside offered only dismay. A dark passage with barely enough room for one person to pass along, led into the blackness beyond.

"Upstairs, but… he doesn't want you here."

Manon motioned into the dark.

"We'll see about that." Catherine scurried along the passage. Antoine paused for a moment, unsure. Faint sobs came from aloft.

"Come on," growled Catherine.

Antoine felt his way down the passage, at the end of which lay a flight of stairs.

At the top, a portly young man paced a dimly lit chamber, containing a large curtained bed. When he saw Catherine he rushed at her. It all happened so quickly. One minute Catherine was entering the chamber and the next, she was falling back into Antoine's arms.

"I've got you," he shouted, supporting her weight, pushing her upright.

The young man snarled, "You've got no right coming here. None. I told that girl. I told her I didn't want you here."

Antoine stepped in front of Catherine and pinned the young man against the wall.

"It's good to see you too, Monsieur Racine," said Catherine.

"Don't you touch her. Don't you dare."

Catherine tore the drapes around the bed aside.

Racine spat out, "If she dies... if she dies it will be your fault. Your fault, you hear?"

"If who dies? Who is it?" said Antoine. He strained to look over his shoulder. Mademoiselle Du Parc! Her eyes were mere slits, her lip dry. A tear, rolling down her snowy cheek, was the only clue she was still alive.

"It's all my fault," moaned Antoine. "I could have stopped her."

"Poisoned." Racine's distress was like a living entity; a strange weeping creature come up from the depths. "I forbid you to touch her. I forbid it. Leave us."

Catherine ignored him and held the candle over Mademoiselle's face. Antoine noticed crimson stains on her chemise and on the sheet. Horrified, he loosened his grasp. Racine lunged forward, knocking first Antoine, and then Catherine away. For a moment Antoine did nothing, so transfixed was he by Mademoiselle Du Parc's bloody state. He could have stopped her. He could have, only he'd been in the tavern, drinking.

Racine bent low over the Mademoiselle, cradled her in his arms, pulling her across the bed, away from Catherine.

"Nothing can save her. Nothing," he moaned. "Leave us be."

Antoine stood, helpless at the sight of true love made desperate by loss.

"She's slipping away. I must have something here. Something." Catherine searched through her bag, bringing out one phial after another. Racine snarled at her like a rabid dog.

Antoine muttered, "I followed her. I saw where she went and now her baby's dead."

Racine, horror-struck, said, "What d'you mean? Baby? What baby?"

"Good God man, you weren't going marry her," snapped Catherine. "She did the only thing a woman can do in those circumstances."

Racine crumpled. "But I love her, and you've taken her away from me."

"You love that she made you money. What choice did she have? What choice do any of us have? You think it easy for a woman to keep a bastard child? How would she have paid her way in the world? Set her up in a house? You can barely keep this one." Catherine snatched up her bag.

A silence fell on the room, punctuated only by the rattle of Mademoiselle Du Parc's breathing. After a while, even that fell silent.

Catherine announced, "Well she's dead now. I'll send Romani with my bill. Make sure you pay it." With that, she went back downstairs.

After a while Antoine said, "Shall I call the maid up?"

"A baby? Why didn't she tell me? A baby. She is wrong. I would have taken care of it… of her. Why didn't she tell me?"

Antoine didn't know what to say, other than, "I'll call the maid. Yes. That's what I'll do."

"She should have told me."

Antoine called down the stairs, "Mademoiselle? Can you come up?"

"Madame is waiting in the carriage," said Manon, hurrying on the stairs.

"Yes. Yes. Please. Monsieur Racine needs your help." Antoine waved her by. Then, with a soft glance back at the dead woman, he went down to join his wife.

Night had fled, towing dawn in its wake. Both Antoine and Catherine sat blank-eyed and mute as the carriage jolted along.

Jolt upon jolt.

The squeak of a wheel, and the faint smell of smoke. A peal of birdsong and the lapping of the river against the bank. The bridge. Antoine screwed up his courage. Hadn't he just watched a woman die? And what of that final bridge, from life to death? Bridges were nothing compared to a lost love. The Pont Neuf came and went. Antoine dared to peep at his wife. The sun stretched early fingers of light through the carriage window to stroke the tears held captive in Catherine's eyelashes. She sighed, long and deep; a stone heart softening.

"If anyone asks, we were never there."

"But…"

"We were never there. Do you understand? The last time I saw Mademoiselle Du Parc was in the afternoon at the party. She seemed to be in fine health. We did not attend her later."

"But I followed her to that woman. The woman you sent her to."

"No, you didn't. You were at the party all afternoon."

"But she got rid of her baby and she died."

Catherine brushed away tears. "She was unlucky. La Lepère is old and grown careless. Monsieur Racine was right; it was my fault. I should have known better. I should have done it myself."

"Yourself?"

"I'm not good with my hands. I prefer… Potions."

It was so hard to tell what was on her mind.

"And our garden? Why bury the babies there of all places? You must have known I'd come across them sooner or later."

Catherine shrugged. "La Lepère usually handles the disposal, but sometimes the unfortunate woman wants to hold her child and give it a proper burial. It can't be buried in sanctified ground. Not when it's never been baptised. So, they come to me." Catherine drew herself up. "You say 'sooner or later' but twenty years we've been man and wife and in all that time, you've never once asked me about any of this. How so?"

Antoine stared into her darkest of dark brown eyes and wondered about that mystery. It was like plumbing the depths of a well on a moonless night… and not a sign of a smile on Catherine's lips, nor in her eyes.

"I woke up and there you were, burying a baby. I thought of Balthazar and wondered if…"

"How could you? You think I would do that to my own child?"

"But how can you do it to any child?"

"Needs must, is all."

"Needs must. Men are meant to be strong and take it all without emotion. I can't do that anymore. You've broken my heart."

"Huh. Broken your heart. You aren't easy to live with. You know that?"

"You aren't either."

Catherine stared through the window. Antoine watched the back of her head.

"God wouldn't sanction such a thing," he said.

"You don't believe in God," replied Catherine to the passing city.

"Of course I do. Everyone believes in God. What does the Priest say about it?"

"Abbé Davot? He's got nothing to complain about."

They sat in silence, Antoine's mind a whirl of heightened emotion and bitter recriminations. She'd been horrified that he might think she'd killed their own sweet baby, but still she'd found a way to minimise what she'd done for other women. After a while the words tumbled out. "I will open a shop you know. It's just a matter of time."

"And money."

"Yes, and money."

"I won't give it to you."

"I never asked you to. Why are you trying to kill me?"

"I'm not."

"Yes you are."

Catherine sighed. "Everyone dies, eventually."

"Why don't you love me anymore?"

"I never loved you."

The knife twisted deep. Antoine bit back a cry. It couldn't be true. She must have loved him once.

"Why did you marry me then? For money?"

Catherine turned her cold eyes on him. "For money, yes. Your father made a reckoning with my mother."

"I don't believe you."

"Fool. Hardly anyone marries for love. Particularly women. Most are betrothed by their parents to men who hold no fascination for them whatsoever."

"What was this reckoning?"

"Your father wanted to live forever." A wry smile lit Catherine's face.

"What?" The idea of it. Preposterous.

"My mother promised him eternity and he believed her."

"No. Not possible. Not my father, and definitely not your mother. She's not capable of anything."

"Maybe not now, but once upon a time, Maman held your father's soul captive."

"But he died."

"Of course he did. I saw to that."

She killed his father? He had no words. Nothing. He just sat there, his mouth open, the knife twisting deeper and deeper still.

Catherine sighed long and loud. "I will spare your life, as long as you don't sell the house."

As long as he didn't sell the house. That was the end to it then. He would stop all this nonsense about a shop. He would stop and she wouldn't kill him. They had a deal.

Chapter Sixteen

The roses shed their petals and the lavender turned a soft grey. Dry patches stained the grass. The apples fell and the hyssop grew leggy. Soon, autumn browned the leaves and winter froze the dew. The uncollected apples mouldered, growing ever more soft and brown. Catherine made no further attempts on Antoine's life, and he stopped worrying about it, but the idea of the shop nagged away at him. One frosty morning he donned a velvet doublet and bashed out the crown of his favourite old hat. He'd made up his mind; he'd open his shop and Catherine would smile.

Sandwiched between an establishment selling the finest escargot and another promising the best ale in all Paris, the building housing the offices of the corporation of marchand-merciers on the Rue du Petit-Lion, was double-fronted, with a large oak door and somewhat sagging window frames. He entered the waxy, wood-panelled front room, cautiously, feeling like an intruder.

"Hello?" No one answered.

A closed door to the left. A staircase dead centre. A further door to the right, and a narrow corridor leading to who knew where? He knocked the left-hand door and tried the handle: locked. He put a foot on the bottom tread, but thought better of it. He didn't want to be caught wandering. He knocked on the door to the right and received a 'come' by way of reply. He took it as a sign his mission would succeed.

"Monsieur?"

Antoine removed his hat and clutched it with both hands like a small boy come to apologise. The hat had a thin place on the brim where the felt had been rubbed almost through. Antoine tried to force a hole in it with his thumb. The last time he'd visited the corporation, he'd hidden behind his father. He'd been naught but a gangly apprentice then, with a shock of dark hair and bitten fingernails.

Monsieur Bertrand Faverolle glanced up. His spectacles fell off the end of his nose. He had been pouring over a ledger, though the quill, clutched in his right hand, was quite dry of ink. Faverolle's white lace cuffs, Antoine noted, were so full of flounces as to impede the man's ability to write anything much.

"Monsieur? I've come to enquire about my reinstatement."

"Reinstatement? To what?" Monsieur Faverolle rotated the quill between finger and thumb, his face devoid of expression.

"Ah, I should introduce myself." Antoine gave a little bow. "My name is Antoine Montvoisin and I had a shop on the Pont Marie. I inherited it from my father. I am a master, registered with the corporation. My name is in the book."

Monsieur Faverolle put down his quill and licked the index finger of his right hand, before flicking through the ledger until he reached the page he was looking for.

"I see no Montvoisin on the Pont Marie. Montvoisin? Are you sure?"

Antoine fidgeted. "I know my own name sir." He almost blurted out that his wife was La Voisin, "It was some time ago. Before the flood."

"So, six years? More?"

"I was apprenticed twenty-two years ago now."

"And you are a master?"

"Yes. I want to open another shop."

Monsieur Faverolle sighed. "You aren't in business at the moment?"

"Unfortunately not."

"Do you have your papers?"

"Papers?"

"Your indenture? Your release?"

"No. I lost everything in the flood."

Monsieur Faverolle closed his ledger, dust escaped from between the pages like myriad souls giving up unto the heavens.

"Then there is nothing I can do. I might find you in our records, but unless you can prove you are who you say you are…" He shrugged again.

"What if I can get someone to vouch for me?"

"Yes, that's possible. If this person is known to us. Another marchand-mercier. That would be best."

"I can do that." But who could he ask? Monsieur Valmont? He was probably dead. Monsieur Carrier? He'd always hated him. Said he was nothing more than an insect. Monsieur Michel then, on the Rue Saint-Honoré? An illustrious address and high-level clientele. Monsieur had been a friend of his father, though Antoine had not seen him for many years. It was worth a try, though he too may have passed on.

"I have someone in mind. Monsieur Michel? Would a word from him suffice?"

Monsieur Faverolle arched his eyebrows in surprise.

"If you think Monsieur Michel will come here for any other reason than because he had been accorded some great accolade, you are much mistaken. They do say he has the ear of the King. There is much to do in that new palace at Versailles." Monsieur Faverolle shook his head. "No, I doubt Monsieur Michel will vouch for anyone." He waved his hand dismissively.

Antoine felt miffed. "We'll see about that."

There was always something to test him. He stuck his hat back on his head and left Monsieur Faverolle to his dry quill.

Chapter Seventeen

Even in the hottest weather, it felt cold inside the barrel-arched halls and long stone passages of the Monastery of the Grand Augustins. The monks might be long gone, and the empty cells turned over to the newly formed Gendarmerie, but there were still some who said the clerics' supernatural presence could be felt by those of a sensitive disposition. Sergeant François Desgrez paced outside the closed door of his superior's office, clearing his throat and sending up echoes. He didn't like the old Monastery. He felt watched. He'd far rather be out in the city air, for all its foul miasma.

Footsteps. The door opened and an apple-cheeked clerk peered out.

"The Lieutenant General will see you now."

Desgrez swept through the door, his cloak all a-flutter from the zephyrs within. He'd make his report and get out; he'd not stay a moment longer than need be. In that instant he was reminded of his father lying in wait for him to return from his studies, the lash in hand ready to administer correction. An uncomfortable memory if ever there was one. Desgrez shuddered. Some attempt had been made to make the forbidding cell he now stood in more comfortable: an old tapestry on one wall, leather-bound books on the vault-high shelves, a couple of chairs in front of a huge blazing hearth, and a sturdy oak table behind which Lieutenant General De La Reynie sat, sifting through a pile of papers. Desgrez doffed his hat and waited in silence. De La Reynie looked up. He was a steady man; someone you could depend on. At least, that was the impression the Sergeant had got when first they'd met some two years earlier.

"You brought me the report?"

Desgrez winced. He wasn't sure how to discuss the King's amorous escapades without it seeming like the rantings of a gossip. He pulled a roll of paper from his satchel.

"Well? What does it say?"

"Madame de Montespan visited with a certain Dubuisson, sometimes called Adam Coureret, but more frequently known as..."

"Yes, yes, what's his damned name?"

"Lesage."

"And?"

"Our informer claims the Abbe Mariotte was paid by Lesage to officiate at a black mass, and that the lady in question asked that the King's mistress, Madame De Valliere, be..." Desgrez searched for the right words. "...be put aside. Apparently, Lesage in exchange for his freedom. Says Lesage has a den down by the tanneries where he dabbles in alchemy. The two of them have been at it for some time."

"And this is... this is this man with three names? Lesage? What have you done about him?"

"Nothing yet."

"Then do so. Arrest him and force him to tell all."

Desgrez frowned. "It's a delicate situation sir. Do we really want to investigate Madame De Montespan? Won't it incur the King's wrath?"

"Very possibly. Then we must tread carefully Sergeant. Very carefully. You have your orders. This three-named crook. Arrest him. Press him for details."

"And the priest?"

"Him too."

"Yes sir." Desgrez took himself from the chamber, glad to be free from the mysterious spirits and chilly emanations.

***

Lesage had his nose buried deep in a grimoire when the gendarmes burst through his scuffed, pentacle-scrawled blue door and into his laboratory.

"Mon Dieu! What...You have no right. Get out of here."

The gendarmes swept aside the ambit, cucurbit and retort, upturned the buckets of entrails and knocked the dog's head flying. Lesage reached for his hazel staff, only to have it snatched from his grasp. This was unthinkable! Never in his life had he been so outraged. Who were they? What did they want? Two burly men grabbed him by the arms and forced him down onto the table. He lay there, face pressed sideways into the wood, feeling the grain mark his skin.

"Adam Coureret, you are arrested on a charge of sorcery," said Desgrez.

"You've got the wrong person. My name's not Coureret."

Gendarmes charged from the room, their boots loud on the stairs and then overhead.

"I hear tell you have many names."

"No. No. Not me." Damn him, but this gendarme had done some digging. What else had he found out? That he was really a bankrupt wool merchant, with no more magical power than his lover's stupid husband? No, not possible. No man could connect him to his old life. Desgrez yanked Lesage's head back by the hair.

Lesage hissed, "Who are you?"

"Your man Mariette has already given the game away."

"Who?" Lesage played dumb. They'd get nothing from him.

The gendarmes thundered downstairs.

"Well?" said Desgrez.

"Nothing," came the reply. "Just a load of old rubbish."

Lesage grunted in anger. Rubbish? How dare they? The sanctuary was a sacred space. His devilish collection contained irreplaceable items of great value.

Desgrez shoved Lesage forward.

"Right then. Let's hear what you've got to say for yourself when you meet the Comte d'Avaux."

"Who?"

"The President of His Majesty's parliament, that's who."

"No." squeaked Lesage. "No, no, no. I'm innocent. I was pardoned by the King. I was. Whatever it is you think I've done, you're wrong. I dabble in… I… it's just herbs. That's all. Herbs… that's all I've got. A little something for the stomach, or the feet. Yes, terrible trouble with my feet." This fellow had said Mariette had given the game away. He worried that the fool had told them about Madame and the black mass, and then there was Davot. Had he been arrested too, and if so, what of La Voisin?

"I… I wouldn't rely on anything that priest tells you. He's not right in the head. You, on the other hand, have a fine-looking head. Rounded, with plenty of room for your very distinguished brain. Perhaps I can tell you your fortune? Phrenology? My fingers can unlock the mysteries of the personality." Lesage's hand snapped out, fingers flexed to test the air around the Sergeant's head.

"It'll wait," said Desgrez and he marched Lesage out into the street.

Chapter Eighteen

"They've been arrested," cawed Abbé Davot, as he flew into the house on the Rue Beauregard.

"Arrested? Are you sure?" said Catherine.

Digging at the end of the garden, Antoine cocked an ear. What was that? Who'd been arrested?

"As sure as God sits in judgement," said Davot. "They came for Lesage first thing this morning. Mariette too. They've locked them up in the Bastille."

Antoine upped spade and moved closer to the voices. Keep it easy. Don't let them know you're listening. He stopped when he reached the well. The bucket was empty.

"Who told you? On what charge?" barked Catherine.

"Who knows? Sorcery? Conspiracy? Treason? The hearing's in three days' time. They'll come after me next. I know they will. I'm doomed. You have to hide me."

Treason? Doomed? Now what had Catherine got herself in to? Antoine set his spade aside and dropped the bucket down the well. It banged on the side, the rope snaking down and down.

"Hide you? Where, and what about me? Don't you think they'll come for me too?"

Pain fizzed beneath Antoine's breast bone, like a taper to a slow-burning fuse. He wound the bucket back up. The handle squeaked.

Round. Squeak.

Round. Squeak.

The raven glared. "Can't you get rid of him? Poison him or something?"

Antoine started. His eyes locked on Davot, the pain in his chest burning stronger. Damned Priest, sticking his nose in where he wasn't wanted.

"Who?" said Catherine.

"Your oaf of a husband, that's who."

Antoine hefted the bucket onto the wall and sluiced his hair and face. Oaf? The raven called him an oaf? How dare he?

"Don't think I haven't thought about it."

Catherine's words struck Antoine like a fiery arrow, right where the pain gripped him the most. He knocked the bucket off the wall. Three-quarters full, it dropped like a stone, the handle spinning and squeaking, spinning and squeaking. Fuse well and truly lit, Antoine took up his spade and marched towards the kitchen door. He should have done something about all this nonsense long ago. He'd wasted time wondering and planning and…. and what was a plan if you didn't put it into action? The devil had taken up residence. Time for action. Davot took flight, his vestments flapping as he disappeared through the garden gate. Antoine didn't stop in the kitchen. He strode straight through, his spade over his shoulder.

"Where are you going?" said Catherine.

Antoine took the stairs two at a time, his anger so hot he had no thoughts but to…

"What are you going to do?" Catherine shouted. She tripped on her skirts as she hurried up the stairs after him.

…destroy everything. Smash it to pieces. Take away her power. Stop her from harming another soul. Save himself.

Yes, that was it: save himself, but what about love? What about the smile? The long desired smile? Look where it had got him: dedicated to a feckless evil woman. Just like his mother.

"You're all in league with the devil," he shouted and strode into Catherine's bed chamber, hefted his spade and brought it down on the sconce, cleaving it from the wall.

"Stop. You can't do that," shouted Catherine.

The hidden door swung open. Wielding his spade like a sabre, Antoine charged inside. Glass shattered. Papers flew. Wood splintered.

"Stop it, now. Stop," shouted Catherine again.

"Two peas in a pod you are. My mother and you." He couldn't help himself. "I love you and you murder people. Babies. Husbands."

"No. Stop it."

Antoine ignored her. He knew only one thing: he would get rid of the sorcery before it annihilated him.

"I've given you everything. Everything."

"Please," screamed Catherine. "Stop this madness. You're destroying my life's work."

Antoine felt her hand on his raised arm, but he shook her off. For a moment, the sound of his own heart came quick in his ears, and then Catherine's growling sobs and vituperative screeches. He dropped the spade. It hit the floor like a lead weight. Marguerite, on the threshold, peered in.

"Maman? Papa? What's going on?"

An iron fist squeezed Antoine's heart. "Stop," he moaned, echoing Catherine's pleas.

Catherine snarled, "Get out my sight. Go on. Go."

Antoine stared with blank eyes, seeing and yet not seeing. He had no words for how he felt. He should have done something when he'd first found out about the moles. Yes, then. Not now. Then. It was too late now. The desire for a love-filled smile was a fantasy; a pathetic fantasy. No one married for love. No one cared if their wife smiled or if their husband was kind. He shoved Catherine aside, and ignored Marguerite as he stomped downstairs after freedom.

"Papa?"

Outside the clouded sky seemed bright after the dark room upstairs. Antoine walked and didn't stop until he reached the end of the Rue Beauregard. Here, he threw a backward glance at the house, then took the alley to his right. He dipped his head beneath the fan-maker's sign, the walls closing in; funnelling him down the old paths towards the now ruined Court of Miracles. He stepped in a pile of dog shit, swore and took the next left. The iron fist in his chest had become a kid glove, but thirst now crawled up his throat like hot sand.

The Court of Miracles, once a great festering city within a city, stood empty. The canopies covering the square, beneath which the thieves and vagabonds plied their crooked trade, had been torn down. The windows in the surrounding houses were all smashed, the doors broken on their hinges. A legless beggar scooted past on his board, propelling himself with blackened hands, and disappeared into the dark maw of dereliction. Somewhere water trickled. A great black bird let up a mournful cry from its rooftop eerie.

Antoine shuddered. Someone had trampled on his grave.

"Not a pretty sight, is it?" came a man's voice. The whiskery grandfather sat on a box in the corner. "A few people still hide out here, but it's not the same as it was. They're going to raze the place to the ground. Build new houses. Everything changes." The grandfather struggled to his feet. "You're drinking again."

"Hard not to."

"The Angel-Maker getting under your skin?"

"I thought, if I didn't make a fuss, it would all go back to how it was."

"And you'd be happy with that?"

"Yes."

The grandfather raised his eyebrows.

"Alright, no. I wouldn't be happy. Not exactly. I want her to stop it. I want to open a shop. I want her to smile as she used to when we first met." There it was: the foolhardy hope of a lost man.

"You were melancholic the last time I saw you." The grandfather squinted. "You're a little more choleric now. There's a fire in your belly that wasn't there before."

A philosopher, thought Antoine. Such learning wasn't the preserve of an ordinary man.

"And that means what?"

"Yellow bile? Black bile? It's all dry. Too dry by far. It's the reason for your thirst."

"You're wrong. It doesn't feel like fire. It feels like a broken heart. What's it got to do with anything, anyway?"

"Does it matter? In the scheme of things?"

"In the scheme of things?"

"You love her." The grandfather started to walk away, across the square. Antoine trailed after him. The smile was what mattered, even though he knew he was being stupid.

142

"I just need to see her smile, and mean it. She's got to give up the killing though and she won't do that. There's too much money in it. Too much, and she loves it. She does."

The old man stopped. "Love conquers all." His voice echoed.

"But it doesn't, does it? And it hurts."

"You think you'll be fulfilled if she loves you?"

Antoine nodded. "I suppose so. I suppose it will feel like I'm worth something."

"Ah. You are basing your self-worth on how others feel about you. You should concern yourself more with how you feel about you."

Antoine frowned. It didn't make sense. How he felt about himself? He felt terrible, that's how he felt.

The grandfather smiled. "Love is better than hate. Hate eats away at you. You start out thinking it will protect you from their slights and offences. You think you have the moral high ground and that hatred is the only way, but really, what you're doing is turning on yourself." The grandfather stroked his beard. "You say you love her? Then you have to stop hating her."

The great black bird flew overhead. Instantly, Antoine thought of Abbé Davot. He spun, face raised skywards, trying to see where the bird had come from and where it was going.

"I don't hate her," he said. "I don't."

"You hate what she does. You said as much."

"Yes." Would the pain ever stop; the frantic, tortured ache of it all?

"But you've tried to reconcile yourself to it all the same."

"Yes." Where had all the air gone?

"But it still eats away at you."

"Yes." Eats away like a ravenous dog, feasting on entrails thrown out by the butcher. Antoine clawed at his shirt; his belly growled.

The grandfather shrugged. "There may be a way to win her love." He ambled off.

"What?"

"Apologise," shouted out the grandfather. He'd not walked fast and yet he'd almost reached the other side of the square. "If it doesn't work then come and find me." He waved a hand; a nonchalant gesture. He looked like a monk, not a philosopher. Were they different things? Perhaps not.

"Can you help me raise the money for my shop?" he shouted. "A buyer for my house? A loan? I don't know where you live or even what your name is."

The whiskery grandfather had all but disappeared into the shadows. A disembodied voice drifted back to Antoine: "Other days, other ways."

***

The kitchen was empty, the fancy receiving room too. The adjoining chamber and the sun room: all empty. Antoine listened to the house sigh and creak. All manner of drafts found their way under the doors, and through badly fitted window frames. The timbers were rotten in places and the roof needed patching. Even if he could find a buyer, he'd not get a good price for it.

Footfall overhead. Antoine glanced at the ceiling. Not the wind. Not the breathing house. It was her. Catherine. Only one other person had ever sparked such a confusion of feelings: tenderness, devotion, revulsion, dread, and anxiety, all rolled into one. He remembered cowering in the corner of the shop when he was little, his arms protecting his head, his feet drawn up underneath him, while his mother unravelled: the shrieks of fury and a thousand intimidations as her thread of sanity drew out thinner and thinner. At its worst, he thought he might die; snuffed out like candlelight between finger and damp thumb. At best, she would gather him up and promise it would never happen again.

"Let me love you better," she'd say, as if he'd been the one to cause the maelstrom, and now, here he was caught in the very same eye, the storm raging all around. He hung his head in shame and climbed the stairs slowly, rehearsing his apology.

"Forgive me. I am beside myself with sorrow."

Other days. Other ways.

"I didn't mean it."

She killed for a living.

"I beg your forgiveness"

She loved no one but herself.

"I love you."

She returned nothing of his love.

Angel-Maker.

For whatever reason, God had seen fit to give him a loveless mother *and* a loveless wife. Perhaps they were no more than he deserved. Apologise the grandfather had said. He could try. It couldn't harm. It might win him the prized smile. It might not.

Antoine found Catherine in her secret room, now no longer a secret. She held a shattered glass flask in her hand, the shards of her clandestine life having been swept into a pile in the corner. She froze as he entered. His spade leant innocently, against the wall. He felt sheepish and not a little stupid.

"You've come back then," she said. Her voice sounded hollow; sound and no sound, like dead air in a deep cave.

Antoine explored Catherine's face for an indication of pleasure; the smile, always the smile. Finding none, he muttered, "Yes," but that was all. Ashamed, angry, confused, contrite, he fidgeted and wanted to run out to the bottom of the garden, but he stayed put. Apologise, the grandfather had said. Apologise. The words wouldn't come.

"Well?" Catherine tapped a foot in annoyance.

"It was wrong of me to lose my temper, but it was equally wrong of you to listen to that bastard priest telling you to get rid of me. As if you need the encouragement." Damn it, but it had come out all wrong.

"Blasphemy." She turned away.

"I was a merchant once, with a beautiful wife and shop on a bridge."

"You can't set foot on a bridge without dirtying your breeches and I am still beautiful." Catherine turned back, drew herself up, head held high, nose in the air.

"I made a good living, and it bought this house. You have much to be thankful for, and yes, you are still beautiful, though much good it does me to say so." It wasn't an apology, but it was something.

"I won't let you sell the house."

"You can't stop me."

"You want to die?"

"Of course not." Antoine leaned towards her, one eye screwed up to inspect for any tell-tale signs of love: a certain spark, an insouciant quiver of the lips? Both absent.

Her lips had tiny, vertical lines from too much pursing and pouting in disapproval, and her eyes…

Antoine fell into their bottomless pit of despair. A few hours later, after sulking at the bottom of his garden until he could sulk no more, Antoine pushed through the door to the church and stood in the silence.

Forgive me Father…

He whipped his gardening hat off.

… for I have sinned. But not as much as my wife.

He glanced at the confessional in the corner.

My last confession was…. When was it exactly? He couldn't remember – a long time ago and then some. His mother hadn't been big on church. His father more so. He'd carried him on his shoulder all the way once. Antoine had been no more than a toddler, but he remembered it. He'd felt like king of the world that day. King of the whole bridge-wide world.

He took a step towards the confessional, imagining the smell of its musty interior and that of the dismal priest. The raven would sit in the dark box and scratch at the wood. His beak of a nose would poke through the latticework. Davot hated him; wanted him dead. He'd be damned if he was going to die just to satisfy that old storm bird.

Antoine glanced at the ceiling, where rampant angels stretched out their hands to beckon him heavenward: the ferocity of an all-powerful God in gaudy colours.

He muttered, "I am truly sorry for my sins and for those of my wife. In choosing to do wrong and failing to do good, I, we, have sinned against You, whom we should love above all things. I should. She should."

He sighed. "I firmly intend, with the help of Your grace, to sin no more and to bring Catherine to a place of purity and…" What? She was still a murderer.

He sighed again. He'd said it all; no need for the confessional proper. "In the name of Jesus Christ our Lord. Amen." Best add that for good measure.

He backed out. The door closed quietly behind him, the latch giving a determined click. He couldn't go to the authorities. He didn't want to see Catherine incarcerated, or worse, executed… and what if the long finger of the law was to point at him instead? What then? No, no, like the grandfather said, other days, other ways.

He paused at his garden gate to glance up and down the street. Perhaps God would intervene with all this… this witchcraft. Well, that was what it was. No point in pretending it was anything else. Then again, perhaps God… Antoine barely dare think it. Perhaps God didn't exist. It came like a whispered thought. Catherine had accused him often enough of not believing in God, and he was always telling her he did, but…

There was a chance, an outside chance that God didn't exist. It was heresy to say so. Heresy. No, no, no. He'd been to church. He'd hedged his bet. He'd confessed his sins, so everything would be alright. Besides, he had other things to worry about, such as would Monsieur Michel vouch for him, and should he go hunting for the right premises now or later? No, he had plenty to occupy his mind without worrying about God.

Chapter Nineteen

The Rue Saint Honoré stretched from beyond the city wall in the west, past the palace of the Louvre, all the way to the old market at Les Halles. For the most part it was a narrow and unremarkable street of tightly packed shops, but behind each dull façade, lay some of the most exclusive establishments in all of France, or so it had always seemed to Antoine. He stopped at the corner of the Rue Saint Honoré and the Rue du Four to gaze longingly at Monsieur Michel's establishment. It had overhanging upper storeys and a fine view of trade in both directions. Montvoisin Senior had been something of a regular here, and Antoine had often listened to Monsieur Michel wax lyrical about the needlework of Marseille, and why the taxes were so high on imported fabrics. The shop had been warm and had a new wool smell. The illustrious proprietor had a passion for forest green and the walls had been hung with thick tapestries depicting the hunt, the like of which Antoine hadn't seen elsewhere.

He wiped his hands down the front of his jacket. Things had changed. He'd changed. Monsieur Michel would have changed too. Grown older and forgetful. Antoine picked on his worn cuff. He'd wait a bit. That was it; he'd wait. He crossed the street, narrowly avoiding an old crone, and installed himself in the entrance to an alleyway in the wall opposite. Here, he watched the door, intrigued by his memories, but confused by the feelings that accompanied them.

The shop had been wonderful, but as often as Antoine had listened to Monsieur Michel, he'd also spent many an hour in this alleyway. He threw a soft gaze into the dark unknown. He'd always been afraid to go any further in. He'd often waited here for his father, throwing pebbles against the wall, imagining all manner of monsters.

Antoine put his back to the gloom and, just as he had all those years ago, watched the shop door. A fine rain started up. He was a child no more. No one was going to come out and beckon him forth. He had to take the initiative. He'd come this far. Why, only a short while ago he'd been full of courage and five times as confident.

Right then.

The door did not creak on entry. Quite the opposite, it opened smoothly, the warm woolly air greeting Antoine just as he remembered. A young man looked up from behind a long countertop covered in bolts of bright silk, his face screwing up instantly, as if a bad smell had just wafted in. Indeed, a sour aroma may well have accompanied Antoine, for Paris was not a particularly savoury place when the wind was in the wrong direction.

"You have brought the weather with you Monsieur," the young man said looking at Antoine's wet footprints. Ah, so that was it. Not a smell, but the rain.

"I'm looking for Monsieur Michel." He removed his hat and gave a slight bow, all the better to ingratiate himself.

"He's not here." The young man's reply came with a sneer.

"I can wait." Yes, he could wait. Inside preferably. Out of the rain.

"He isn't… I'm sorry, what business do you have with Monsieur?" The young man came out from behind his counter. He didn't look old enough to be left in charge of such a grand shop. His feet were small and encased in slippers. His hose, blue silk. Antoine stood his ground. Sweat dripped down the nape of his neck, that or perhaps the rain? His stomach burned.

"Is there someone else I might speak to?" Monsieur Michel had a son, Charles. They'd never been friends; Charles had been sent away to school.

"No."

"Ah, and you are?"

"Monsieur Michel, the younger…"

A grandson. A pretentious grandson.

"Your father perhaps? Is he here?"

"My father has been dead these last five years, not that it is any business of yours. Monsieur, I would ask you to leave now. Unless you wish to purchase something?" His look indicated that he doubted this very much.

Antoine stepped back, surprised by young Monsieur Michel's forcefulness.

"Your grandfather then. He's still alive?"

The boy took a step closer.

"Yes, but he is otherwise occupied."

With what, wondered Antoine, but he didn't say as much. Instead he said, "Right. Well, please, tell him I called. I am Monsieur Montvoisin. He will remember me, and if not, then he will remember my father."

Antoine placed a hand against the solid silent door.

"It's a matter of importance. Great importance."

The young man blinked once and turned away. Antoine stepped out into the drizzle. He lifted his face to the sky and allowed the fine, sharp drops to prick his skin and dampen his courage.

"Antoine?" came a voice from behind. Not Michel the younger. Not him, and not the elder either. This old man was grizzled and bent and wore an apron over his rust-coloured jerkin.

"Leclerc? Is it you? Is it really you?"

"Antoine. Where have you been? You stopped coming. You stopped." Leclerc cracked a toothless smile and opened his arms wide to embrace Antoine like a long lost son. "I heard about what happened. What a disaster."

"I lost everything. Can we get out of this rain?"

"Of course. Come back inside."

"I'd rather not." Antoine nodded towards the door. "He does not deem me worthy enough."

"Guillaume thinks too highly of himself. Come then." Leclerc led the way into the alley. "Ever since the old man retired, he's been impossible."

They sheltered together in the lee of the wall, Antoine leaning his back against it.

"Retired? Monsieur Michel?"

"When you are as rich he is, you can afford to retire, no?"

Antoine thought of his own situation. Some might call him retired, though he had no money of his own.

"I need a favour."

"What kind of favour?" Leclerc's eyes narrowed.

"I need someone to vouch for me with the Corporation. I can't find my papers. The flood took everything."

"Ah, well, you need Monsieur Michel for that and he is…" Leclerc shrugged.

"Retired. I know, but would he see me, do you think?"

"Maybe. Maybe not."

"Or you? You could vouch for me. You've known me all my life. You must be as old as…"

Leclerc raised his eyebrows. "Yes?"

"Well, could you?"

"They wouldn't listen to me. I never got my papers."

"What? But I thought. All these years and you…"

"I never learned to read. I could count, but not read. You were a lucky boy to have the father you had. All those wonderful stories of his. I remember the one he told about Jason and his golden fleece. What was it?"

"The fleece was kept by a King. He promised to give Jason the fleece if he sowed a field for him."

"That's right." Leclerc chuckled. "But he fell in love with the King's daughter. What was her name?"

"Medea."

"Medea. Hah. I remember now. And your father used to call your mother Medea. His little witch. Ah, but it was a long time ago. My father died before I knew him, and my mother… Ah, well best not speak about her." He offered up a knowing look. "You still married to your witch?"

Antoine pushed away from the wall. The rain had let up.

"Yes."

"Monsieur Cinq-Mars might vouch for you. He's opened a new shop on the other side of the street."

"Him? He hated me."

"The rest are dead."

"Ask him will you?"

"Who? Cinq-Mars?"

"No. Monsieur Michel. Ask him?"

"He's not been well."

"You said he'd retired."

"Because he's not been well."

"You said it was because he'd made a lot of money."

"That too. I'll ask him. When I see him next, I'll ask him."

"When will that be?"

Leclerc shrugged. "I can't promise when." He glanced up at the sky. "The rain has stopped. Don't be a stranger."

The old man stepped out of the alley. Antoine thought he cut something of a forlorn figure, with his crooked back and hobbled gait, but it was true: the rain had stopped.

Chapter Twenty

The high-ceilinged, wood-panelled courtroom filled slowly, the press of bodies such that a great stink issued forth and caused Catherine to cover her nose. She sat at the back, with Davot at her side, the hood on her cloak pulled down low over her face. He was disguised as a merchant and she as his corpulent wife. Catherine guarded her clients' identities jealously, and with good reason; many were members of the court, with complex kinships and money aplenty. Her charms, potions and advice crossed moral and criminal boundaries. Some of her actions might even be considered treasonous. There was but the slimmest possibility the court would see the light and let Lesage go. Stranger things had happened.

The defendants, prodded by their guard, hobbled into the court and took their seats. Lesage and Abbé Mariette were bedraggled, perhaps even ill-used. Catherine's heart leapt like that of a love-sick young girl. Quietly, she cursed her stupidity. To have fallen for his charms, and he a complete charlatan.

The entrance of the eagle-like Comte D'Avaux prompted the clerk of the court to bark, "On your feet." The gossiping crowd stood up in a cacophony of scraping chairs, coughs and chatter.

"Be seated."

A sly smile played on Lesage's lips, his tongue flicking in and out to taste the air. Catherine leaned in towards

Davot and said, "They look rather better than I thought they would."

Davot flashed a warning look. Catherine hrumped her annoyance as calm descended on the courtroom's unruly occupants. It was now that the man on whose order the Court of Miracles had been cleared, Lieutenant-General Nicholas De La Reynie, strode in. He doffed his hat and bowed low.

"If the court will forgive my tardiness."

"Yes, yes, be seated," said the Comte. He waved, dismissively.

De La Reynie took up position behind the defendants, which made those he pushed by mutter in annoyance.

"Who's this?" whispered Catherine, her attention shifting from Lesage to the new arrival. His well-made presence did not go unnoticed by some of the ladies. Catherine, jealous of their excitement, fluffed herself up; raising her head and throwing back her hood.

"Take care. He's in charge of the gendarmerie," said Davot.

"Ah." A man to court; to charm. Who knew how useful he might be? "His name?"

"De La Reynie. He bought his position."

"Really?"

"He married into money."

"The right marriage is so important," Catherine said, thinking of her own. She'd been young and foolish. She should have waited. Antoine was a wastrel. He'd not done a stitch of work since the flood. She'd never have married him if her mother hadn't been so set on it – and yet, that was a nonsense because Maman dearest was also the one to tell her to get rid of him.

The Comte rifled through his papers, and shoved his wig back to scratch at his bald pate.

"These men stand accused of sacrilege."

The clerk consulted his notes. "Sir, you interrogated them yesterday. They did make a Black Mass and pray over the body of Madame de…"

A volley of coughs from the courtroom made the clerk to look up, mid-sentence.

De La Reynie shouted out, "My Lord, if I may approach?"

The clerk gave De La Reynie a withering look. The Comte beckoned him forth.

"Make haste sir, we do not have all day."

De La Reynie extracted himself from his seat, with much apology to those he disturbed for a second time. He bowed his head close to that of the Comte's, and spoke in a low whisper.

"The lady in question is a relative of yours. The Abbé Mariette too, a distant cousin I believe. As much as I wish these crimes prosecuted the King would not be best pleased if Madame were to become the subject of common gossip."

The Comte eyed the defendants.

"A relative you say?"

"Yes sir."

"Which relative?"

De La Reynie hooked a finger and bade the Comte closer. A hush came over the crowd as all strained to hear the secret. Catherine leaned forward.

"Ah," came the Comte's reply. "I hadn't realised. Please, return to your seat."

De La Reynie did as he was told, all eyes following him, all mouths open.

"We're safe," hissed Catherine to Davot. "The fool of a judge's daughter is married to De Montespan's brother."

"You can't possibly have heard what they were saying." Davot gave her a pointed look. "But you knew about it already."

"Of course I did."

"He'll still pay for his deeds," said Davot. "Both of them will."

"This De La Reynie fellow seems mindful of unwarranted intrigue. That bodes well, don't you think?"

"Let the accused stand," said the clerk.

This time the serpent-like prisoner needed no prodding, although Mariette struggled and groaned as he drew himself up.

"It is the verdict of this court that you, Adam Coureret, sometimes known as Adam Lesage, and you, Abbé François Mariette, are guilty of the crime of sacrilege. You did willingly and with much malice cause a Black Mass to be said on behalf of…"

De La Reynie gave a sonorous cough.

"…which is punishable by death."

The crowd gasped. Catherine stifled a cry. She'd expected some form of punishment, but nothing like this.

"However, on this occasion, the court is minded to be lenient. I thereby commit you, Abbé Mariette, to the prison at Vincennes for a period not less than twenty years, where it is hoped you will pay penance by ministering to the prisoners."

Twenty years? Call that lenient?" Catherine shouted. Heads turned.

The Comte ignored the interruption and continued.

"As to you, Adam Coureret, or Lesage, whichever name you prefer. You are to be despatched to Marseille and thereafter will serve a sentence in the galleys."

"The galleys?" This time Catherine stood up.

"Don't draw attention to yourself," hissed Davot, pulling her down. It was too late. Lesage had seen her, and so had De La Reynie.

"But the galleys?" she hissed at Davot. "To be treated like a common criminal? That's not lenient. It's certain death. They might as well have burned him at the stake."

"Shh," urged Davot. "Many with influence must owe you favours."

"Yes, yes they do," she said, quieter now.

"Then call them in. If De La Reynie fears a certain lady's involvement you must use it to your advantage." Davot raised his feathery eyebrows. "No?"

Catherine considered. It was possible. Anything was possible. It would be difficult though. Who knew what Lesage or Mariette had said about her?

The guards took hold of the prisoners, ready to haul them away, but in that instant Lesage lunged across the crowded room to bay at Catherine: "This is your bastard husband's doing."

Catherine fell back in alarm and let the onlookers crowd around her. The gendarmes grabbed Lesage forcefully by the scruff of his neck. The swarm tried to follow, but were quickly shut out. Eventually the door opened again and all vied to be first to carry the news of the trial to the gossips on the street. Catherine allowed the wave of humanity to carry her forward, out of the building, and into the smoky, somewhat liquid, late morning air. She stood in the lee of the monastery wall, the anger of it knotted in her stomach. A man spat at her feet.

Lesage: gone to the galleys.

Mariette: incarcerated.

How had Davot escaped such persecution? How had she? They'd both been there. They'd both been part of it. She was about to ask as much, when Davot piped up: "He's right you know. Your husband is behind all this. Always skulking around. Who knows what he's heard and what he's passed on?"

"I don't know." She'd been soft with Antoine; allowed him too much leeway.

"You should do something about it, before he gets you arrested too." Davot touched his forelock and walked off. Catherine watched him, her heart full of hatred for those who had done her wrong – and there were just so many of them. A whiskery old grandfather caught her eye. She bit the quick on her nail. He seemed familiar. When she risked another glance, both Davot and the grandfather had gone.

A short while later Catherine sat at the table and weighted a curling sheet of paper down with a small limestone sculpture of a hunting dog. From her position close to the window she could see the length of the garden and even glimpse the city wall. It was an idyllic spot. She didn't want to leave this house. She wouldn't leave it. It *was* hers. It didn't matter what the law allowed. It didn't matter what Antoine said to the contrary.

Antoine: he must have betrayed them. He hated Lesage; hated Davot too so why hadn't he been arrested? Curious.

She brushed the paper gently, feeling its silky smooth surface. She could have chosen French, English, or even

Italian paper, but no, it had to be Dutch for its whiteness and obvious quality. Only the best would suffice for a letter to the King. She said a silent prayer for the nuns of St. Sulpice for teaching her the fine art of reading and writing.

"Rely on no man to tell you the contents of a document," she whispered, in echo of the words used by her mother many years earlier. "Few women can read, let alone write, but it will stand you in good stead," the old lady had said. Catherine couldn't agree more. Quill in hand, she considered the right way to begin. False starts would waste words and words were so very precious; words could change the course of a person's life. Then there was the matter of delivery. The best way was to travel to Saint-Germain-en-Laye and wait in line to present the petition to His Majesty himself. This was by far and away the best choice. The others being to give it to someone to attend on your behalf, or to ask someone close to the King to pass it on.

She dipped the quill into the ink and began:

Your Majesty…it has been brought to my attention…

No, it was too business-like. The Sun King was no merchant.

Your Majesty. I am but a humble woman…

Too meek, too mild.

Your Majesty. A certain person has been incarcerated unjustly.

But why should the King read on? The tone was too abrupt; too aggressive. He would throw it aside. Perhaps she shouldn't address him at all, nor bother to travel to Saint-Germain to deliver it into his hands, but instead write to someone with influence. After all, a letter was so readily cast aside, but a mistress… Madame De Montespan, for instance? That might work. She was far gone with child and rumour had it now living in close quarters with the King at Saint Germain en Laye. Madame Des Œlliets passed from court to city and back again with fair regularity. She might be persuaded to take the letter straight to her friend and ensure it opened and read. Yes, Madame De Montespan was a better choice of addressee than the King, particularly as this was a matter of the heart. The lady would understand and would come to her aid, but how to couch it in favourable terms?

Catherine dipped her quill into the ink and the words came to her in a flurry of maternal sentiment.

Madame, my prayers are with you for the speedy and safe delivery of your child.

Yes, that was a good start.

Forgive me, but there is a matter of the highest importance I would broach. It is somewhat delicate.

Madame de Montespan would understand. She would see that the writer meant every word.

Monsieur Lesage has been despatched to the galleys. I am sure you will understand when I say, I have developed the very closest affinity with him and am quite distraught at his departure. I beg you Madame, if you are able to intercede on my behalf with He who has the power to commute his sentence, you would be assured of my utmost discretion. Madame, I am sure I do not have to explain further, for this is a matter that affects us all. I am not someone who readily throws herself on another's mercy, but I do now throw myself on yours, in the hope that you will comprehend the danger we are all in.

I am your most humble servant.

Yes! The perfect letter. Catherine signed it with a flourish. There was nothing incriminating in it. Another might read and discover only that she was a foolish woman lost in love. She had not alluded to anything underhand or criminal. She glanced out of the window. Antoine crossed the grass, heading towards the bottom of the garden. Interfering old... Damn him to hell. She folded the letter carefully. It must be delivered at once. She couldn't trust it to Antoine.

"Marguerite? Come here."

The girl thump thumped up the stairs.

"What is it?"

"Take this to Madame Des Œlliets. No one else. Only her." Catherine thrust the folded letter at her daughter.

"I don't have time Maman. She's not even in Paris."

"I know very well where she is. Give it to Romani. He's to deliver it into Madame Des Œlliets and no one else. Understand?"

"Of course." Marguerite lifted a petticoat and shoved the letter deep into her pocket.

"Tell him he must go immediately."

"He'll want paying. He won't do it without."

"There's money in the box on the shelf. Go." Catherine shooed her daughter away. It was probably better that Romani went. He would know how to get in and out of the old palace without being seen. He'd been a guard. He would have friends who would turn a blind eye. Yes, it was far better.

Marguerite took the box down from the shelf and opened it up. Catherine gave her the briefest of glances and then allowed her gaze to fall through the window. Curled apple leaves; dry brown and ready to fall. The summer drawing to a close. The lavender spent of blossom and the roses a flutter of falling petals. She'd been too soft on Antoine. He'd survived all three attempts on his life. He would not - nay, could not, survive the fourth.

Downstairs, the door banged. Marguerite, gone to find Romani.

Catherine tapped her fingers furiously on the table top. She would send Antoine on an errand... a long errand that would take him away from the house for a day or more. She'd pack him some food: pastries, bread, cheese, fine cuts of cold meat. She'd make sure it was all well-seasoned with... Wolfsbane? Hemlock? It might work. Monkshood would be best, but so dangerous to handle. There was only one thing for it, it would have to be an old favourite, *Poudre de Succession:* sugar of lead, ground glass, a little *Aqua Tofana*, and a lot of arsenic. Yes, that was it. She need never see Antoine alive again. He would die on the road. Roll into a ditch. Perhaps never to be found. Oh, what joy!

Chapter Twenty-One

The very next day Catherine asked Antoine to go and buy the herb Savin from a certain Monsieur Raymond, who lived in the town of Deuil La Barre.

"It's a day's journey, there and back," she said. "Take the north road."

Antoine considered: go or stay? Catherine was up to something. He knew it. He felt it in his water. He ought to refuse, but then again it would get him out of the house. A jaunt into countryside might do him some good. Catherine pressed a purse of coins into his hand, together with the merchant's address.

"Don't let him palm you off with anything but the best," she said, and frowned.

Antoine buried the purse deep in his leather satchel.

"Can't you buy it here?"

"You can pick it in the garden, but Monsieur Raymond's is of a superior quality."

Superior quality indeed. "In the garden? My garden?"

"The one we grow isn't…"

"Poisonous. That's what you mean isn't it. Ours is just the ordinary kind. You want the poisonous one."

Catherine didn't answer. Instead she held out a parcel of food: offcuts of meat, an apple and three sweet pastries. "The sooner you go, the sooner you'll come back." She pecked him on the cheek.

Antoine touched the dampness that lingered on his skin and searched her eyes for the tell-tale spark. Nothing. He shoved the parcel of food deep inside his satchel and set off.

***

"Where have you sent him?" said Marguerite. She'd been picking herbs in the garden and carried an armful of long borage stalks topped out with tiny drooping heads, and aromatic sage. She dropped them on the kitchen table.

"Don't put them there," said her mother.

"Maman, tell me. Where have you sent him?"

Catherine snapped, "Deuil La Barre. Don't worry. He won't feel a thing."

"Won't feel a thing?" Her mother was up to something.

"We're better off without him."

"Without him?" Marguerite shouted. "What have you done?"

"He does like those pastries so. They'll say he choked on them."

"Maman you can't kill Papa. You can't. He's Papa."

Catherine wrinkled her nose. "He won't be able to resist those pastries."

Marguerite flew from the room. The wind had whipped up leaves hard against the garden gate. They crackled as she opened it. In the street she noticed Romani and quickly turned away. Her father had been gone a while. Long enough that he would be walking the main road between the fields, the sun beating down on his head.

"Where are you going?" Romani caught her by the arm.

"She poisoned the pastries. Can you believe it?" Her hair fell soft across her face and Romani reached out to brush it off. Marguerite slapped his hand away.

"If he dies it will be easier for us." Romani's smile was crooked, his eyes sly.

"How can you say that?"

"You know he wants to sell the house? When he dies it'll be ours. Yours. Mine, if we're married. What d'you think of that? We'd be set for life."

Marguerite shook him off. "Did you take the letter?"

"What letter?"

"To Madame Des Œillets."

"Of course. She's where you said, at Saint Germain-en-Laye with the King's whore."

"Don't say that."

"Why not? It's true."

"I'm not sure I want to marry you."

"You have no choice. I've already paid your mother for the privilege of bedding you."

"You bastard." Marguerite had heard enough. How dare he? Paid for her. If it were true, then… then she most definitely would not marry him.

***

Walking the road north through the Montmartre fields, and on into the dark, tangled forest, Antoine took no notice of the lurking fox and the rummaging boar. He walked in a daze, the wind whispering through the trees.

She's never loved you.

She's full of hate.

She wants to kill you.

Kill you.

Kill you.

Antoine stopped in his tracks. It wasn't just the attempts on his life. It wasn't just the house and the shop, or the dead babies.

Dead babies.
In the garden.
The garden.

Catherine meant the world to him. She'd been his first and only love. Her cruelty grieved him so, but he couldn't abandon her. He pulled his jerkin tight and put his head down. All he really wanted was to love and be loved. It wasn't such a terrible thing. He detoured into the undergrowth, set his satchel down and sat beside it. Love took some pondering. How close it was to hate, and how exactly do you make a woman love you when she's set on an altogether different course? Those days they'd spent dropping stones off the bridge to see which made the biggest ripple, and Catherine's joy when she won. Such innocent fun. Yes, and watching her delight as the boats passed beneath the arches and came out the other side with sails to the fore, men at the bows and hands to the oars. Walks in the moonlight, silver threading the wind-ruffled river. Achingly beautiful memories from a time long since passed. Surely they'd meant something more to her than merely a way to ensnare him? And look, now he had nothing, other than the house and his love - always his love He rubbed his aching chest. His heart knew the torment. His belly too. He fished in his satchel and pulled out the parcel of food. He wasn't an unreasonable man; he could have refused this errand.

He stuffed the offcuts of meat into his mouth. He'd do anything Catherine asked... or would he? The sweet pastries were next. They smelled delicious.

***

Marguerite begged a lift with a carter and, when he dropped her a league outside the city walls, she hitched up her skirts and continued on foot. Anxious for her father's safety, she stumbled on the rutted road, alternately cursing and praying. Papa was an innocent; a fool; a useless lump of nothing but gristle. There really was no point in killing him. None at all. Besides, she loved him. She didn't care what he did or didn't do. Love was the thing. Love.

The forest tried to ensnare her; stray brambles prickled, and a swirl of last year's leaves softened her footfall and threw her into ankle-twisting ruts. He wasn't the best of fathers, of that she was sure, but he was the only one she had. No one could replace him.

***

Antoine sank his teeth into the pastry and a few crumbs dotted his jerkin front. Instantly, his mouth fizzed with the taste of honeyed almonds. He swallowed and stuffed the remainder in whole. He was greedy. He knew it, and these were just so good.

"Papa! No! Stop. Don't..."

Antoine squinted. Who was it? He swallowed. Marguerite. Now what was she doing following him?

"Please, Papa..."

Antoine shoved the second pastry into his mouth. And that was another thing: she needn't think she was going to have any of his food, oh no.

"Papa! Spit it out." Marguerite stumbled, turned her ankle and swore.

Children shouldn't swear, no matter how old they were. "What?" he said.

"Papa. She's poisoned them!"

"What?"

Antoine spat. A great gob of masticated pastry landed on a tussock of grass at his feet.

"Are you sure?" He rubbed his belly and hiccupped.

Marguerite dropped to her knees.

"I knew you wouldn't get far. You walk so slowly."

Antoine had to admit he did amble rather than walk with purpose, but then it had never been his intention to actually go to Deuil La Barre, only to make it seem that way. He'd had it in mind to double back at some point and tell Catherine that there'd been no savin.

"How many have you eaten?"

"One? Two?" Antoine pointed to the gobbet and gave another hiccup. His tongue cleft to the roof of his mouth. He gagged.

"Water?" said Marguerite.

"Bottle of wine in my satchel. I wasn't going to drink it though. I swear."

"I don't care. Drink it. Now."

Antoine wasn't so sure. Marguerite was always telling him off for drinking too much.

"How did you find me?"

"There's only way north from our house. Go on. Do it. Drink it fast. Then make yourself sick."

"It's a waste of good wine that is." Antoine stuck out his bottom lip like a petulant child.

"Do you want to die?"

"No."

"Then do what I say." Marguerite arched her eyebrows.

"Are you sure?"

"I'm sure."

Antoine gulped the wine down, pausing only to hiccup halfway through and mutter, "She poisoned me." He touched his cheek. "But she kissed me."

Catherine wasn't all bad. She couldn't be. His mother had been bad. His mother would have killed him given half a chance. She'd more or less said as much – tried it too. That time when she found him fishing from the stock room window with a spool of thread and a bent needle. He'd been six, maybe seven years old. She'd grabbed and shoved. It had only been the intervention of his father that had saved him, yanking him back from the brink by the scruff of his neck.

"You could have killed him."

"He needs to be taught a lesson," his mother had said.

"He's a good boy."

"What I could have done with my life if I hadn't had him."

"He was fishing. It's nothing to kill him for."

Monsieur Montvoisin senior had smiled down at his son, the corners of his mouth crinkling beneath his heavy moustache, his smell all tobacco and spirits, wrapped up in linen and linseed, and sprinkled with sweat.

Antoine, caught in the past, briefly wondered if he'd died. Then Marguerite's voice came to him. "Put your fingers down your throat."

"She kissed me. Damn it but that's the fourth time she's tried to kill me." He belched. He'd been such a fool. Such a fool. Of course she'd tried again. Of course she had. Like mother, like wife.

"Papa?"

Hiccup.

"Papa! Please!"

The poison, or maybe the wine, took his senses away. A while later, a cold wind ruffled his hair and urged him awake. He cracked an eyelid and spied a shadow. Heaven was a might chillier than he'd expected. The shadow let out a long sigh.

"Ah," said Antoine.

"You snored for hours," said Marguerite.

A light mist sat in the hollows and ghosted the trees. Apart from the ever present ache in his chest and a thumping headache, he was none the worse for his poisoning. Perhaps his mouth was a little dry. A drink wouldn't go amiss. He glanced at his daughter and struggled to his feet. His breeches were damp, and his bones ached.

"What are you going to do?" said Marguerite.

"Do? Leave her of course. Leave her." He really should. But then it would mean leaving the house and his darling daughter too.

"Papa? You can't do that."

Oh but Marguerite was making it so difficult for him. Leave. Stay. It was all the same in the end. He couldn't wait around to be killed. He couldn't. He set off down the road.

"Are you coming?"

Marguerite groaned. When Antoine dared a look, she'd grudgingly fallen in step. It made him feel better; his daughter walking with him like this. He felt protective and proud. It wasn't a precise thing. He just knew he didn't need to prove himself to her.

"Smile for me," he said.

"What? Smile? What for?"

"Just do it."

Marguerite made a jocular smile. "Is that good enough?"

Antoine saw the light in her eyes. "Yes, it tells me all I need to know." He turned back to the path. His daughter loved him through and through. He could ask no more of her.

Eventually, the forest released father and daughter into the soft afternoon light. A gentle breeze ruffled the long grass and blew the mist away to reveal an azure-streaked sky. Birds competed noisily. They reminded Antoine of the caged linnets his neighbour used to sell on the bridge: bright little things, always chirruping. Life was better then, despite his mother and the endless hatred.

"If I still had a shop it would be like the old days. Well, not exactly, but…"

Marguerite stopped. "It wasn't Maman's fault," she said.

Antoine carried on walking.

"Whose was it then?"

Marguerite caught up. "Lesage?"

"Huh? Him? I hear he's been sent to the galleys."

"Abbé Davot, then?"

"That raven has a lot to answer for, but what can I do about it? Kill him?" It was an interesting thought.

The road ahead fell down the hill. The air smelled of fresh grass, delicate white hawthorn, and manure.

"I suppose you're going to tell me there is no Monsieur Raymond?"

"No. Yes, I mean… there might be, but she doesn't need savin. She can get it from the market."

"Thought as much."

Antoine stared at the ruts.

"It'll start getting dark soon. Let's go home." A little while later he added, "I'm hungry."

Chapter Twenty-Two

Some distance across the city, in her beautiful, hidden apartment in the Chateau of Saint-Germain-en-Laye, Madame de Montespan went into labour. The shutters were closed and the candles lit. A fire roared in the grate, and midwives and physicians flustered and fussed, fidgeted and fretted. In the adjoining room Madame Des Œillets paced back and forth, back and forth. Her dear friend, her only friend, was about to give birth to the King's bastard. She should be at her side. She should be pressing a damp cloth to Madame's fevered brow and uttering words of encouragement, not lingering in an antechamber with the daylight fast disappearing, and the sound of bats in the attic and mice in the wainscot. As it was, she'd been denied entrance by the dreadful midwives, who were at pains to hide the birth from prying eyes.

Footsteps.

A door opened.

Not *the* door, but the one immediately opposite. A guard entered, bowed imperceptibly, and thrust out a letter.

"If it pleases Madame. Correspondence for Madame de Montespan."

"Not now." Couldn't he see how distressed she was, and he wanted her to take delivery of a letter? Impossible.

"I have instructions to see it conveyed into her hands."

Madame Des Œillets snorted her anger. "Instructions? Whose instructions?"

"I am not obliged to say, save that it would not be in Madame's best interest to refuse."

"Such impudence! Madame is in labour and in no fit state to read."

The guard inclined his head slightly.

"Nevertheless."

Madame Des Œillets snatched the letter from his outstretched fingers.

"You may go."

The guard bowed again, lower this time, and backed away. The door closed with a click. Madame Des Œillets fanned her face with the letter, but didn't open it. Instead she went back to her pacing until, some hours later, a midwife opened the other door and hissed out, "She asks for Madame Scarron."

"The widow? Why? Has she had the child?"

The door closed.

"Confound it, but…" Letter still unopened, Madame Des Œillets followed after the long-disappeared guard until she reached the top of a magnificent staircase. Here, she stared imperiously into the dusty dark well. The depths below gave off naught but the occasional echo. Distant doors slammed and far-off footsteps reverberated. Not for nothing had the Sun King secreted his pregnant mistress in this out-of-the-way mausoleum; it was as silent and empty as the grave.

Finding no servants or guards, Madame Des Œillets hurried back the way she had come, not stopping in the corridor or ante-chamber, but instead bursting into the birthing chamber and startling the assembled midwives, who rushed to stop the intrusion.

"Get out. How dare you enter uninvited?"

Too late, the intruder had already caught sight of her dear friend lying sweat-strewn and bloody on her bed, her face contorted, her energy spent.

"Oh my dearest," Madame Des Œillets cried and pushed the midwife blocking her path aside. The cry of a newborn baby filled the air. A second midwife turned, the baby cradled in the crook of her arm.

"Praise be the Lord." Madame Des Œillets fell to her knees, the letter forgotten.

"Did you send for Scarron?" muttered the new mother.

"You are delivered of a beautiful..." Madame Des Œillets glared at the midwife. "Boy or girl?"

"Girl."

"Yes, a beautiful baby girl, and she's perfectly healthy." Madame Des Œillets searched the face of the midwife for reassurance but found nothing by way of response. The other midwife made to place the baby in the new mother's arms, but Madame de Montespan turned her head away.

"Give her to Scarron. Where is she? Is she here yet?"

Her friend didn't understand. "Are you sure you want her? You should keep the child with you, don't you think? Or at least, send her to the nursery with your other children. We'll find a wet nurse for her."

"I can't. The King... The Queen... I can't. It has to be this way. Scarron comes with the very best of references."

The fire spat an ember out onto the floor and made everyone jump. Madame de Montespan beckoned her friend to come closer.

"He doesn't love me. He's already bedding someone else."

"You can't be sure of that." Madame Des Œillets herself had given way to the King's charms on more than one occasion. Perhaps her friend had found out.

"Who with?"

"The bitch Fontanges." The new mother scowled. "What have you there?"

Madame Des Œillets stared at the letter briefly, then threw it in the fire. "It's nothing," She said, relieved that her secret was still safe. "It's nothing at all."

Chapter Twenty-Three

Father and daughter sat on the wall at the end of the Rue Beauregard and watched the sun rise softly in the east.

"What will you do?" asked Marguerite. "I'll talk to her if you want. She'll come round." Fingers of light touched her toes.

"It won't make any difference." Antoine rubbed his breast bone where the pain nudged at him. Marguerite was a good girl. She'd come after him. She loved him. He glanced at his daughter. The dawning light had reached her knees.

"It comes to us all in the end," he said, and he got up and walked past his house to enter the church next door. The confessional loomed on his right, the aisle stretched out into the gloom. Daylight penetrated only as far as the gallery. Dust, like the very souls of the dearly departed, lay heavy in the dead air.

It didn't make sense. He and Catherine had rubbed along in the shop for years without a problem. It was only when she'd moved into the big house that the trouble had started... and then there was the flood, always the damned flood, and that priest. Don't forget him. Antoine looked round nervously. The raven, Davot, and that snake, Lesage: charlatans. Yes, that was it. Catherine would never have tried to kill him without their interference.

Stay away from my wife.

Not strong enough.

Stop putting ideas in her head.

Better.

Meddle in my affairs and I'll...

But what would he do? What exactly? Would he commit murder? Could he commit murder? Even if he did he'd have to kill more than once; he couldn't just stop at Davot. Lesage was out of the way, serving time in the galleys, but there were others. The grandfather had told him so. He might have to get rid of Catherine as well. It wasn't as if she didn't deserve it, but no, he couldn't do that. He couldn't kill her. He loved her. He still wanted to see her smile.

Footsteps echoed. Abbé Davot knelt at the altar rail, his head bowed in prayer. Antoine flattened himself against the stone. The priest had God on his side, and who knew what the Almighty had in store? Didn't the faithful gain comfort in the notion that no matter the terror visited upon them, God would be there at the end? Yes, they did. They did.

Antoine dared another look. One swift blow with a candlestick would do it. He held his breath and his chest tightened and mutated into the familiar, knife-sharp pain. He couldn't do it. It wasn't right. He couldn't rail on about the corpses littering his garden and then go and add to their number by killing this man. He'd be no better than his wife – and for a moment there, he'd even thought about killing her. No, he couldn't do it. Ashamed, he tippy-toed out of the church. Catherine had made a mistake. She didn't really want him dead, despite all her talk of unwanted husbands, and he definitely did not want her dead. He loved her and she loved him. She had to love him. It was all he had left. Well, Marguerite, but when she got married he'd be left with no one. He glanced back at the church and then at his house. He still couldn't face Catherine. Not yet, at least. Where then? He spotted the whiskery grandfather at the far end of the street. The old man ambled along, seemingly without a care in the world. The two nodded to one another from afar. For all Antoine wanted the grandfather's company, he didn't think he could face another conversation of riddles and profound wisdom. It all took too much fathoming. He took off for his shrubbery. It was as good a hiding place as any.

***

The dawn light stretched long into Catherine's bedchamber to fall across her face as she slept on her back, mouth open; a runnel of spit dribbling down her chin. A dog barked outside. Early morning dreams caught her halfway between wakefulness and slumber: Lesage, tethered to his oars, a demon bearing down on the ship. The wind beat the sails back and forth and a trail of rope hit the deck, thump, thump, thump.

Catherine snorted, swallowed, coughed and sniffed. A door slammed. Her eyelids flew open. Marguerite. Her meddlesome daughter couldn't be relied on to do anything quietly. She'd been on a fruitless escapade, chasing her father. Stupid girl, staying out all night. Catherine pulled the sheet up to her chin. Antoine was dead and this was her first morning of freedom. An involuntary sob crawled up her gullet. This wouldn't do; crying for a man she'd never loved. She threw back the covers. The floorboards were cold. She glanced out of her window. It was a lovely garden. She could credit Antoine with that at least. With him gone she'd have to find someone else to tend the plants; someone who wouldn't worry too much about the 'molehills'.

And then Antoine walked across the grass.

Antoine?

Yes, Antoine.

He disappeared into the shrubbery. His shrubbery.

Catherine clenched her hands so tightly her knuckles turned white.

"How?" she muttered. Then, louder, "Marguerite!" She should never have let her daughter chase after him. She should have… she should have stabbed him in his bed. She should have put a pillow over his face. She should have killed the pig and …

"Maman, Madame Leféron is here."

"Yes, yes." But no, Madame Leféron shouldn't be here. Not now. Her appointment wasn't until later. Catherine pinned her hair. Both father and daughter had to be taught a lesson, and soon. This sorry state of affairs could not go on.

***

Antoine crouched beneath the laurel's sturdy stems to hide where garden met wall. The soft tilth was rich with fallen leaves, the canopy still verdant. Mid-bush, a blackbird set a beady eye on him as he leant back against the lichened stone wall.

He was such a coward.

To stay.

To go.

To hate.

To love.

The grandfather parted the branches and entered Antoine's hideout.

"There you are."

"Are you following me?"

"Not at all."

"Why are you here then?"

"I can go if you want."

"No." Secretly, Antoine was pleased. He wasn't getting anywhere on his own. Decisiveness wasn't his strong suit. Yes, yes, the grandfather talked in circles and yes, he'd run from him out on the street, but he could change his mind, couldn't he?

"Papa?" Marguerite called, from beyond the green curtain. "Maman is sorry."

The pain in Antoine's chest impaled his anger. The grandfather opened his mouth. Antoine shushed him, finger to lips.

"Papa? I know you're in there."

Antoine's rage surged, but he remained silent.

"Papa? Maman's sorry. She wants to make it up to you."

No she doesn't. Damn it. Interfering women. Yes, yes, even Marguerite. Even her. Perhaps especially her. No, no, she loved him. Her smile had proved it. He couldn't include his daughter. Then again, if he'd died out there on the road, he wouldn't have to make the heart-wrenching decision to leave his wife of... of just how many years? Too many, that was what. Too many... and he wasn't leaving was he? He was here, in the shrubbery. Hiding. Pathetic as ever.

The grandfather barely got the words "what are you going to do" out, before Antoine shushed him again.

"Papa? Are you there?" The leaves rustled, but Marguerite didn't move beyond the edge of the path.

Antoine could see the tips of her silk shoes in the soil. Where did she get the money for them? She hadn't come to him on the road in silk shoes. No. They'd been sturdy work-a-day shoes, not these. These were... what were they? Harlot's slippers. Yes, that's what they were. His daughter wore harlot's slippers around the house.

"Go away. I'm busy." He felt guilty for being angry with her, but that made him even angrier.

"She says to tell you she's sorry."

"I'm still busy." Women tied a man in so many knots he didn't know which end to pull to untangle the mess, and that was a fact.

Marguerite huffed and puffed. Antoine held his breath. The silk slippers paced back and forth, back and forth... and then disappeared.

After a while the grandfather hissed, "I think she's gone."

"Do you have any money?"

"Not on me."

"Me neither."

Antoine's rage had subsided a little. Both men stared at the jigsaw of light filtering through the leaves. The problem was... what was the problem? The problem was the dead babies and...

The grandfather said, "The problem is not that your wife tried to kill you. The problem is that you love her."

"I'd call death a problem. Love is love. I can't stay here." But if he left he'd be walking away from the longed for smile, and that meant everything to him. Without it he might as well be dead. Perhaps it would have been better if he'd never been born. His mother should have done away with the contents of her belly, like all those mothers who'd left their poor babies beneath his soil, and then the flood wouldn't have happened and all would be well with the world.

"Where will you go?" asked the grandfather.

"I don't know." The Church promised life after death, but Antoine wasn't sure if it would be life in the sense that he knew now, or some other kind of life… and what about how he died and the feeling of being dead, and then there was the atonement of sins. If he didn't know what they were, then how could he atone for them?

"You need a plan. You can't go off into nowhere, you know. You did that once before and look where it got you."

Antoine stared at the blackbird. It stared back at him, its eyes as bright as polished ebony.

"Right back here again."

"Exactly."

"Then it's simple. I'll walk and not stop. I'll walk day and night for as long as it takes to get right away from here. And I won't sleep. When I sleep I forget what I'm doing and… do you think that's what death is? The forgetting? The non-existence of thought?"

"These are big questions. What if you walk in a circle?"

"I won't." He wouldn't. He'd walk himself into his grave. He'd walk and walk and walk and walk.

The grandfather shook his head. "Distance doesn't diminish love."

"So what should I do?"

"What do you want most in all the world?"

Antoine sucked in a breath, long and deep. He wanted…

"The smile. The one that says she loves me. Oh, and a shop. A little shop would be nice. It's what started all this. She might smile if I had a shop. I've been to the corporation. Did I tell you that?"

"You have no money, remember?"

"And no one to vouch for me." He'd work something out. He thought of Monsieur Michel, old and infirm, and the younger Monsieur, lording it over all, and then there was Leclerc. He'd promised to help.

"I know someone who might help. There'll be a price to pay, but..."

"I told you, I have no money."

"It won't cost much."

"Will I have to sell my soul to the devil?"

"The devil doesn't want your soul."

"He doesn't?"

"He's got his hands full with these damned priests."

"Ah, yes. That's probably true."

"Follow me." The grandfather pushed aside the foliage and peered out.

"Where are we going?"

"You'll see."

***

Catherine, standing in the kitchen, watched her daughter come in from the garden. That girl was too rosy-cheeked for her own good. A beetle, charting a course up the wall, came to a halt at eye level. Catherine flicked it away. It landed on its back on the floor. She squashed it underfoot, grinding it into the floorboards. Antoine would die that night. She'd see to it. She wouldn't countenance his presence in the house a day longer. He couldn't go on surviving her attempts. He just couldn't. It wasn't possible.

"You told him I'm sorry?"

"He doesn't believe me," said Marguerite.

"You should never have gone after him." How could he still be alive? He should be lying in a ditch, his tongue lolling out of his mouth, his eyes rolled up into his head, not cowering in a bush at the bottom of the garden with some old man… and who was he? He looked familiar.

"He doesn't understand why you did it and neither do I," hissed Marguerite. "He's Papa. You can't kill Papa. He loves you."

"Who is that greybeard?"

"Who?"

"The man out there with your father."

"Him? He's always hanging around. I thought you knew him."

"Why should I?"

"Because he's La Bosse's father that's why."

Of course. That's who he was. The old fool wasn't any friend of Antoine's. He was a spy for his charlatan of a daughter.

Marguerite said, "You won't do it again, will you?"

"Where God has his church the Devil will have his chapel. People die every day. Every single day." She'd have it out with that old devil. Coming here, wheedling secrets out of her husband. She pushed past Marguerite and ran down the stairs. She passed through the kitchen at speed, knocking a dish of apricots off the table as she went. Outside, the grass was still soft with dew, but the air was warm. She flew at the shrubbery.

"I know you're there. Come out." She shoved through the leaves. A blackbird gazed back at her from low in the foliage. Antoine and his aged companion had gone. All that was left as proof they'd once been here was an old hat.

Chapter Twenty-Four

Far across the city, De La Reynie covered his nose against the foetid stench of death and entered the dank mortuary. The vaulted ceiling and high windows did little to alleviate the decrepitude. Stretched out on a central wooden table lay the corpse of one Jean-Baptiste Gaudin de Sainte-Croix. Behind the table stood Sergeant Desgrez, seemingly inured to the putrid aroma. De La Reynie arched an eyebrow.

"No doctor?"

"He was called away."

The new arrival gave the corpse a cursory inspection. "What do we know about him?"

"He was overcome by fumes."

"Fumes?"

"Poisonous vapours."

"What kind of poisonous vapours?"

"You remember the D'Aubrays? It was a while ago."

De La Reynie frowned. "Them? I've been a fool Desgrez."

"Sir?"

"This business with Madame de Montespan and the black mass. I tried to protect her reputation, for the sake of the King, but..."

"You weren't to know it would escalate."

De la Reynie shook his head. "The city is abuzz with gossip and we do nothing because we're afraid to distress the King? No Desgrez. It can't go on."

"I'm not sure I follow."

"The poisoners. The D'Aubrey's were her brothers."

"You're right. They were."

Desgrez stepped to one side and revealed an open red leather trunk. Beside the trunk lay a sheaf of papers, several of which had been pulled out and flattened for ease of reading.

"Sainte-Croix was the Marquise's lover."

"Was he indeed?" De La Reynie peered inside the trunk. A cluster of phials lay inside. "You've inspected these?"

"Briefly."

De La Reynie reached inside the trunk, but thought better of it and instead, picked up one of the letters.

"And the correspondence?"

"That one was meant for the lady in question upon this gentleman's death. The others are hers to him. There is mention of killing her brothers, so she can inherit her late father's estate."

De La Reynie grabbed at a memory. "The stomach and entrails of each man were black."

"That is so."

"The liver was gangrenous and burnt, but Monsieur Gramond, our good doctor, deemed it natural. I argued the opposite. I said we had a killer on our hands and my God, so we do!"

"Indeed sir. Indeed."

De La Reynie stared at the corpse.

Desgrez pulled another letter from the pile. "There is also mention of the Marquise consulting the fortune teller La Bosse."

A fly landed on the dissecting table. It skittered this way and that. De La Reynie wafted it away. "La Bosse? Is there anything that directly links her to the D'Aubray murders, or the death of this... this unfortunate?" He indicated the corpse.

"Nothing specific as such, but she is linked to another woman. A fortune teller by the name of La Voisin. People say she's the devil in a dress."

"No man can die these days without the womenfolk applaud their inheritance. Poison has become the remedy for whatever ails every desperate creature out there. These so-called fortune tellers are the conduit by which such remedies are procured. We must stem this rising tide of villainy or it will consume us all: King, court and populace." It wasn't just that. De La Reynie wanted to prove himself. He didn't like being thought of as the man who had bought his post. He was made of better stuff than that.

"Well?" he barked. "What else do you know?"

"The Marquise de Brinvilliers has been seen on the road going north the low-countries."

De La Reynie sniffed. "A person often meets his destiny on the road he takes to avoid it. Issue an arrest warrant."

"And the fortune tellers?"

"Not them. Not yet. We must make sure the evidence is sound. We don't know how far their web of deceit stretches. I would sweep them all up at once."

"And Madame de Montespan?"

"I'll speak to Louvois and get an audience with His Majesty. As to these others… Watch them closely. If we amass enough intelligence the King can't refuse a special investigation. That's what we hold out for." That's what would make his name. He'd cleared the Court of Miracles. He'd clear the city of poison. The gossipmongers would not dare to talk about him in derogatory terms if he headed up such an enquiry.

"Sir."

De La Reynie gave a cursory glance around the repulsive mortuary, swept his cloak up over his shoulder and left Desgrez to his ruminations.

Chapter Twenty-Five

Paying no mind to a brief but fierce storm that washed the city stones clean and swept the detritus all the way down to the Seine, the whiskery grandfather led Antoine hither and yon, until they reached the well-worn step of La Bosse's house. Antoine wiped his nose on the back of his damp sleeve and slicked back his hair. The grandfather knocked on the door and waited quietly, patiently, for the maid to open up. Antoine followed the grandfather meekly through the first chamber and thence into the rose-redolent courtyard. The clouds chose this moment to part, and the sun appeared overhead. Stunned by the intensity of the blooms, Antoine barely knew which way to turn. He spotted a pink-tinged white blossom, and one with petals crowded in so completely, it appeared like pillowed silk, while beneath, on the stem, the cat-claw thorns offered their warning, and all the while, the heavenly damp aroma filled his nostrils. He was reminded of the old palace gardens and his youthful explorations. If only he could grow flowers as beautiful as these.

"It's quite something, isn't it?" said the grandfather.

"But who's done all this?" If nothing else, Antoine would find out about the gardener and learn the secrets of this horticultural oasis. Flowers soothed his aching soul.

"The woman of the house. Madame Marie Bosse."

The grandfather swept his hat off his head and bowed low as La Bosse, dressed head to toe in pink damask, stepped out from the cloister. Antoine's heart leapt. She turned her dark eyes on him and he was instantly lifted to the heavens. It was an extraordinary sensation. Not love. At least, not like that he felt for Catherine. No, this was something else. He struggled to name it. Was it lust? It had been so long. No, it couldn't possibly be that. Enchantment, or perhaps, witchcraft?

"Sir, you are most welcome." Her honeyed voice sent a shiver down Antoine's spine.

"Madam." He gave a slight bow. Unlike the grandfather, he had no hat to doff. He'd lost it somewhere in his shrubbery. He felt underdressed. His brown fustian breeches and leather jerkin were alright for the garden and for running errands for his murderous wife, but not for visiting a lady of such inestimable horticultural talents. Besides, they were wet. *He* was wet.

"Madame is aware of your situation. It was she who suggested I bring you here. She has a solution to your problem." The grandfather chuckled. "Yes, a solution."

A vague sense of uneasiness prickled at Antoine. He liked the grandfather, and this woman was a wondrous creature, but something wasn't quite right. He couldn't put his finger on it.

"You've suffered much pain," said La Bosse. She gave Antoine a sidelong glance and he noticed the high colour in her cheeks and the way her lips parted very slightly to display small white teeth like pearls. Catherine had bad teeth. Those in her lower jaw had almost entirely rotted away. Not that he minded; his own teeth weren't that marvellous. He looked away. It was rude to stare.

"Pain. Hmm."

"Your wife has tried to kill you." La Bosse was nothing if not to the point. She touched his arm and with it came a chilly tingle.

"Nothing ventured, nothing gained," said the grandfather.

How to reply? "All I want is her love. Nothing to kill a man for."

"Love is precious. Very precious." La Bosse took the path through the rose beds to a now sun-blessed seat set against the wall at the end of the cloister. Here she lay out a handkerchief to soak up the raindrops, and sat down on it.

"Come," she said, patting the empty seat beside her. Antoine squeezed in, feeling decidedly uncomfortable, both in body and mind. The dampness of his breeches felt cold now against his buttocks. He raised his eyes to the sky, relishing the sun's warmth. The grandfather melted away so completely it was as if he didn't exist at all. Antoine sat, hands on his knees, waiting like a small child, for chastisement or praise, and all the while something nudged at him. Something wasn't quite right. What was it?

After a while La Bosse said, "Tell me everything."

Antoine gave her a nervous glance. Where to start?

"At the beginning," came the grandfather's voice from the cloister.

At the beginning. Very well, thought Antoine. "My wife is Catherine Deshayes. At least, that was the name her father gave her. I never met him. He died before... before... We were happy. I thought we were happy. Then I lost the shop on the bridge. I... well, the flood came, but she'd already moved out. Catherine I mean. Gone to the Rue Beauregard. I bought the house. I had money then, but now? Now there's nothing save what she earns, and she doesn't share it with me." His words tumbled out. He doubted he'd made much sense.

A delicate blue-winged butterfly hovered above a white rose. Antoine wished he could fly away with it.

"But you live under the same roof?"

"Yes."

"And you eat the food she prepares?"

"The maid cooks it. Sometimes my daughter."

"All the same, your wife provides the food?"

"Yes."

"And you…"

"Vegetables. From the garden. And we used to have a pig." But it was slaughtered, he thought. Slaughtered and eaten and the pigsty's roof fell in. He really ought to repair it.

"But essentially, her income is shared with you."

Antoine knew it. He'd be homeless if it wasn't for… Wait a minute. The house was his. As long as he stayed he'd never be homeless. He was about to say as much when La Bosse spoke up again.

"You're married to La Voisin and she's tried to make an Angel of you."

La Voisin; the neighbour; the Angel-Maker. He shouldn't have come. A dove alighted on the cloister roof. A light breeze ruffled its feathers. Antoine shifted in his seat. He'd been brought to this house under false pretences. Duplicity made for a treacherous friend.

"The old man has become your confidante?" said La Bosse.

Not after this, but Antoine didn't say so.

"You fear being ill-used?"

He gave the briefest of nods. So, she could read minds. He must be careful.

"I will say it plain and simple. You want your wife's love, but she has hardened her heart against you. She has hardened her heart against everyone. It has to be this way or she couldn't withstand the pain and suffering of those who ask for her help." A bee hovered above La Bosse's head. She brushed it away. "She is guardian of a knowledge older than time."

"She is?"

"We all are."

"We?"

"Myself, La Voisin, La Lepére…" Antoine's ears perked at that name. "La Vigoureaux, La Joly. La Filastre. La Trianon."

"So many of you." What confusion.

"A city full. But the best…" La Bosse's eyes glazed for a moment. "Well, there are those who say I am the best, and others who say your wife." She blinked, slowly, very slowly, before refocusing on Antoine. "You think if you open another shop, she will return to your loving arms, full of joy at your entrepreneurial spirit."

Antoine shrugged. It had seemed like such a good idea, but the way this woman described it, it sounded pathetic.

"Four times now. Four times she's tried to kill me."

"Where will she live if you sell the house?"

"Above the shop, with me." He couldn't see what was wrong with this idea. They'd done it before, at the start of their marriage.

"And where will she see her clients? Surely there won't be enough room? Wasn't that why you bought the house in the Rue Beauregard in the first place?"

"I bought it as an investment. You make money and you invest. Everyone does it."

"And you know who her clients are?"

"The Countess of Soissons is one. I met her. In the garden. At the party." He clapped his hand to his mouth. He'd said too much. La Bosse gave a little laugh that made her head nod slightly and her chin jut out.

"And you honestly think a Countess will climb a narrow flight of stairs to a pokey room above a haberdashery?"

Crestfallen, Antoine shook his head. "I might set the house against a loan. Then I wouldn't have to sell it." It was a thought. It might work.

"A loan?"

"Yes." Why not a loan?

"And has anyone come forward to help in this regard?"

"No, not yet, but they will, soon enough."

La Bosse gave him a sly smile. "And this is your plan? To purchase a shop with money borrowed against your house?"

"Yes." At least… what if, even after all his efforts, Catherine still didn't smile? What then?

"You're nothing if not determined. I can help you, but you must give me something in return."

He didn't know what he could possibly give this terrifying creature. The grandfather had led him to the witch's lair and deserted him. Catherine might still kill him, and he had nothing save the house.

"Are you saying you'll lend me the money?"

"Something better. You want the shop because you think that it will mean La Voisin will give you her love." La

Bosse inclined her head slightly. "That's the case, is it not, Monsieur?"

Antoine didn't reply. He was afraid of giving the wrong answer.

"Am I right in thinking Madame De Montespan consults with your wife?"

"Madame de Montespan?"

"The King's mistress."

"Oh, I don't know."

"I think you do. I think you're very good at closing your ears and your eyes to what goes on under your roof, but you know well enough."

It was true, he'd lived for many years knowing and not knowing. He'd only really woken up when that business with the moles happened, and even then... well, he'd tried to push it away. He'd tried to ignore it. It hadn't worked though. It had eaten away at him and now he'd allowed himself to be led to this viciously beautiful garden to sit before this diabolical woman, and all because he wanted another shop; because he thought his success would buy him Catherine's approval and yes, her love. It was a hopeless prospect. Catherine had never really loved him, not like... not like his mother, but wait... she'd not loved him either, and in any case love was nothing but your heart twisting and aching. As to the shop, there was just so much to do. Every time he thought he'd made progress, another stone blocked his path. He turned to La Bosse and in that moment her eyes filled with light. The world became a pinprick of nothingness in which Antoine drifted, mindlessly, blissfully. There, that's what he wanted from Catherine: to drown in her love.

La Bosse clapped her hands and broke the spell. "Bring me information. Names, dates and what her clients want from her. It doesn't matter how insignificant or unusual their demands. For this, I will give you the gift of La Voisin's love."

"Not a loan then?"

"The shop is nothing more than a means to an end. You don't need it. It's very simple. I want La Voisin's business and you want her love."

Ah, so there it was. This woman was Catherine's rival.

She went on, "You don't want to die, do you?"

"No." At least, not until God ordained it, and he couldn't believe that God had agreed to murder, so...

"Then you'll do as I say."

Where Antoine had once seen a magnificent woman he now saw a wholly different creature. Her face was threaded with fine blue veins, her hairline balding and grey, and her lips pinched. She grabbed his hand. He tried to pull away, but her claw-like grip held him fast.

"You know how many men she's killed? Hundreds. That's how many. And those babies? Their deaths were the price we pay for the gift of a life lived to the full. We are all born to die. Some sooner than others. Ask Monsieur Guillaume, the executioner, if you don't believe me. He knows better than most how fleeting life is."

Antoine stood up so quickly La Bosse's nails gouged marks across the back of his hand. He had to get out. Overwhelmed by a surfeit of venom-filled words, he couldn't remember how he'd got here or who with.

"She will kill you and get away with it," hissed La Bosse.

There in the corner of the cloister - the door.

"She won't," Antoine muttered. "She won't." Poison. Poison everywhere: words, thoughts, deeds.

"But if she does?"

"I'll make sure that if she kills me, they will investigate my death and she'll pay for it."

"And how will you accomplish this feat, if you are dead?"

"I will ask this Monsieur Guillaume to examine my body. I will tell him that if I am declared dead, he is to consider me murdered." Yes, yes that's what he'd do. Where was that door? There. He ran.

Outside, the overflowing conduit greeted Antoine with its great stink. It was a marked difference to the heady aroma of the damp rose garden.

"You shouldn't have done that," said the grandfather, coming up behind him.

"You told me she could help," he said. "You lied."

"It's no lie. She can help, if you let her."

"She's as bad as my wife. Worse." Worse because La Bosse was evil dressed in a smile. Not *the* smile, but certainly very alluring. Antoine remembered something his father had once said to him. They'd been sorting buttons; mother-of-pearl from silver. His father had held one of the former up to the light and had showed Antoine how, where the shell was particularly thin, he could see the light shining through. "It looks so perfect doesn't it? But hold it to the light and see? There's nothing to it." There was nothing to La Bosse, but an illusion of beauty.

Antoine crossed the street and took a narrow alley beneath an overhanging house. The grandfather dogged his footsteps, until Antoine stopped dead in his tracks. The walls closed in on him. His heart skipped a beat, and then started up again, ragged and terrifying.

"Go home old man. Go."

"And what are you going to do?"

Antoine waved the grandfather away and started down the alley once more, the thump of his irregular heart loud in his ears. The alley opened into a courtyard, where washing hung on lines and the screams of a baby echoed. A woman stood on a step, beating a mat against the outside wall. Dust billowed out in dirty grey plumes making her cough. She rubbed the back of her hand against her nose. She stole Antoine's stare and returned it with a scowl.

"Where you go is none of my business, of course," called out the grandfather.

Oh Mon Dieu! The old man waited for him to catch up. The woman went inside. The dust settled.

"You know, you've been a thorn in my side since the moment I set eyes on you." Fagioli's wine cellar felt like a lifetime ago.

"I think not. I think you need me."

Antoine wrinkled his nose. He'd loved his father, but hated that he'd drunk himself into an early grave. He'd hated his mother, but loved her too. He loved his wife, but hated what she did. Hated her duplicity, her conniving, her lies and treachery. He enjoyed the grandfather's friendship. Love was too strong a word for it, but certainly, he hated the old man's interference. Hated the way he was always there and always right.

"So, what *are* you going to do?"

Antoine let out a long sigh. "Go to the executioner."

"Monsieur Guillaume? Is that wise? You know what will happen if they find your wife guilty?"

"I'm not dead yet."

"But when you are?"

"It won't matter then will it?"

The alley narrowed, ready to spit the two men out onto the bright street beyond.

The grandfather nodded. "I'll come with you."

"I'd rather go on my own." It was a delicate matter; he'd rather not have someone looking over his shoulder.

The grandfather uncurled a hand from beneath a voluminous sleeve and placed it gently on Antoine's shoulder.

"You've nothing to fear from me. Nothing at all."

Chapter Twenty-Six

The great *Palais du Louvre* stood close enough to the River Seine to dip its feet in the swirling waters. Behind the confectioned south façade, in a suite of rooms that had only recently been remodelled, his Majesty, the Sun King, had amassed a collection of paintings the like of which could not be equalled anywhere else. Today was particularly notable because he'd decided to hang works previously kept in storage. A number of paintings purchased many years earlier from Jabach the banker would now take pride of place on the walls of the *Petite Gallerie.*

The curators fussed over the correct position for each piece, arguing with each other in hushed tones about height and prominence. The King observed with head cocked first this way and then that, while his entourage, including his mistress, Madame De Montespan and various ladies of the court, scurried to keep up with him.

At a little past noon a door opened and three men, one of whom was the Minister of War, Marquis de Louvois, approached. The ladies broke out in a flutter of fans and low-voiced comments. The men stopped short of His Majesty by a good margin and waited. The King extended an arm, unrolled his long fingers and beckoned him proceed. Louvois was a plump young man who'd somehow managed to win both the Sovereign's ear and his confidence.

"What news of the Spanish?"

Louvois bowed low. "Your Majesty. The Comte de Vivonne has brought us another victory. Our galleys engaged the Spanish off the Isle of Lipari."

"A hot bed of pirates."

"We dealt them a harsh blow."

"But that is fine news! And we must reward our men. They fight all the more readily when they go after a boon. What do you suggest?"

"Your Majesty. It is not for me to say."

"You're not usually so bashful." The King looked Louvois straight in the eye and tried to read his Minister's mind. When he failed, he tried to catch the gaze of Madame De Montespan. When he failed the King turned his attention back to Louvois.

"Well.. free... fifteen galley slaves."

"Your Majesty?"

"I'm feeling generous. The prisons are overflowing with reprobates ready to take their place. Free fifteen men from whichever galley you choose."

"Your Majesty is indeed most generous."

"Make it so." The King waved his hand, dismissively, and Louvois backed away, bowing long and low.

Chapter Twenty-Seven

The executioner's old wooden house was commonly known as the Mansion. It was a dark, octagonal structure in the marketplace of Les Halles. A visitor to Paris might say it was an unfortunate location for such a house because of its proximity to the market and also because it served as the pillory; a giant cage revolving beneath a sharp steeple. Those who lived in its vicinity gave it little thought, save when some poor unfortunate was executed. Then the spectacle could be quite something.

Antoine had passed the Mansion many times. There was always someone in the cage, and always plenty of rotting vegetables to throw. Today was no different. The man imprisoned aloft was dirt-smeared and rake thin. Antoine winced and tried hard not to look, spotting instead the grandfather, who had trailed him all the way, pausing only to test the air for the direction of wind and to watch the clouds scud overhead. A storm threatened. Shaking his head at the old man's antics, Antoine noticed the executioner coming out of his outhouse. Monsieur Guillaume had a shock of red hair and the look of a fox caught in a culvert.

"Monsieur? A word if I may?"

The executioner squinted across the market place.

"What is it?" he said out of the corner of his mouth.

Slightly out of breath, Antoine drew in a lungful of air before continuing.

"It's a matter of importance. Great importance."

Monsieur Guillaume frowned. "Robbery? Someone has been kidnapped? A murder?"

"Not yet." Antoine threw a glance at the grandfather, feigning interest in a stall selling wooden toys. "Can we talk somewhere more private?"

Monsieur Guillaume leaned forward. Antoine caught a blast of his garlicky breath.

"Makes no difference what you got to tell me. No one listens to my conversations for fear they'll be next." He pointed at the cage, rotating creak upon creak.

"All the same." Antoine didn't want to take any chances.

"Oh, alright." Monsieur Guillaume led the way round the back of the Mansion to an alcove under the eaves, where he could watch the cage and observe the market, whilst remaining relatively unseen. If ever there was a time for Antoine to feel uncomfortable it was now, pressed into the space between this house of death and the man who knew a hundred ways to kill you, and all legal. Panic suddenly spread through Antoine like a wild fire, leaving him feeling weak and pathetic. Barely able to breathe, he leaned back against the wall and gulped in the air.

"So what is it?" said Monsieur Guillaume. He pulled out a clay pipe and stuffed the bowl with odoriferous tobacco.

Sweat trickled down the back of Antoine's neck. His scalp itched, and his palms too. This wouldn't do. What was he, a man or a mouse? He tamped down his fear. He'd done nothing wrong. No charges had ever been brought against him. He'd never suffered the ignominy of being incarcerated in the executioner's cage. He gazed out over the cobblestones. A bit of old cabbage leaf, caught in a crevice, waved at him like a green flag. A dirt-smeared boy, leading a mule with overloaded saddlebags, skipped past. A hoof caught the cabbage leaf and ground it to a pulpy smear.

"My wife's trying to kill me." It came out with a gulp. He thought of his terrible mother. She haunted his every thought.

"Your wife?"

"Yes. My wife."

"Why haven't you gone to the gendarmerie?"

"The gendarmerie? Oh, them. I can't prove it. Not yet. No, not yet, but I will." He should have been collecting evidence; proof of Catherine's attempts. All he had was supposition and his daughter's word. Perhaps that was good enough.

"So why are you here?"

"I heard... someone said..."

The fox arched his eyebrows. "Yes?"

"If it looks like I've been murdered, well... you can examine my body. See what you find. You can do that can't you?" It came to him that the executioner might not learn of his death until he was in the ground and they'd have to dig him up again. Catherine would never allow that.

"I'm not a physician. I don't have the authority. Monsieur Gramond is the man you need. Tell a gendarme."

Antoine twitched and shook. His nerves were frayed with the worry of it all. Talking to this man was a mistake.

"But I'll be dead. The thing is... I can't prove anything, save she's tried four times now. Four times. You have to help me."

"Four times? Who? You said 'she'. Who is this 'she'?"

"I told you. My wife. My wife is trying to kill me, and she'll succeed, if I'm not careful, and I'm very careful... well, sometimes I'm not, but..."

The executioner pointed at Antoine's chest with the stem of his pipe. "Look. I don't even know who you are so how would I know if your wife was trying to kill you?"

"She's La Voisin."

The executioner's eyes widened.

Antoine went on, "You must know who she is. Everyone else does. I can't go anywhere, say anything without someone gives me a sideways look."

The calls of the hawkers on the market, the creak of the cage overhead, the moaning wind through the cracks and crevices in the old Mansion house sounded out loud and clear, but not a word came from Monsieur Guillaume.

"She kills for a living," Antoine continued, after a decent period. "That's how I know, she's killed others and now she's tried to kill me, and she'll go on trying until I'm dead and buried."

Still no reply. A thread on Antoine's cuff started to unravel. He picked at it.

"Four times. Four times. Do you hear me? I don't know what poison she used... well one time she tried with toad poison, only I threw it away, but I'm pretty sure...my daughter will confirm it. She knows."

Antoine peered out of the alcove like a rabbit caught in the briars and the fox right there, next to him, ready to pounce. The frayed cuff annoyed him.

"This was a mistake." It all sounded so contrary. "If an investigation shows I was poisoned then my wife will be executed won't she?"

"Not necessarily."

"What d'you mean, not necessarily?"

"Thieving'll get you strung up. Murder's not so easy to prove."

"Not so easy to prove. I'm telling you. You have to do something. It's driving me mad." Antoine looped the cuff's thread tight around his forefinger and tugged at it. The end of his finger went white, but the thread didn't break.

"Go home and prepare yourself."

"Prepare myself? What for?" Antoine tugged at the thread again. The cuff frayed some more, but the thread finally gave. Antoine waved his thread-pinched finger.

"I don't want to bring about her downfall, but I can't let my death go unpunished."

The briar patch tightened its grip. His mother had once caught him behind a stack of cotton and backed him into a corner, but then she was always doing that. Standing in the alcove with the executioner felt the same.

"Quite." Monsieur Guillaume smiled sourly, nosed the air and glanced up at the cage. The wind rattled though the bars. "What's in it for me?"

"I don't…"

"What will you pay me?"

"Pay you?

"Investigations cost time. Time costs money. I've got to earn a living. In the normal run of things, I'm entitled to take whatever's on the body, or what they've brought to the jail with them. In your case, I'd expected a hundred livres."

"A hundred...? I don't have that." It always came down to money.

"Can't help you then."

Antoine blew his cheeks out and set his head to nodding up and down, up and down.

"I understand. You're a businessman. I thought perhaps I could... appeal to your sense of right and wrong."

"Right and wrong don't mean much in my business. If you aren't serious, go home."

"Home. Right. Well, I don't have a hundred livres so that's it then." Nodding and bowing like a maniac, Antoine backed out of the alcove.

***

The grandfather, observing all from afar, watched Antoine weave through the stalls, avoiding the wind-borne debris. When the moment was right, he stepped alongside and pressed his lips close to the younger man's ear.

"You got what you came for?"

Antoine jumped, his hand going automatically to his chest.

"Oh, you gave me a start. I thought you'd gone."

"What did he say? Will he do it?"

"Will he do what?"

"Investigate your death." The grandfather tugged on his beard and sniffed the air.

"Not unless I come up with a hundred livres. I need a drink."

"Ah. Then let me accompany you to the finest of inns and there we will celebrate your imminent demise."

"Cheery fellow, aren't you?"

The grandfather smiled, dipped his head and spread his arms wide, as if bowing to his audience. Inscrutable, that's what he was. Inscrutable.

***

They drank in the old tavern close to Les Halles all afternoon - all afternoon, with a north-easterly wing tearing tiles loose from the rooftops, and buffeting the cage atop the Mansion so that it sounded like some hellish kind of monster. Antoine, in no mood to talk, supped his vinegary wine slowly, his mind spinning stories to tell the devil. Four attempts on his life. The fifth might be the one that killed him. He wasn't a cat. He didn't have nine lives to waste. If he had, what life would he have reached? His first life would be from birth to the first attempt...

...the second... he scratched his calculations into the sticky table top...

...the third...

...and then the fourth.

He reckoned he was on his fifth life.

The grandfather eyed the scribbles. "Trust me, she'll not stop until you're dead."

"I thought La Bosse was going to help."

"You walked out on her."

He had. He had indeed. He couldn't sit here drinking himself stupid. He needed to act. He'd spoken to the executioner and much good that had done. Next up, a visit to the money lender on the Pont au Change to try and raise the cash for his shop. For one brief moment he toyed with the idea of setting some of it aside to pay the executioner, but if he did that it would mean less for the shop. Oh, but what was the moneylender's name? Antoine stared at the innkeeper; a wiry man with the look of a stoat. Monsieur Tournier. That was it. Monsieur Tournier on the Pont au Change. He'd go there immediately. He exchanged stares with the grandfather.

"Can you read minds?"

"I read people not minds." The grandfather closed his eyes.

Antoine traced a line of spilled wine on the table. It meandered with the grain of the wood, came up against a knot, and pooled. He'd used the flood as an excuse for not doing anything. He'd been upset and confused and done nothing for too long. He'd been forced into a slothful life, but no more. Catherine didn't hate him. She hated his apathy. She hated what he'd become. Goodness, he hated what he'd become. Things would change once he had the shop. She would smile. It was only a matter of time. What did he need the executioner for? Nothing. It had been a stupid idea. Catherine would be all love and smiles once he had the shop.

The grandfather's head nodded, chin to chest, grizzled beard trapped, his breathing ponderous. Antoine eyed the door. He might just be able to slip out from behind the table without the grandfather following him. Right on cue, the old man's head bobbed. Antoine froze. The grandfather's breathing settled. Antoine chanced it, pushed up from his seat and was gone.

The wind rampaged through the streets, chasing debris into corners, forcing people to either go home, or take shelter in doorways and alleys. Antoine ignored the gusts and hugged the wall, heading towards the Rue St. Denis and then straight down to the Pont au Change, where a flotilla of light ships bobbed up and down on the swell.

The wind sang through the rigging and unfurled sails to flap like wild ghosts in the gloom. Night had crept up unannounced and pushed the billowed storm clouds aside. A biting chill crept beneath Antoine's jerkin. Winter closed in with every step.

The Pont au Change.

As with all bridges it was topped with houses and shops; an assortment of life; a continuation of the city and yet as distinct a place as to be another country. It wasn't the Pont Marie - his very own Pont Marie, but it was a bridge all the same and gave him much trepidation. Now or never. Antoine took a step, and then another, and another and before he knew it had passed onto that strange, not-land world.

"Monsieur?" Antoine touched the sleeve of a passer-by. The man glanced round. "Do you know where I can find Monsieur Tournier?"

"Who's asking?" The man disappeared in the gloom.

Caught up in a surge of noisy people, Antoine sailed forward, only to be deposited outside a ramshackle shop. The crowd dispersed. Antoine stepped closer, out of the flow of foot traffic. The door had several layers of thick varnish, chipped and scratched. The window had small panes of opaque glass. A worn sign read: "Tournier and Sons, Moneylenders by Appointment to His Majesty". A lie, of course. The door opened and a woman stepped out, bumped past and continued on her way. Antoine stepped inside. Tournier was busy lighting candles. With each, a globe of light grew bright in the murk, but did little to illuminate the whole.

"Monsieur?" said Antoine. The man started and the lit taper almost flew out of his hand.

"Who's there? Who's there?" Tournier craned his neck to peer more closely at Antoine. "We met, I believe. Yes, yes, we met. On the bridge, or not on the bridge. Hah, well we're on the bridge now aren't we?" He beckoned Antoine forward, waving the taper. When it failed to extinguish he blew on it, almost setting light to his tight white curls in the process.

He sang out, "I am the best. The best. The best. Come inside." His hands fluttered over papers laid out on the table. He rolled, folded and whisked all into drawers and onto shelves. Antoine followed hesitantly, marvelling at the man's dexterity.

"I need a loan."

"If you have the right collateral then anything is possible. Yes, that's it. Collateral. Here, come here. Here," and Tournier ushered Antoine into a chair with a view through a green-glass window to the swirling waters of the Seine. The shop was small and dark, and the air rich with the aroma of boiled mutton.

"Sit. Sit. We'll have a nice chat. Yes? Now how may I serve you?" Tournier settled into the chair opposite, steepled his fingers and smiled over the top of them. Instantly, Antoine felt at ease. The years of anxiety and lack of gumption dropped away and the marchand-mercier he had once been re-emerged. He knew how to strike a deal. He must be cautious though, these moneylenders were all charm and glib praise. He would start slowly; create rapport. Yes, that was it. Before he was done he would have this moneylender eating out of his hand. He felt sure of it.

"I have a very nice house in a better part of town." It wasn't exactly the truth. The Rue Beauregard was situated in the enclave of Villeneuve Sur Gravois, which some said festered indolently on the proceeds of its inhabitants' dishonourable income. Never mind, it was as good an opening gambit as any.

Tournier's gaze didn't waver. "Go on. Go on."

"Do you remember the flood of '58?"

"Do I remember? I remember it all right. We had a night of it. The waters rose, yay high." He put a hand up to indicate the level. "We thought we might be next, but God in His infinite wisdom thought to spare us." Here Tournier pulled a crucifix out from betwixt his garments, and kissed it profusely.

Antoine continued. "I had one of the shops that was destroyed on the Pont Marie. In fact, I was brought up there."

"You were?"

Antoine sighed. "A long time ago now."

"And what happened? What happened? Tell me. Tell me."

"I lost everything, that's what. The shop, my stock, my livelihood. Gone in an instant."

Tournier's hand went to his mouth. "What horror. What unimaginable horror."

"Yes, well. I'd had the good fortune to have earned enough money to buy a house, so I simply moved there and…"

"Continued business? Yes? Business is everything."

"Ah, well it didn't work out that way. My wife you see…" He couldn't say it. He couldn't say that his wife was La Voisin. Not to this man. He'd told the executioner because he'd had to, but he really couldn't bring himself to keep spreading the news of his unfortunate coupling.

"My wife has enough money to keep us both."

"You were lucky. Lucky indeed."

"But the problem is, she wants me out from under her feet, and so I have it in mind to go back into the trade."

"The trade? What trade?"

He frowned. "Didn't I say? A marchand-mercier. One of the best, in my day."

"And you want to use your house as collateral?"

"I do."

"And its value?"

"I… I'm not sure."

"How many windows does it have? Yes, windows? How many?"

"Seven, I think. A lot. It's a big house, with a fine garden." Antoine didn't mention the molehills, the babies and the dread that came with digging up another poor little corpse.

"Hm… I'd need to look at it. I would. I'd need to look. I can't possibly say until then. What do you need? How much? How much?"

"Enough to take out a lease on some premises and buy stock. No more than…" How much? A good question. "Two, three hundred livres?" A fortune. More than the executioner wanted. Antoine felt stupid; asking for money from a complete stranger. The thought of it.

"So much, and where? Where? On the bridge? On that bridge?" Tournier pointed through the window to the distant Pont De Notre Dame with its high-built houses. Antoine followed his finger.

"No. Heavens no. I couldn't…." The thought of it confused him. It wouldn't be right. The Pont De Notre Dame was far too grand, and besides, he'd been on dry land for too long now to spend any amount of time once more marooned mid-river, no matter how comfortable he felt on the Pont au Change. No, he wanted someone closer to the main thoroughfare. Then again, he rather liked the idea of picking up where he left off, bridge and all.

As if he'd read Antoine's mind, Monsieur Tournier ventured, "There's a shop empty three doors down from here. Nice little place, tucked a bit back, but watertight. Yes, watertight. Got one room out back, and the upstairs is leased out to a jeweller. Might suit you. And I happen to know the landlord. I do. I do."

Three doors down. "Ah, could I look at it?"

"Now? Not now. No. Too dark. Too late. I need my supper."

Antoine hadn't been keeping track of the time, but his belly had. It rumbled.

"When then?"

"When I've… when I've appraised your property. Then I'll know if you can afford it." Tournier twirled his hand with a flourish.

"And who is the landlord?"

"You're looking at him."

"I see. Well, very good. Name your time and day I will endeavour to…" to get rid of Catherine for long enough to show Tournier around the house without argument.

The moneylender consulted an imaginary calendar, counting the days and time off with a finger poised mid-air, flipping and flicking and counting.

"Ah, three days?"

"Not earlier?"

"Best I can do. Unless I get a cancellation."

"A cancellation?"

Tournier shrugged. "That's the way of it, in my business. It is. It is." He tapped the side of his nose. "Your name sir. I didn't catch it. Nor your address."

Antoine bit the inside of his cheek. "Monsieur Montvoisin. My house is the one next to the church on the Rue Beauregard."

Tournier raised eyebrows. "I thought you said a good part of town. No?"

"It's got a good view." Antoine put his head down, desperate now to be out of this dark place and halfway home.

"Of that mud hole the old Court of Miracles maybe but…"

Antoine didn't hear the rest. He'd gone. The wind flattened his breeches to his thighs and tested the hat on his head. Three doors down he pressed his nose against the windowpane of the empty shop and tried to see inside. Nothing came to him but a ghostly haze. He backed off and let the wind gust him along the bridge in a daze. His new shop was within grasp. He just needed his papers and all would be well.

Chapter Twenty-Eight

Catherine, napping on her bed, one shoe on and one off, her hair tangled, her eyelashes fluttering dreamily, heard nothing of the storm, nor even her daughter's insistent voice urging her to wake up. The dream snared Marguerite, along with a door banging, a staircase creaking, a dog barking and the sensation of rocking. Catherine cracked an eye.

"There's someone here to see you," said Marguerite. "A man."

"Hmm? What did you say?"

"A man. Downstairs. Says he's Monsieur Guillaume. He says it's urgent."

"Who? Guillaume? Guillaume who?" Catherine pulled herself upright. A man, at this hour? What was the hour?

"Monsieur Guillaume."

"Oh my goodness, why didn't you say?" Catherine lurched off the bed. She broke down the back of one of her shoes as she pushed her foot inside. She hobbled across the chamber. Monsieur Guillaume! How often she'd tried to snare him and failed, but wait... She froze.

"Did he say what his business was with me?"

"No. Who is he?"

"The executioner, that's who."

Marguerite's mouth fell open. "The executioner?"

Catherine was already halfway down the stairs. She called back, "Don't gawp. Bring us some wine."

On the bottom step she licked her few good teeth and patted down her hair. Monsieur Guillaume's wife had left him. He was fancyfree and wealthy to boot. His job often brought him surprising boons, but he was not a man to be trifled with.

"Things are looking up," Catherine muttered, as she entered the fancy receiving room.

"To what do I owe this very great pleasure?"

Monsieur Guillaume, sitting in the shadows next to the shuttered window, rose to greet her. His was the grubbiest of professions, and yet here he was in all his finery. Catherine's eyes travelled to his fingers. As far as she could tell, they were clean, and the nails neatly cut.

"Madame. I have information that may be of interest to you, but first I must assure myself that your husband is not at home. The girl said not. Is that the case?"

"I don't know where he is. What kind of information?" Catherine, smoothed down her pink silk skirt and sat opposite him, endeavouring to hide her feet from view.

"I'll come straight to the point," said Monsieur Guillaume. "He paid me a visit."

"Antoine? Visited you, but why?"

The executioner leaned forward, as if to impart a secret. "He wants me to investigate a murder." He glanced round at the door and then back again.

"Whose?"

"His own."

Catherine barked out a laugh. "He isn't dead." But he would be soon enough.

"Not yet, no, but he has some concerns and he thought I might be able to help him. Are you sure he's not at home?"

"He's… somewhere. Did he tell you who he thought might do the deed?"

"You."

Catherine noticed a flicker of amusement on his face.

"And you believe him?"

"He'll be your undoing."

Catherine wasn't sure what he meant. It could be a threat. "Monsieur, what do you want from me?"

"You're a fine looking woman. You can't be without your admirers."

"I am well received, it's true. What of it?"

"I might be persuaded to remain silent."

"Blackmail? You of all people. It's a crime."

"It's nothing of the sort Madame. Not when all are agreed." He held her gaze for a moment and then allowed his eyes to linger over her décolletage before bringing them back to her face. A flicker of understanding passed between them.

"But not here," said Catherine. It wouldn't do to be seen with this man, no matter how much money he had. It would have to be somewhere out of the way.

"And not at the Mansion," he said.

His voice held a darkness that raised the hairs on the back of Catherine's neck.

"I hear you have a house on the outskirts of the city."

"In the country. It's private enough."

The idea came to her in a flash. "Monsieur, do many murders remained unsolved?"

"Unsolved? What has this got to do with my house?"

"My husband has an uncanny knack of survival. If he were found guilty of murder, he would be executed, would he not? He couldn't possibly survive an execution, and I would have nothing to do with it."

Monsieur Guillaume's eyebrows danced.

Catherine continued, "I will deny it if you bring charges against me."

"You realise what you're suggesting is…"

"Wrong? I think we are both long past wrong." Catherine's hand went to her breasts. "I can be most accommodating. Discreet. Your wife has left you and the whores you visit are pathetic creatures. Wouldn't you like a real woman?" She licked her lips. When it came to it, most men were stupid for sex.

"Can you find a freshly murdered corpse?"

"Of course," said Monsieur Guillaume.

"And the evidence?"

"A bloody knife, hidden in personal belongings should do it."

"And he'd be executed?"

"He'll have to stand trial, but yes, if someone is found guilty of a crime for which the penalty is death, then I would carry out the sentence to the best of my ability." He flexed his fingers. "You realise murder is not frowned upon as much as, say, theft? It would be easier to try him for theft. Get him sent to the galleys or such like."

"No. He'd still be alive. How soon can you arrange it?"

"An arrest? Or execution?"

"Either. Both. How soon?"

"There's any number of deaths to choose from. It's a small matter to tip-off that hound Desgrez. Your husband can be arrested tomorrow morning if you so desire."

"I can't have them take him here."

"Where then?"

Catherine wasn't sure. Where? An errand? That might work. She lifted her petticoats. Monsieur Guillaume drew in an audible breath.

"My shoes need repairing. I'll send Antoine to the cobbler. Monsieur Petibon on the Rue St. Denis. It's busy there. Plenty of people will witness it. Do we have a deal?"

"It'll cost you more than a night's romp."

Catherine held her poise. "How much?"

"Your husband was ready to pay me a hundred livres."

"I don't believe you. He's not got a sous to his name."

"What do you earn?"

"It's none of your business."

"Two hundred livres and I will bring you his head."

"Impossible!" She had no doubt Monsieur Guillaume would do as he said, but the thought of paying out all that money when she should have been able to do the job herself galled.

"Then, forgive me, but I must decline."

Monsieur Guillaume stood up, gave a slight bow, took one of Catherine's hands in his own and pressed his lips to it. He started towards the door. Catherine's thoughts tumbled over one another.

"Wait. I'll match his offer. One hundred livres."

Monsieur Guillaume half-turned. "One-fifty, three nights, and you have a deal."

Catherine gave a curt nod.

"Madame." Monsieur Guillaume placed his hat on his head and left Catherine clenching both fists and teeth.

Why was it men were so... so... Argh, she had no words for it.

***

The church of Notre Dame de Bonne Nouvelle. A whisper of wind through the cracks. Just a whisper, though outside the storm raged like no other. Without warning the doors banged open and the gale entered like a howling demon. Abbé Davot, on his knees at the altar, looked up, a prayer for deliverance from gluttony on his lips. Lesage stood halfway down the aisle, his clothes no more than tattered rags, his eyes crazed, and his beard long and unkempt.

Davot struggled to his feet. "You! I thought you were…"

"Dead?"

Davot sensed menace. "They sent you to the galleys. What happened?" Had he escaped? Were the gendearmes after him? Or worse still, the musketeers?

"The King, in his wisdom, saw fit to release us."

"But you were…"

"Fighting the good fight in Lipari, though down in the galley's bowels I saw precious little of it." Lesage pulled off a long-cuffed glove.

"And the King just set you free? Just like that? Why? Why would he do that?"

"We won the battle. Seems he was pleased with us. Who was it?" Lesage drew in closer, picking at a whitlow on his index finger. The raven took another step back.

"Who was it what?" Davot didn't like the look of this fellow. Lesage had changed. Become, somehow, wilier, if that were at all possible. The man had always been a trickster.

"The tattletale. The one that informed on us. Do you know? Was it the haberdasher next door?"

Davot put a finger to his lips to shush the interloper.

As a priest he'd done so many bad things; ungodly things. He'd pay penance, but right now he needed to get rid of this dishevelled criminal. He felt Lesage's breath on his chin; the smell all bilge water and faeces. Lesage stroked Davot's face.

"I haven't got any money if that's what you want." Davot knocked Lesage's hand away and took another step back, feeling the uneven stones beneath his feet and the weight of his draw-stringed purse against his thigh.

"Did she kill her husband in the end?" Lesage threw a nod to one side. "Madame Montvoisin. Well, did she? Got a guilty conscience have we?"

Davot grabbed at his purse and spread its mouth wide. "How much to go away?"

"You said you had no money."

"I have enough. What do you want?" Davot emptied it into his palm.

Four?" Lesage's eyes widened. "Maybe five livres?"

"Two, and that's all I can manage."

"You have at least five there."

"Three."

"Give me four."

"I can't. I won't have enough."

"Enough for what? Give me four and I will leave you to your guilt."

Davot sighed. Those who want to be rich fall into temptation and become ensnared by many foolish and harmful desires that plunge them into ruin and destruction. This he knew to be true. Lesage grabbed up the coins and spun away, laughing.

"What is it the Bible says? Put to death your earthly nature: sexual immorality, impurity, lust, evil desires, and greed."

Davot watched the snake walk towards the open door where outside, the wind took up a swirl of leaves to flirt with the grimacing stone cherubs.

"You should never have come back."

Lesage waved a couple of fingers without turning and put the wind to his back.

***

Catherine, closing her shutters against the storm, saw her former lover stride down the road, and did a turn and turn about. Her heart leapt. It couldn't be. In an instant she banged through the door to run after him, never minding that the wind greeted her like a vicious dog, snapping at her heels, swirling her petticoats and hobbling her with every step. She fought for her footing as her prey got away. Her letter had worked. He'd come back. The young girl she'd once been told her everything would be alright now. The woman she was in that moment cautioned her to take care. The aged crone she'd yet to become growled she was a fool and no good would come of it.

"Monsieur!" The gale took her voice away and brought tears to her eyes. The man in question didn't stop, nor even glance round. Perhaps it wasn't him. After all, why would he walk down her street if he wasn't going to visit her? But it must be him. He had the same slouch. The same nonchalant gait.

"Monsieur Lesage!"

Still nothing.

"Adam Coureret, you stop right there."

At the sound of his real name, Lesage spun round. Catherine came to a halt and stood hands on hips, her face like thunder, the wind crusting her tears. Lesage took a step towards her, and then another.

"I was going to come to see you, but…" He shivered. "Can we have this conversation inside?" He danced foot to foot.

"Of course. What am I thinking?" The sarcasm in Catherine's voice rung out. The old crone had won out; she'd been a fool to fall for this rogue. She'd be an even bigger fool to throw her lot in with him again. Lesage came closer still.

"You shouldn't have called me by that name. Not out here. Not on the street."

"Which name?"

"You know which one." Another step and he'd almost reached her.

"I wrote to the King you know. I wrote asking him to have you released. You wouldn't be here otherwise." Nasty snivelling man. She should have left him to rot at His Majesty's pleasure.

"I don't think it had anything to do with any letter." Lesage looked off down the street and then back at Catherine. "Business good is it?"

Look at him, she thought. All skin and bone. What had she ever seen in him?

"Madame Brisard came this afternoon. You killed a dove for her once. Read the entrails." The wind whipped Catherine's hair across her face. There were better men than Lesage. The executioner sprang to mind.

Lesage took the last step.

"Not here," said Catherine, smelling Lesage's foul odour, putting a hand out to stop him. He was as pathetic a creature as Antoine.

Lesage pressed his face in close to hers, but didn't touch her, didn't do anything save inspect her.

"Inside?" he said.

"Antoine is at home."

Lesage walked away. Back to her, he said, "You've had ample time. You should have let me do it. You talk about entrails? I would have read his in an instant." He clicked his fingers.

"He will be, soon enough." She'd waited a long time for this man's return. She had written a pleading, whining letter, begging for his release. She'd placed herself at the mercy of the King's mistress and for what? This ragamuffin? Time apart had not made her heart grow fonder. She picked up her petticoats and left Lesage standing in the street.

Chapter Twenty-Nine

The following morning, with rain sleeting sideways, the gendarmes, mob-handed, pushed into a small cobbler's shop on the Rue St. Denis and pinned Antoine to the back wall. He dropped Catherine's broken down shoes and exclaimed, "What? What am I supposed to have done?" He'd lived as blameless a life as possible. He didn't kill people for a living, not like his wife. He didn't confuse them with potions and powders, or take their unborn babes from the womb. Lord, but perhaps they'd dug up the garden while he'd been out, and Catherine had told them it was all down to him. If he could have genuflected he would have, but the bindings bit into his wrists and the stench of last night's ale came heavy from the gendarme who now leaned hard on him.

"Murder. That's what," the stinking man muttered.

"Murder? Me? Never." Not him. Catherine yes, but not him.

The crowd pressed their faces to the window and huddled so close they prevented the gendarme from removing his prisoner without something of a tussle. Antoine hung his head. The shame of it. If the corporation heard of this there'd be no reissue of his master's certificate. No chance of opening his shop again.

Monsieur Petibon, the cobbler, seemed as concerned as Antoine. He fretted and fussed.

"Gentlemen, please, think of my customers. My wife. My livelihood."

The gendarmes forced their way through the crowd, ignoring the cobbler's pleas.

Antoine said, "Where are you taking me?"

No answer came. The gendarme at his back bundled him into a waiting tumbrel. The wood was black and splintered and the boards slippery. Antoine shivered, lost his footing and came down hard on a knee. Pain shot up into his thigh. The gendarme yanked him upright and shoved him onto the bench. Antoine could see the surface of the road between the slats in the bottom. Better men than he had gone to the gallows in such a cart. His mother had always said he'd end up on the wrong side of the law, and here he was. What did it matter what the corporation thought; he'd be lucky to get out of this mess alive. He was nothing more than unspun wool; roving they called it. No substance. Raw unspun roving. He broke into fragile tears, his pent up emotions tumbling out with his words.

"I haven't done anything. You have to believe me. You have to." He was as innocent as the day he was born. If he'd been an obliging child and died at birth, like the garden babies, poor little molehill creatures, then none of this would have happened.

Stone-faced, the gendarme tied Antoine's hands to the backboard. Old blood had stained the wood a bitter black. Antoine's heart skipped a beat, nudging the old torture, knee and heart both in agony. A hollow sensation tore at his guts. He needed the outhouse. He didn't want to soil his breeches. The shame of it. He fidgeted uncomfortably, and one of the gendarmes gave him a slap that said 'keep still'.

If he'd have died at birth then he'd not have lived to see his mother die, nor married the most beautiful woman in all Paris, who had also turned out to be the most evil, nor lost his own little son, nor suffered at the hands of... he couldn't remember. It was all jumbled up. Truth and fiction, warp and weft and the soft foolish roving.

"I haven't done anything." He glanced at the sky, half expecting to see God glowering at him from the heavens. A fat blob of rain hit him in the eye, and then another, and another. He blinked the drops away and brought his gaze back down to earth. The grandfather stood in the crowd of gawpers. Rain plastered the old man's grizzled hair to the sides of his face so he looked like some latter-day holy man.

"Tell Catherine," Antoine shouted. "Tell her I couldn't get her shoes mended. Tell her I love her." Nothing mattered anymore save the love he felt for his terrible wife. Yes, and his mother too. Miserable old sow she'd been; eaten away with hate from the inside out. He had to stop hating or he'd go the same way... if he lived that long. It was love then. Love or nothing.

Monsieur Petibon stood on his doorstep, the offending shoes in hand. The driver cracked the reins and the horse jolted forward.

"Wait," the grandfather shouted, breaking into a haphazard run. "Wait. He's innocent. Listen to me." The old man couldn't keep up; the cart left him behind.

The passing streets blurred as despair got the better of Antoine. The pain in his chest grew and grew, sapping his strength and threatening to knock him out cold. His guts strained to hold onto their load. He couldn't think straight. He hung his head and felt the crowd's eyes on him, stories running between this man and that; a thousand lies for every truth. Antoine dreaded the idea of gossip more than death itself. And murder? Well, they'd hang him for that and blather endlessly about it in the taverns and wine cellars. He closed his eyes and tried to blot everything out, but the sound of the wheels, squeaking and groaning, the horse's hooves on the cobbles, the muttering city and cold rain forced him further and further into his memories.

A curl of thread, silver against the darkest of velvets. He'd thought it silk, but his father said not. His mother had slapped his hand away and sent him outside. The air had been crisp and the rime on the window-ledge thick. He'd leaned over the bridge's parapet and thrown pebbles at the ice caught against the lee of the abutment below. Then had come the clip around the back of his head and his mother's voice, as sharp as the brightest shards of broken ice. "Get back inside. You'll catch your death. Not that it would be any great loss."

A rising tide of sorrow welled up. Antoine opened his eyes and glimpsed a beetle, caught between the tumbrel's baseboards. He closed his eyes again and dived down deep.

"You're the only family your mother's got." His father sucked at the end of a thread and, with one eye screwed up, threaded a needle. Antoine had watched him do it a thousand times. "She's afraid she's going to lose you."

"But Papa, she hates me."

"She doesn't hate you. Not you. She hates the life she's never had."

"I don't understand."

Montvoisin Senior had laid down his sewing and sighed, long and deep. "The thing is, your mother never had a family. What you've never had, you can't give."

232

"I don't understand."

"Love, boy. Love. She's been a good wife, and she's looked after the shop and fed us both, but there's no love in her. Never was. Never will be. I blame her mother. Abandoned her she did. It's not anyone's fault."

Back then, Antoine hadn't understood what his father had meant, but now, with his own wife just as spiteful as his mother had once been, it made more sense: the endless web of pretence, woven by day and undone by night.

The tumbrel lurched to a halt. Antoine felt his arse pucker as tight as a whore's lips. He opened his eyes and a hand reached out, grabbed him up and hauled him down. The guards frogmarched him through heavy oak doors and down a long, vaulted corridor. On and on they went; now descending steps, going deeper, ever deeper, into the bowels of the old fortress. An acrid smell came to him, the air bitter, and the sound subtly different. Cell doors clanged and keys rattled. Voiced echoed. The floor, slippery at every step, ran with sewage.

"You've got the wrong man. I'm innocent," Antoine pleaded, his guts ready to explode if they didn't let him use the pot soon.

"They all say that." The words echoed: "say that, say that."

They pushed him forward and slammed the door. A tiny slit of a glassless window, high in the slime-greened wall, offered the only light. A stone bench and a bucket – thank the Lord - greeted him. With the greatest of haste Antoine pulled down his breeches and squatted over the receptacle. His bowels responded, not with a whimper, but with a roar.

Relieved somewhat, he shouted, "I'm innocent."

Laughter rang out, followed by a volley of coughing. Antoine stood up, righted his breeches and wrinkled his nose at the foul smell he'd created.

"God damn it."

He was caught between gendarme and execution, imprisoned for nothing more than being in the wrong place at the wrong time. And Catherine? He couldn't die without seeing her smile. It was all he'd ever wanted: her glorious, wonderful, love-filled smile. He sat down on the cold stone shelf and tried to ignore the foetid icy air and the other inmates' desperate cries. He'd give anything to see the smile and yet Catherine had tried to poison him time and again. How stupid did a man have to be to love a woman like that? Fine kettle of fish, and it was all down to those moles. If he hadn't sat up in wait for them in the garden…

… the garden. He should plant more roses. He'd been particularly taken with La Bosse's arbour. Oh, what the hell was he thinking, La Bosse was another viper, as poisonous as his own sweet Catherine. His gut, his malodourous gut, told him they were almost one and the same creature, and that being the case, what lay beneath La Bosse's marvellous roses? More babies? Antoine shuddered. The contents of a woman's belly was as much the property of her husband as the woman herself. Maybe 'property' was the wrong word. Responsibility was better. Yes, both mother and father were responsible for their offspring. That being the case, no woman had the right to do away with the unborn infant without agreement. Antoine hrumped his conviction at this thought. He had that right, at least.

What then to do in the case of a woman who found herself with child, but for whom no father stepped forward? Or the husband wasn't the father? Or what if she had been raped? What was this poor woman supposed to do? Give birth to a child that reminded her of her attacker? Antoine hung his head. It wasn't the baby's fault. It wasn't, but no woman could be expected to live with such a thing.

And then, there was the question of God, who surely must have the last word on matters such as this. The Bible said... ah the Bible. The church had a rule for everything. The good Lord surely hated hands that shed innocent blood, and what could be more innocent than an unborn child? Yet, Catherine would undoubtedly argue that God acted through those who took away the infant before the light had come into it. A strange conundrum. Antoine couldn't say his corvine wife was Godlike in her piety, though she knelt often enough at her prie-dieu, her hands pressed together, her head bowed, a prayer for who-knew-what on her lips. Yes, and she went to confession often enough, but then what exactly did she confess to? Her sins were so... so immense and...

Instinctively, he rubbed his chest. He couldn't go on debating it this way and that. Death solved all manner of problems. The death of his mother, for instance. Hers had come one morning when the light had barely crept across the threshold and his father was away in Lyons. Antoine had lain in bed listening to the dawn chorus on the roof's ridge, immediately above his bed. Even as he marvelled at their song, he realised that the rest of the house was as quiet as the grave. He tippy-toed down the threadlike steep stairs to his parents' chamber below, ever fearful he would wake his mother and suffer for it. His feet were cold and his eyes still crust filled, as he captured a vision that had stuck with him all his life. His mother lay uncovered on her bed, her eyes glassy, her skin a blue-white. The cancer, which had eaten away at her breast for over a year, showed bloody and pus-filled through her flesh-stuck gown. Antoine had crawled to the bed, touched her cold arm, recoiled in fear, touched it again and let his hand rest there. He'd cried, but they'd been dry tears. He'd covered her with a sheet and watched her shrouded body for hours and hours, half expecting her to rise up and come for him, threatening blood and thunder.

"You'll get a chill sitting on the stones like that and you'll deserve it."

The Bastille walls echoed with his mother's voice, though he was all alone. Insanity had caught up with him. He vaguely remembered an aunt who'd gone mad. He hugged himself and cried softly into his sleeve. No one loved him. No one had ever loved him. Knit together with bones and sinew and yet life was so pointless.

"That's not true," said Marguerite. He looked up, wiped his nose with the heel of his hand. Neither mother nor daughter; just his mind playing tricks.

"Go away," Antoine mumbled. "Go away." He buried his face in his hands and let the pain of it all overwhelm him.

"There are three things that amaze me—no, four things that I don't understand: how an eagle glides through the sky, how a snake slithers on a rock, how a ship navigates the ocean, how a man loves a woman. No, make that five. How you can be so stupid as to allow your wife to get you arrested?"

Another voice. More madness. The hearts of the children of man are full of evil, and madness is in their hearts while they live, and after that they go to the dead, and so... Antoine looked up. The last voice had seemed different.

"Can you hear me? Are you paying attention?"

Perhaps he wasn't alone after all. Perhaps someone lurked in the corner and even now, played tricks.

"Who are you? Where are you?"

"Here. Up here."

Antoine struggled to his feet. A hand reached down from the tiny window.

"You're more phlegmatic than you were. Watery. It's the wrong way round."

"You," said Antoine, recognising the bony digits, and then the rectangle of face that squashed into the slit once the hand had been retracted: the grandfather.

"It took me forever to find which cell they'd put you in. I worried I wouldn't find you. Round and round the perimeter I went, praying they hadn't put you in the tower. Listen carefully, I don't have much time. They're saying you killed an old woman in the churchyard of St Saviour. Dame Habonde. They have a bloody knife with your initials scratched on the hilt. I'll give you an alibi and get you out of here. If they ask, say you were with me."

"Alibi? I don't need an alibi. I don't have a knife and I haven't killed anyone, least of all this Dame..."

"Habonde. I know that. Leave it to me. Do you have any money?"

"You know I don't."

"Well, I'll pay them myself, but you'll owe me."

"Pay them? You just said, you'd provide an alibi."

"Money oils the wheels of justice. Don't you know this?" It seemed to Antoine that the grandfather was put out, disgruntled even.

"Money. Always money." Antoine bit back the frustration. "Get me out of here and I'll gladly give you whatever you want." But he wasn't sure where he'd get the money from. Perhaps the moneylender? The one who was going to help him. Monsieur Tournier. Him.

The grandfather pulled away from the window and didn't return. Antoine walked the cell: six steps up and six steps back. Dame Habonde? Who had a name like that? He toed the bucket and instantly regretted it.

Catherine.

It was all her doing.

She'd scorned his attempts at love. She had scorned his attempts to better himself. She'd scorned his very being.

"You're a witch my love. A witch who captivated my heart with one glance. I'm no man. I'm a worm. A worm."

A voice shouted out from beyond the thick stone walls of his cell: "Stop blathering on you idiot."

***

That same morning Monsieur Tournier, the moneylender from the Pont au Change, turned up on the doorstep of the house in the Rue Beauregard, asking for Antoine. The maid told him her master wasn't in, but Tournier put a foot inside and although she tried to close the door, the man's toe got in the way. In the end the maid gave up on the door and went in search of her mistress, leaving Tournier hovering on the threshold, gazing at the substance and structure of the building. Catherine cracked the kitchen door and watched him. He was surely an insect. His eyes roved in every direction and his bony, claw-like fingers tested the air. Catherine shuddered.

"What did he say he wanted?"

"He said he'd come to look at the house."

"The house?" Catherine, bristling with anger, pushed the kitchen door full open and hurried towards her visitor, the maid in tow, still wittering on: "He wouldn't go. He wouldn't let me close the door."

"Monsieur," said Catherine, fixing a closed smile on her lips. She offered her hand. She would be civil. You never knew who might bring business. Tournier swept his hat from his head. His corkscrew hair sprung out manically, like a hundred insectivorous antennae. He pressed his lips to her hand and Catherine hastily withdrew it, her fixed smile replaced with a grimace approaching disgust. His lips had been moist to the point of slobber.

"I am come on a most important errand to see the master of the house. Yes, the house. I told him a week on... well it doesn't matter. I had a cancellation. I came straight away. Yes, straight away. Is he at home? Is he?" Tournier ran his eyes over the ceiling, the walls and back to Catherine.

Again, she shuddered. "I'm afraid my husband isn't here this morning. Nor perhaps ever again." She could but hope. "When did you meet him?" Tournier smelled of camphor.

"Ah, yesterday," he said. "Yes, yesterday. The storm. Oh, but it is as Monsieur said. It is a fine house with many windows. Windows. So many. Seven I believe?"

Catherine frowned. "Seven. Yes. A fine house." It came to her in a rush. "He's told you about his scheme, hasn't he?"

"Scheme? Scheme? What scheme? Shop, he said. He wants to put the house against a loan for a shop. That's why I'm here; to appraise the property. Yes, that's right. Appraise it."

"No. Not this house. Not ever." Catherine shooed him towards the door. The nerve of the man. Coming here. Thinking he could just walk in. How dare Antoine go behind her back and talk to this … this… she had no words for him…without telling her; without so much as a by-your-leave. Well, Antoine would pay the price now all right. He'd been arrested and he wouldn't escape his fate this time. So what if they were trumped up charges? No one knew save Monsieur Guillaume. No one. Not even Abbé Davot. Ha!

Catherine practically spat in Tournier's face. "Get out and don't come back." Invincible, that's what she was. Invincible. She growled at the moneylender and he backed away, bumped the wall, found the door and fled.

***

Footsteps echoed hollow, followed by the rattle of keys. Antoine cracked an eyelid. He'd not really slept, but then he'd not really lain awake either. The heavy door opened and two burly prison guards dragged him up and along the corridor, his feet barely touching the ground, his head aching; the smell of fearful sweat on his clothes, his skin, and in the very fabric of the building. Briefly, hands reached out to him from between bars. He glimpsed dirty, emaciated faces. Some shouted at him, but he couldn't make out the words. It was a house of chains alright; a place of vengeance and there was none as vengeful as his wife.

"Catherine!" he shouted. "Catherine."

A volley of laughter and an echo: "Catherine…Catherine…"

They dragged him along the rank corridors like a sack of onions and deposited him on a stool in the middle of a high-arched chamber. A soft golden light, filtered in through a small window and graced a table set some distance from his resting place. Alone, save for the sentinels now standing either side of the closed door, Antoine allowed only his eyes to rove this way and that. He was too weak and too tired to attempt an escape. One of the guards shifted and the door opened and in strode Sergeant Desgrez, followed by two gendarmes. Desgrez carried a sheaf of papers, which he threw onto the table. Motes of dust sprang up into the golden light. Antoine squinted, unsure if he should plead his innocence straight away or wait for the inevitable interrogation. He decided on the latter and watched Desgrez pace, realising only when the Sergeant turned that he'd met this man before, in Fagioli's wine cellar. Would it be a sudden punch to his kidneys, or a knife in the ribs? The excruciating fear of his imminent demise froze Antoine to the seat. His life was nothin but year upon year of misery. He'd tried to be a good man, but he knew he'd been a burden. He'd been cursed with bad fortune. Cursed. It wasn't an easy thing to dodge.

Desgrez pressed his face in close to Antoine's. "An old man came to me this morning. Said you couldn't possibly have killed that poor woman as you were with him and his daughter. What do you say to that?"

"Who? What?"

Desgrez sent him sprawling with a sudden backhanded thwack. Antoine tasted blood and attempted to push up from the grimy floor, but Sergeant's boot found a fleshy place between his shoulder blades and thrust him back down. The pain in his chest and stomach, seared through like a poker, hot from the hearth. He didn't want to die like this. He noticed an empty chrysalis wedged between floor and table leg, where the stone slabs met and formed a crevice. Whatever had been imprisoned inside, moth or butterfly, had flown free. The boot ground down on his back.

"We have your knife. We have a statement from your wife."

"I… My wife?" Desgrez's boot had forced all the air from Antoine's lungs; he could barely snatch a dry breath. "Please," he croaked.

The chrysalis case turned red, the floor too. Then the pressure let up and Desgrez retreated to the other side of the chamber. One of the gendarmes took hold of Antoine and dumped him back on the stool. His vision cleared slowly as he massaged his chest. A trickle of blood tested the skin on his cheek and dripped onto his lap. If he'd killed someone, and he hadn't - no, he hadn't, but if he had, there should be a witness. Not his wife, no not Catherine. And they couldn't prove it was his knife. They couldn't. Come to think of it, he didn't carry a knife. A pair of dressmakers shears maybe, from time to time, but then… He stared blankly at Desgrez, trying to fit the pieces together.

"Tell me about Madame Montvoisin."

"Madame…?" Antoine thought of his mother, all snide remarks and bitter emotions, dead, long dead, but then realised this man meant Catherine.

"A man or a woman who is a medium or a necromancer shall surely be put to death. They shall be stoned with stones; their blood shall be upon them. Come on, everyone knows who your wife is and what she does. She's La Voisin, the fortune teller. I've heard she drinks the blood of newborn babes."

"What? No," but Antoine couldn't be sure it wasn't true.

"What will we find if we turn your house over?"

Dead babies. He'd play dumb. It wasn't so hard.

"Nothing. Nothing at all." Antoine's gut rumbled. "It's like you said, she tells fortunes. That's all."

"And what of her relationship with Madame De Montespan?"

"Who?"

"The King's whore."

The guards sniggered. Desgrez shot them a look. Antoine fidgeted. This man knew everything. Everything. So the game was up. No point in keeping quiet now, but then… why make it easy? An idea began to surface. He'd make them a deal; an exchange - his life for information on Catherine's nefarious deeds. It would be as simple as that. He'd leave Paris. Go to the mountains in the south. He'd cross over into Spain. He'd be free. Answerable to no one. He'd miss Marguerite of course, but she didn't need him anymore. She was a grown woman and about to marry.

Romani.

Antoine tasted bile. He couldn't let his daughter marry that repulsive little weasel.

"Without shedding blood there is no forgiveness of sins. If I were a vindictive man I'd interrogate you until you broke." Desgrez stepped away.

Antoine swallowed. His throat hurt. He'd kill for a drink. He couldn't run. Love shackled him as surely as it did the sorry prisoners lingering in their foetid cells. It wouldn't matter where he went or for how long. Spain? He couldn't speak the language and it was oh, so far away. In any case, this brute wouldn't let him go. Not in a hurry. Not ever. He'd swing on the gallows before the week was out. Probably before the end of the day.

"You're a fortunate man."

"I am?"

"You have friends." Desgrez turned to the guards. "Get him out of here." And just like that, it was over.

"I'm not going to… you aren't… I'm free?" Antoine couldn't believe it. The guards came forward to lift him from his seat.

Desgrez sniffed. "A word of warning. We'll be watching you." He seemed about to leave when he turned back and said, "Your wife is La Voisin."

Antoine's bowels groaned. The man played a cruel game indeed; promise freedom and then deny it. He sat back down.

Desgrez nodded. "I'll be watching you both." The Sergeant strode from the chamber. The guards dragged Antoine up and frogmarched him out. The poor haberdasher wasn't sure what had happened. Imprisoned? Freed? Threatened? What?

They ascended a flight of stone stairs, passed through a set of dark double doors, which banged back against the wall noisily, and carried on, out in the bright white afternoon.

"I'm… this is…" Antoine had been sure they'd hang him, or shoot him, or cut off his head. He'd been sure, and now this mention of 'watching you both'.

The guards retreated back inside the Bastille, and closed the door. The bolts hammered home and Antoine stood in the dazzling sunlight, blinking, trying to focus, trying to stop shaking, the sounds of the city more melodious than he remembered. He sheltered his eyes, a wave of relief and confusion washing through his tired bones. He'd been that far from death. In his mind's eye he saw his finger and thumb measure the distance. That far. He almost fell over, but a hand came out to steady him. The grandfather whispered in his ear.

"You don't look well."

"He said… he said he's going to be watching me. Us."

"Us? You and me?"

"No. Me and my wife. He knows."

"Knows what?"

"What do you think?" Antoine lowered his voice to a hiss. "The babies. The poisoned husbands." He took a hesitant step forward. "How much do I owe you?"

"Nothing. They found the man who killed that woman."

"They did?" They walked together, the grandfather supporting Antoine with an arm around his shoulders. A dog cocked a leg against a pile of baskets. The piss steamed warm. A boy careened past, a screaming woman at his heels, stick raised to bring it down on the child should his steps falter. The sound of a delicately plucked lute rang out and a voice picked up the song. Never had the world seemed so vibrant. They made their way slowly back to the Rue Beauregard.

"So what happened?"

"I went to see that Sergeant, but he was otherwise occupied."

"With me."

"No doubt. They dragged in some poor unfortunate who'd tried to kill himself by jumping out a window, only he was as drunk as a Lord and didn't go high enough."

"What do you mean?"

"You can't kill yourself by jumping out a ground floor window. Anyway, he tried again. Hanged himself in the outhouse." The grandfather leaned in, conspiratorially. "Was still alive when they cut him down, and hauled him in front of the Lieutenant General. Confessed all he did. She'd a tongue like a pig wife."

"Who had a tongue like a pig wife? Who are you talking about?"

"Dame Habonde."

"The dead woman?"

"Her."

"So I don't owe you anything?"

"Maybe your life." The grandfather shrugged. "At some point or other."

"Can we go home now?" Antoine pushed away from his saviour, teetered for a moment, but then found his footing. When he chanced a look over his shoulder, the Bastille frowned back at him, stern and forbidding. He must have been there for months. Months and months.

"You shouldn't go home."

"I have to."

"She won't be pleased."

"She's never pleased."

"Come with me." The grandfather stopped. A bale of straw, fallen from a passing cart, blocked their path.

"I have to go back," said Antoine. "I want to open my shop again." He had to focus on something. The shop would take his mind off things; distract him from the mind-numbing torture of Catherine's evil heart.

"She'll not stop at five."

"You think I don't know that?" Antoine shoved the bale of straw aside.

"She meant you to die by execution. So that's five times she's tried to kill you. You're on your sixth life now. You've only got nine you know."

"Pah. I'm not a cat. Sixth life. I've only one life. This one. The one I'm living." But the grandfather was right. Catherine wouldn't stop until he was dead and buried. They walked in silence for a while.

Eventually, the grandfather ventured, "How's your bowels?"

"What kind of question is that?" The idea of it provoked Antoine's buried fury.

"You're full of phlegm."

"Phlegm?"

"Explosive phlegm."

Appalled, Antoine remembered his moment on the pail. Not months inside then, just hours. Oh, the horror of it.

The grandfather went on. "Phlegm is nourishing. It clears the humours. It's a good sign."

It didn't feel like a good sign. The old man was a crazy old bird. Phlegm indeed. What nonsense.

Antoine spotted the end of his road. "We're nearly there."

247

"It's your funeral."

The grandfather wandered off. Antoine watched him for a moment, feeling drained of energy and full of scornful self-hatred. Then he headed down the Rue Beauregard, pushed open the garden gate and made a beeline for the well. He pulled the bucket off the wall and doused himself with the contents. He slicked back his hair and wiggled a finger in his ear. Crazy or not, the old man was right: she'd try again. Time to go find that moneylender. There was a decent enough shop on the Pont au Change and Antoine meant to put his name against it. He'd be the underdog no more. Yes, he was tired beyond belief, and disoriented by the day's events, but he had to take action before the fire in him died completely. He poured a jug of sour wine from the vat by the door and supped it long and slow. Voices rumbled from further inside the house. He froze, jug in hand, ear cocked.

"She can't have him." The voice rumbled low through wood and walls.

Have who? Antoine set the jug down on the table and quietly approached the fancy receiving room's closed door. Here he leaned in close, ear to wood.

"This Mademoiselle de Fontage is no one. You are so much more gracious than she."

"Catherine," whispered Antoine. Up to her tricks.

"I'd rather see His Majesty dead than in the arms of another," came a second voice.

Catherine replied, "I can provide a remedy for your rival. I will send someone to pose as… I have it… as a glove merchant. She won't be able to resist. It will be a simple matter to dust the inside of each glove."

Dust the inside of each glove?

"And the King?"

"A petition, delivered into his hands."

The second voice said, "A petition? To request what?"

Catherine replied, "Does it matter what, other than that paper will be tainted? People will say the King simply wasted away."

Antoine listened in horror. He could hardly believe it. He heard footsteps and shrank into the shadows. They were planning to kill the King. The Monarch was divine. He ruled by no earthly edict, but by God's grace alone.

A voice said, "I'll pay you handsomely to deal with both His Majesty and his fancy woman. What do you say to one hundred thousand écus?"

Antoine dropped the jug. It broke into three pieces, the wine finding crevices in the floorboards. His heart leapt. He heard footsteps and then the door opened. Terrified, he screwed up his eyes, thinking that if he couldn't see them perhaps they couldn't see him.

"You!" Catherine snarled. "Why are you here? Weren't you arrested?"

Antoine dared to look. Catherine's face was creased into a thousand evil lines.

"You can't kill the King," he said. "It's treason. You've gone too far. You might kill a hundred, or even a thousand pathetic husbands, me included, but not the King. Not him. No."

He heard flutter of skirts and two faces appeared over Catherine's shoulder: one had almond eyes, and the other the most perfect golden skin and soft hair. The nose on the taller of the two ladies wrinkled and Antoine realised that, fresh from the Bastille, he probably didn't smell very good.

"Who is it?" asked Madame de Montespan.

"No one," snapped Catherine.

"I should… I have… business to attend to," stuttered Antoine.

"But who is he?" said Madame.

"No one," repeated Catherine.

"I'm her husband." Antoine hopped from foot to foot, his terror turning swiftly to exasperation. He had to extricate himself somehow, but he was frozen to the spot.

"Ah, the mysterious Monsieur Montvoisin." Madame Des Œillets looked him up and down.

Antoine wished he was anywhere else other than occupying the space beneath her gaze, but still he couldn't bring himself to actually leave.

"Monsieur, I am Madame Des Œillets and this is Madame de Montespan. You have doubtless heard of us. We have important matters to discuss with your wife. Your discretion would be greatly appreciated."

Madame Des Œillets held out her hand as if expecting Antoine to take it in his own and press it to his lips. Instead, overwhelmed by both her charm and a surfeit of Flemish lace at her neck, he gave a hesitant bow. Flemish lace. He'd not seen any of that for a long while. It made him think of the shop and his pressing need to resolve matters in his favour. This trouble over the King though; he couldn't let that go unpunished.

"Mesdames, my apologies." He flashed a look of shame at his poor state of dress. "I was in the garden. I will, of course, keep these matters to myself. You can depend on me." He backed away, still bowing, his teeth gritted at the lie he'd been forced to utter. He had no intention of remaining silent. He was going straight to…

Catherine hissed in his ear, "If you repeat anything. Anything."

Antoine hissed back, "You'll what?"

Catherine flashed a glance behind, half-closed the door and came at him. "What's your game?"

"What are you talking about?"

"That man that came this morning."

"Which man?"

"The moneylender."

"He came? Already? He said two days. No, three."

"If you think I'm going to let you beggar me, you've got another think coming." Catherine shoved past him and blocked the passage with her ample girth. "My livelihood depends on the good grace of those women and others like them. You eat because they pay me." She pointed at the door. "And you would prevent me from making an honest living?"

"There is nothing honest about what you do and you know it." Antoine tried to go upstairs, but Catherine wouldn't let him.

"I want you out of this house. Out of my life." Her voice was full of bile and bitter recrimination.

Antoine pushed her gently aside and this time she didn't stop him.

"Where will you go?"

Antoine half-turned. "What do you care? You want me dead. You've tried to kill me five times. Five. And yet, look at me. I still love you and always will. It's madness, I know. What a fool I am."

Catherine gritted her teeth. "You won't tell will you? You can't tell."

Antoine heard the anxiety in her voice. "You'll have to wait and find out." He hurried up the remaining steps, entered his bedchamber and closed the door, fear nudging at him. She might storm in and pick a fight. He listened for a moment, but all remained silent. He stripped off his dirty clothes, pulled out clean hose and breeches from his chest, and found a freshly laundered shirt and one of his fustian jerkins. He'd go and see that Sergeant. The one that said he'd be watching him. If he got in first, and told what he knew, well then he couldn't be arrested. He might even get a reward. A man could hope.

A reward.

He stopped for a moment and imagined how he'd feel. Glad, that's what. His face lit up. A bit sad too. His face dropped. They'd execute Catherine of course… but no, the King's life was at stake. There was no time to lose. The morning had gone. The afternoon too. The rain clouds had lifted and naught but a streak of gold lay low on the horizon. Antoine set his second-best hat on his head and ran down the stairs, paying no mind to the rumble of voices that coming from the fancy receiving room. Catherine would get her comeuppance alright, still it irked him that he'd have to tell on the love of his life; his sweetheart; his darling murderess. When all was said and done, that Sergeant Desgrez was a sly dog.

Outside, Antoine kicked up a stone. He needed moral support. He couldn't tell on Catherine without someone by his side. In his heyday, his father would have gone straight to the gendarmes; he'd have told and not worried about the consequences. Or not. After all, Montvoisin senior had his own evil-hearted wife to contend with. Argh, women.

Chapter Thirty

Catherine watched her guests climb aboard their carriage, and then returned to her own safe and now not-so-secret place beyond the panelling in her bed chamber. With the door closed, and no candle, it was darker than dark, and the silence profound. What a frustrating day it had been, what with Antoine's arrest and that insect, Tournier, come to put a price on the property. Then there was the plan to kill the King, and Antoine's return. Once again, he'd escaped death. She ground her teeth in disgust, and felt for the crucifix that hung around her neck. The good Lord made poor and rich alike. One hundred thousand écus to kill the Monarch. So much money and for such a small thing, and there was Antoine sticking his nose in where it wasn't wanted. She had to get rid of him once and for all or he would be the death of all of them.

She let the darkness sink into her bones, along with the silence. The answer would come when she freed her mind from the mundane and allowed God to work through her.

"We are from the Lord and yet the whole world lies in the power of the evil one."

The answer came in an instant: violence - swift and gruesome. She'd have Romani arrange it. She'd tell him he could only marry Marguerite if he killed Antoine and brought her his head. She'd not accept anything less. Not an ear, nor nose, nor finger, but the head. The same as if he'd been executed by that slippery devil Monsieur

Guillaume. Then and only then would she be satisfied. She'd be Salome to Antoine's John the Baptist. The thought amused her. Hadn't her mother always told her to despatch him quickly? Herodias would have her platter.

"Romani!" she screamed. "Romani!"

A door banged.

Hurried footsteps and anxious murmurings.

"Romani, where are you?"

Catherine beat out a tattoo on the stairs, charging with full force into Marguerite at the bottom.

"Where's that good for nothing man of yours?" When her daughter didn't answer, but instead flung a glare at kitchen door, Catherine pushed her aside. "If you want something done…" She could rely on no one; not even Marguerite, though God alone knew the secrets that girl had been party to over the years.

Catherine caught up with Romani at the garden gate. The moon hung like a silver fish on a line, and the wind soft and damp.

"Where are you going?" Really, men served no purpose whatsoever.

"Nowhere."

"I called for you. Didn't you hear me?"

"That's why I was…"

"Going to the tavern? Wine cellar? Church? You're as bad as Antoine."

Romani kicked up a stone. It hit an unturned bucket by the wall.

Catherine stood hands on hips. "You want to marry my daughter?"

"You know I do."

"Then do what I tell you. If you do, I promise, you'll be married before the month is out, and there'll be something for your pocket." Catherine couldn't see his face properly. She couldn't tell if he was shocked or pleased.

"What?"

"Kill Antoine."

"Me?"

"You heard me."

"I… I'm not sure. Me? Kill him?"

"If not, you can get out of my sight and not come back. Ever." Catherine leaned in close. Romani smelled sour, like cold vomit.

He danced on one foot, the other pressed into the wall. "What's to stop me from just reporting you to that… that new Chief of Gendarmes? The one that cleared the Court of Miracles. Him. What's to stop me? You'd be gone and Marguerite would be mine."

"You could try, but you'd have to watch what you ate or drank for the rest of your short life."

"You'd poison me? You couldn't. You'd be in prison."

Cheeky bastard, thought Catherine. "Perhaps I'd do it before the gendarmes arrived at my door. You're easily disposed of."

"Why haven't you done in Antoine then? Should be easy for a woman like you." He glanced over her shoulder. She followed his stare. Marguerite stood in the kitchen doorway, the candlelight to her back.

Catherine grabbed Romani by the arm and pulled him to her, leaning in close to whisper: "That bastard's immortal, that's why."

"If that's the case, what makes you think I'll succeed where you've failed?"

"Ssh." Catherine didn't want Marguerite to get wind of the plan. She'd only go and tell her father again, and then Antoine would be doubly on his guard.

"Because you'll surprise him, and his guardian angel won't have time to work his magic."

"Guardian angel?"

"Marie Bosse's father. Follows him round like a lost dog."

"I don't know. I'll have to think about it."

"Do it tonight and I'll see you'll not go short," Catherine said, thinking of the money she'd been offered to arrange the King's death. Thinking, soon she wouldn't have to tell fortunes or sell inheritance powders. She'd be set for life.

"How much?"

"Enough for you to buy a house and get her out from under my feet." Catherine nodded towards Marguerite.

Romani looked surprised. "Where is he? Here?"

"No. He's gone to report me for..." She daren't say it: plotting to kill the King. "He won't have got far. I watched him go down to the Rue St. Denis. He'll have gone to find the old man. Make it look like he was attacked by a stranger."

"You'll make good on the promise of a house?"

"I'll throw in enough for a new bed."

"I'll do it."

Catherine gave him a sly smile.

Marguerite called out, "Do what?"

"Never you mind." Catherine sang out the words. To Romani she said, "Go now. If you take the short cut and run you'll meet him coming towards you."

"Won't he..."

"He'll probably get stuck in some tavern or other. Take the short cut and intercept him. Run. Remember, I want his head. Nothing less."

***

Antoine passed inebriates and beggars, tripped over a pile of dung and hugged the wall along the Rue St. Denis to let a cart pass. He should have been hurrying, but his mind was a jumble of thoughts. He'd had a narrow escape. He'd fully expected to spend his remaining days locked up in the Bastille, or dead, yes dead, but, by the grace of God, he'd been freed. He ought to go to church and say a prayer of thanks, but there wasn't time for that. Besides, who knew which priest to trust and which not? He eyed an open door, from which came the sound of raucous laughter and the smell of stale ale and pungent wine. Ah, so tempting, with the faint glimmer of firelight, and the thought of sitting back to the high board of an old bench, his feet warming against the hearth. He could spend a few hours in delicious drunkenness and find the grandfather later, but no, he must carry out his duty. The King ruled by divine right. No one could plot to kill him and get away with it. Not even Catherine.

A hand reached out and yanked him into an alley. Antoine half expected to see the grandfather, but instead he was shoved up against the wall by... he couldn't see. Definitely not the old man. It was too dark. With a great bellow, his attacker thrust a knife between jerkin and shirt to meet skin, sinew and bone. Antoine doubled up in pain.

"She said she'd give me the money for a house."

"You!" croaked Antoine.

Romani sounded like a small boy, desperate for honeyed cake... and oh, but how the honey dribbled and dribbled and dribbled… Antoine, hand to stomach, blood rinsing through his fingers, pushed up from the wall.

"And you believe her?"

He'd not die so this verminous man could take his daughter away. The murderous forces working against him must not succeed.

"Didn't she tell you?"

"Tell me what?"

"I'm immortal," and with that, Antoine launched himself at the younger man, slapped the knife out of his hand and barrelled him to the ground.

They grappled for a moment, fingers gouging and grabbing, fists pounding until Romani brought up a knee and tried to kick Antoine away. The older man landed a punch to the younger man's jaw, knocking a tooth out and with it blood and pus. Flat-handed, Antoine steadied himself against the ground, his legs trembling, his head down; snorting blood; tasting bile. Romani flew up and bit into the haberdasher's nose. As Antoine howled Romani bit down harder still, tearing at the flesh, wild with horror and glee.

An explosion of light filled Antoine's eyes and then he was punching his way free, his poor tortured nose parting company from his face with every thwack, blood draining out of his nostrils until he could barely breathe. When he stopped, Romani careened off the wall, and stumbled into the street. Antoine, dropped to his knees, blood dripping, chest heaving, his heart full of pain. The sound of the drinkers in the tavern next door blasted into the blood-filled air. That, and the snort of a horse in the street. Antoine imagined its hot breath and sweat-sluiced body. His mother had always told him to watch out for horses.

"Terrible, unpredictable animals."

"Go to hell, you old nag," he shouted. "Go to hell, where you belong."

He head-butted the ground, and rolled over. Time did a lazy dance. No one found him. He lay stupefied by his injuries, gore pooling in the back of his throat, slowly drowning him. He coughed and almost choked. He turned his head to one side and spat out the nauseous mess. With shaking fingers he explored his stomach, feeling the clotted blood that had welled up and stiffened his shirt. He forced an entry to feel out the extent of the wound. It hurt more now than it had mid-fight. It wasn't deep. That was something.

He touched his nose and found nothing but tortured gristle. He coughed again and the agony of his complaining heart cut through all other pain. He rolled onto his side and let the stained sputum drain free. Little by little, he brought himself to his knees and then, grabbing the wall, steadied himself; one foot there and one foot there, imagining someone was pointing. "Careful, careful," they said, but it was all in his head.

The ground was uneven, the stones damp and slippery. Upright, he rested against the wall for a moment to get his breath. Then he pushed out into the night, his vision blurred and his footsteps tentative, as if he'd been drinking all night. He took stock of the road and noticed the junction up ahead. Beyond the corner lay the street where the grandfather lived – where La Bosse lived. Doubtless, she'd be there. He balked at the thought, but stumbled on, scanning the sky like an animal testing the weather and judging the rotation of the earth and the rhythm of the night. He'd tell the grandfather about the plan to kill the

King, and he, Antoine Montvoisin would take his revenge by surviving, and by exposing his mother's malevolence. No, no not his mother: Catherine.

The city blurred, his footsteps weaving a tortured dance, and yet somehow he made it to the worn doorstep. He knocked and sank to his knees. The maid opened up and he fell inside. When he woke up he was lying in a narrow cot pushed hard against a wall. It wasn't his own bed, nor his own house. He touched his face and found a damp dressing. Someone swam into view: La Bosse and behind her the grandfather.

"Where am I?"

"Quiet now. You've been injured." La Bosse pushed Antoine back down. A sting of energy passed through him.

"What have you done to me?"

"Nothing. You've been attacked. You're lucky to be alive. Sleep now. It will do you good."

Antoine pushed her away. "No! The King is in danger." His words came thick, obscured by a plug of mucus in the back of his throat.

"What do you mean?"

"I heard her."

"Heard who?" La Bosse leaned in close. "Tell me? Who are you talking about and what's the King got to do with it?"

"That woman, De Montespan. Yes, her, and my wife. They're going to kill the King."

"They what?"

Antoine nodded. It was true. All true. He closed his eyes, relieved to get it off his chest.

"We have to stop them," said the grandfather.

"Yes, but how?" replied La Bosse. "There's talk of an investigation."

"Warn the King," muttered Antoine. "Go to that Sergeant at the Bastille."

"Desgrez?" said the grandfather.

"It might work," said La Bosse. "But we can't incriminate ourselves. That would foolish. We'll send a letter."

"A letter?" The wound in Antoine's chest sent a pain screaming through his tortured body "What good will that do? Their plan involved a letter... no, a petition... yes, a petition."

La Bosse scowled. "You may be right. Petitions are given directly to the King. Our letter would be one in hundreds. He could be dead by the time he reads it."

"What then?" said the grandfather.

"We could enlist the help of a trusted Jesuit."

"One of your devils?" said the grandfather.

"Far from it." La Bosse hurried from the chamber.

Drawing what little energy he had left, Antoine tried to get out of bed. His head spun. His nose throbbed.

"Where do you think you're going?" said the grandfather.

"I can't lie here. I have to do something."

"You have to trust my daughter."

"But a Jesuit? If she fails then the King will die."

"She won't. She'll know the right person."

Antoine sank into the grandfather's outstretched arms. For now, he could do no more.

After a while the old man said, "What you need is a new nose. Silver I think. Looks good. Shiny."

"People will think I've got the pox."

"Have you looked in a mirror?"

"No."

"Then don't. It's not a pretty sight. I'll get you a new nose. Don't you worry."

***

All night Catherine waited for Romani's return; all night next to the hearth, her chair drawn close, her shawl pulled tight around her shoulders, her anger biting at every sinew. As dawn light grew in the eastern sky, the fire died and Catherine fell asleep. It was now that the door opened. A man stood silhouetted in the doorway. He coat was long, his hair wild. Startled awake, Catherine grabbed the poker. This wasn't Romani.

"Not the welcome I had hoped for."

The poker clattered to the floor.

"Lesage! You frightened me half to death."

The garden gate banged against the wall. Romani had come back. Catherine shoved Lesage aside and ran outside.

"Where's his head? Have you got it? I waited up all night for you. Well? Where is it?"

Romani steadied himself against the wall. "What? Bring what? Why are you giving me grief?"

"His head, damn you. His head." Catherine felt Lesage at her back and half turned.

"Would you believe it?" she said. "I send him to do a job and he comes back at cock's crow as drunk as a Lord."

"Me? Drunk? Never," said Romani. He started out over the lumpy grass.

"Come back here."

Romani weaved this way and that, Catherine snapping at his heels.

"I told you what to do. I told you," she said.

"No head."

"But you did kill him?"

"Ohhhh…. Yesssss…" Romani leaned against the apple tree. "Bit his nose clean off." He gestured like a madman with something stuck on the end of his fingers.

"His nose? Is that all?"

"Left him… somewhere…"

Catherine glowered. "Stupid man. I gave you one task. One simple task."

"It's alright. He's not coming back. He's as dead as dead can be. Got him good and proper."

"He's dead?" shouted Lesage. "Who? The haberdasher?"

Catherine shot him look that said 'shut up', and pointed at Romani. "You better be telling me the truth."

Romani sank to the ground. Lesage crept up.

"If it's true and your husband is dead, would you mind if I stayed the night only my home is derelict."

Catherine rounded on Lesage. "One night. That's all, and then only if you help me prepare a petition for the King."

"A petition? What for?"

"It doesn't matter what for. Only that the surface will be covered with poisonous resin."

Lesage's mouth dropped. "You're going to kill the King?"

"For an unimaginable amount of money, yes." Catherine's eyes met those of her one-time lover. He towered a good head and shoulders above her.

"Fair enough, dear lady. Fair enough. You're going to need La Trianon for that. She's the one for petitions."

"I'd rather not involve anyone else."

"You're going to write it then? You? What will you say?"

Catherine picked up her petticoats and recrossed the lumpy grass, Lesage at her heels.

"I'll tell you what it will say. A certain Blessis... you remember him?"

Lesage gave an offhand nod. They entered the kitchen and closed the door, leaving Romani outside.

"It'll say that the Marquis de Termes has taken Blessis prisoner at Fontenay."

"Is it true?"

"Of course not."

"But you will write this?"

"It's what I intend."

"Better La Trianon does it."

"Why for God's sake?"

"Because she has beautiful handwriting. Do you have beautiful handwriting?"

"It was good enough to get you freed!"

"You?" Lesage laughed. "You didn't do anything."

"I wrote a letter to... to..." Not the King; Madame de Montespan. "Well you're here aren't you?"

"Can I stay longer than one night?" Lesage raised an eyebrow.

"You are gone in the morning. Do you hear me? Gone."

Chapter Thirty-One

"You've read this?" shouted De La Reynie.

He threw a crumpled sheet of paper on the table and turned away from his Sergeant to hide the worst of his anger. Reports came in by the hour from every part of the city: a man had dropped dead in the street, foaming at the mouth; another had spewed up a foul mess and choked on it; still others complained of mysterious lesions that ate them away, and no rhyme or reason to any of it. Certainly, it wasn't the usual thing: apoplexy, consumption, agues. No, these recent deaths came with a stench of wrong-doing; with a weakness that floored even the healthiest of young men. It might be plague. The physician said as much, but De La Reynie's money was on poison. The rumour mill had gone into overtime, and now this. The King's life was in danger. It could only be that cabal of poisoners, masquerading as fortune-tellers.

Desgrez ventured, "We've interrogated the Jesuit from St. Antoine, near the Bastille. He says a woman brought the letter to him at the confessional. She told him she'd found it on the path at the Palais-Royal. The priest gave it to the King's confessor, Père La Chaise, who is also a Jesuit. He brought it straight here. Sensible man. I've talked to both of them. They've nothing to gain by lying. Unlike many, they both seem to be pious men. No scandal. No gossip. Live frugally. I trust them."

"You say that but the clergy is at the very centre of this business with the fortune-tellers. Ah Desgrez, it's all around us. Do you know they're putting fatherless babies to death and using their blood as a means to summon demons?" Tears welled up in his eyes. He'd lost children of his own. His wife too. "Little children, for God's sake. This Brinvilliers case was just the tip of the iceberg. We need hard evidence. We have to catch them at it. Someone needs to start talking, and soon. This La Voisin woman. What about her?"

"They say she's the most feared woman in all Paris."

"Will anyone come forward and attest to her deeds in a court of law?"

Desgrez shrugged. "It's doubtful. They fear what might happen if they did."

"We had the Abbé Mariette and that fellow Lesage and neither of them said anything beyond admitting to being paid to administer a black mass to the King's mistress, and look what happened there. The sorcerer has been released."

"No sir. That can't be right. They sent him to the galleys. You were at court during the sentencing."

"True enough, but Louvois tells me the King ordered fifteen galley slaves freed. Fifteen, and this Lesage fellow one of them." De La Reynie thumped the table. "I must beg an audience with the King. We must get to the bottom of this."

"The King? But his life has been threatened. Should we not handle it... I don't know, discreetly?"

"As you've been doing with the Vanen gang? Have you got anywhere with that?"

"About to make arrests, sir."

"And they're linked to the poisoners?"

"To one perhaps. A woman called Marie Bosse. None of the others though."

De La Reynie pushed back his wig and scratched. Infernal itch. Scratch, scratch, scratch. Someone was going to pay. Be sure of that.

"My God man, we know who the main culprits are. It's not as if they're in hiding. Catch La Voisin at it. Catch them all at it. You had her husband, right there. Murder wasn't it? Right there, and what? You let him go?"

"Someone else confessed," said Desgrez.

"When has that ever stopped you?" De La Reynie rounded the table and closed on his Sergeant. "Well?" He snarled. "I want them all, Desgrez. Every last one of these charlatans. Every woman and every man peddling death and destruction. Do you hear me? Take them by whatever means necessary."

Chapter Thirty-Two

Marguerite shaded her eyes as she gazed up at the doves alighting on the outhouse roof. Their wings patterned the bright sky, their cooing and fluttering made her think of high summer and lazy days in the pasture doing nothing but watching the clouds drift by.

"Bring me the whitest dove," her mother had said, not telling her what for or why. Marguerite knew why; they were brewing up a noxious substance with which to kill the King. 'They' being her mother and Lesage. They'd already had La Trianon, another of their coven, prepare the petition. All they needed to do now was to steep it in the poison and deliver it. Marguerite had watched Lesage grind sulphur into a fine yellow powder. He'd given her an angry look and said, "It's for Madame Brisard. We don't want to keep her waiting. Off you go, fetch the dove." It was a lie. Marguerite knew it.

So there she was in the garden, pondering her problem. She wasn't about to climb up and grab a bird off the roof. She'd have to buy one from the birdman at the market.

The sun took a lazy turn in the east and headed for noon. Marguerite hurried along the alley connecting the old Court of Miracles to the market place on the street beyond, where she spotted the birdman and his assortment of wicker cages.

"Monsieur, do you have a white dove by any chance?" she asked, casting her eyes over the assortment of caged birds.

The birdman's face was pock-marked, his nose bulbous, and his hair like string. "A popinjay take your fancy young lady? It'll cost, but they talk. What about it?" He smiled and showed his rotting teeth. Marguerite recoiled at his stinking breath.

"Just a dove."

The birdman ran his hand of the top of cages as if he was caressing a woman, and licked his lips. "A dove. I have one here. To you, twenty sous." He patted the top of a cage.

"Show me." Marguerite bent down and looked the dove in the eye. What would happen if she just walked away and never came back? She could go and find her father and they could run away together to another town. They used to pretend as much when she was little. He'd reach down and lift her high onto his shoulders and tell her she was 'queen of my world' and she'd beam and feel full of love.

"Is it the only one?" she said.

The birdman screwed up his eyes. "Today? Yes. Tomorrow? I can get more."

Marguerite knew she couldn't go anywhere. She had no money and neither had her father. At least, not yet.

"I'll give you ten sous."

"Ah, I can't go that low. They cost you know."

"The price of a child to catch them in the street?"

The birdman shrugged, sniffed and said, "What can I do? You want the bird or not? I'll take fifteen. No less."

Marguerite was in no mind to haggle over a few measly sous. "Fifteen it is. Give it here."

The birdman unlatched the cage and reached inside. Cupping the dove in one hand, he put his other out for the money. Marguerite dropped the coin into his palm and took the dove from him, cradling it close to her stomach. The birdman leered as she hurried away.

The dove breathed soft and warm. Marguerite felt its heart through the feathers. As she reached the kitchen door she glanced at the doves on the outhouse roof. It would be an easy thing to let the captive bird fly free. She held it up. Its coo vibrated through her fingers. All she had to do was…

"Is that you?" Catherine screamed through wood and window.

"I have it Maman," Marguerite replied, pulling the dove close and hurrying inside.

Romani stepped out in front of her. "What you got there?"

"What do you care?"

"Put in a word for me."

Marguerite didn't understand. "About what?"

"She won't let us get married if she knows."

"Knows what?" Marguerite tried to sidestep him, but he wouldn't let her go.

"Your father."

"Yes?" She felt the dove struggle.

"He's still alive."

"Yes… What? What do you mean? Of course he's still alive."

"No, you don't understand. She promised me a house… you… she promised me you. All I had to do was kill him."

"She what? No." Marguerite glanced up the stairwell and then back at Romani, "What did you do?"

Romani took a step back. "Nothing."

Marguerite took a step forward. "You said, she paid you to kill Papa. Tell me. What did you do?"

"Bit off his nose is all."

Marguerite squeezed the dove in anger.

Romani took another step back. "She wanted his head. He's as strong as an ox."

Marguerite could barely believe it.

"His head? She wanted his head?"

"It's not my fault," said Romani, putting up his hands in surrender. "She's going to kill the King too. You know that? The King."

"I don't care what she said. I'll never marry you. Never."

As she took off up the stairs, carrying her feathered bundle all the more softly now, Romani called after her, "Your father's still alive. He's gone to La Bosse's."

"Where've you been?" said Catherine as Marguerite entered the secret chamber. "Give it here." She snatched at the bird, forced its neck down on the benchtop and drew a sharp blade suddenly across its neck. Marguerite flinched.

"Papa's alive. Did you hear me?" said Marguerite. "Romani failed."

"Failed?"

"You sent him to kill Papa. How could you?"

"You know how."

"But kill Papa? Again? And now the King as well? What are you doing Maman? What? It's madness."

Marguerite turned away in disgust. As she did so she heard Lesage whisper "You sent a boy to do a man's job. I know someone who will do it properly. He owes me a favour."

"Today," said Catherine. "Have him do it today."

Marguerite ran down the stairs and out into the street. She had to find her father. She had to warn him.

***

Antoine lay in bed watched the cracks in the ceiling of La Bosse's house breathe. He imagined worlds inside the wood; phantom countries full of sweetmeats and pastries, fountains of fruity wine, and women with long hair and loving smiles. Delirious, he heard whispers and strained to make sense of them.

"Just a moment, but no longer. He's not well enough."

"I have to warn him. He's in danger."

"D'you think I don't know that?"

A face swam into view. Marguerite stood over him.

"He's awake. Papa? Can you hear me? Papa?"

Antoine grunted and tried to rub a nose that wasn't there. Marguerite grabbed his hand.

"No Papa. No."

"Marguerite?" He tried to sit up. Why was it so hot?

Marguerite pushed him gently back into the pillow.

"You've got a fever. You have to rest."

"No, I'm..." He glimpsed the whiskery old grandfather at Marguerite's shoulder. "I'm alright. It's nothing. I was dreaming that's all."

Marguerite didn't look convinced. "No, Papa. He bit off your nose. He was going to kill you. They're still going to kill you. I heard them."

"Rubbish. I'm as fit as a fiddle. There's no one going to come after me again." He said it, but didn't believe it.

"It's true. You have to hide."

Antoine sniffed. "Where? Here? You found me."

"Romani told me where you were."

"And how did he know?"

Marguerite shrugged.

"Hmm… well." He glimpsed the grandfather, hovering in the background. "Did she go?"

"Go? Who? Where? What are you talking about?" said Marguerite.

The grandfather nodded. "The deed was done. The King is safe."

"Not so," said Marguerite. "They've sent Romani and one of his friends with the gloves for Madame Fontanges. When they get back Maman will go with them to Saint-Germain to deliver the petition to the King."

Antoine let out a long sigh. "I knew I should have gone to that Sergeant myself. I just knew it."

"And risked them taking you a second time?" said the grandfather. "You're better off out of it. She's right, you should go into hiding."

"Listen to him Papa. Listen."

Antoine grunted, and shuffled up the bed until he was upright.

The grandfather retreated to the other side of the room and poked the fire with a stick. "That woman will be the death of you. Mark my words."

274

"Find me my jerkin and shoes." Antoine put one leg over the edge of the bed to test the floor. He felt shaky, but he couldn't lie here feeling sorry for himself. Marguerite snatched up his jerkin and held it close

"Where will you go?" she said. "Not home I hope?"

"I still own that house. She can't take that from me. Not until I'm dead, but no, I'm not going home."

"Where then?"

Antoine stared at the grandfather. "Is it true? The gendarmes know about the plot to kill the King? You aren't just telling me lies to shut me up?"

The grandfather stirred up the embers and grunted, "It's as I said."

"Then there's no more to be done. I've got a shop to open." Antoine's mind was made up. He'd find the moneylender and arrange the deal. Before that though, he had to visit Monsieur Michel and persuade him to talk to the corporation. Without that there really was no point in opening the shop at all, unless he intended on selling something other than haberdashery. He shook the thought away. He couldn't possibly sell anything else. Jewellery maybe. He'd always dabbled in trinkets. Catherine had liked trinkets. In the early days.

"You're in no fit state to go anywhere," said Marguerite.

"Either I'm in danger or I'm not. Make your mind up."

"A shop? Now?" she said. "How can you think of it when Maman is…"

"Is what? Going to be arrested for treason? Should be murder. Will be murder if she succeeds in killing me." He thought back to his conversation with the executioner.

Much good that had done. "I don't want her arrested, but what can I do?"

"Warn her."

"Warn her?" Antoine stood up. The chamber whirled. Too soon. Too soon. He sat back down again. "Haven't you worked it out yet?"

"Worked what out?" Marguerite blinked.

An innocent, thought Antoine. She feels but doesn't comprehend. She acts out of love, yes love, but she didn't really understand any of it.

"You were the one that warned me about the pastries. About how she was trying to kill me. You came after me. Don't you remember?" He tried his feet once more. Better. The dizziness had passed.

"Yes but…"

"And you wanted me to leave her then because you said she was trying kill me."

"No. I didn't."

"You did. You said she would kill me and I should leave."

"But I didn't mean it. She didn't mean it. She doesn't mean it now. She helps people. She doesn't want to hurt them."

"But she does. You know she does. All those babies in the garden. All those women she's helped get rid of their husbands. All those daughters who want to free themselves of their father." He gave her a pointed look. "I'm not saying you. I didn't say that. Your mother wants me dead. As dead as she wants the King dead. As dead as she's ever wanted anyone dead and I've loved her and loved her and it makes no difference." He let out a strangled sob.

"She doesn't want you dead. She wants her freedom."

Antoine stared open-mouthed at his daughter.

"Her freedom? Have I kept her a slave? Have I forced her into this life, where she kills for money? Have I? Well?"

Crestfallen, Marguerite picked at a thread on her bodice. "No Papa, but there have been times when…"

"What times? Tell me."

"Times when we didn't have enough money and she had to go out and tell a fortune so she could put food on the table."

Antoine frowned. "Tell a fortune. Any money she's ever had she's gambled away."

"No Papa. That's not true."

"Money runs through her fingers like water."

It was Marguerite's turn to frown.

"Come here. Come." Antoine took her in his arms and cradled her close. "My baby girl. So grown up and yet you know nothing."

Marguerite tried to pull away. "No Papa, it's you who know nothing."

Antoine's heart skittered. He wished she was the tiny babe he'd once watched sleep: butterfly eyelashes and rose petal lips.

"For a long time, I was like a blind man stumbling around in the dark, but not anymore. I see your mother for who and what she is now. I thought I could change her. I thought, if I was a better man, then she'd love me. I thought it was my fault because It was always my fault. My own mother… she taught me that everything was my fault… but I'm good enough the way I am, if your mother can't see that…" He kissed the top of Marguerite's head. It wasn't entirely true; he still longed for the smile; the special love-filled smile. If he saw that, just once… just once… then he could die a happy man. "…if she can't see that then… the shop will do it. The shop will make everything all right again. You'll see." He'd open the shop and Catherine would be wooed just like she was all those years ago. It couldn't fail. It wouldn't fail.

Marguerite's cheeks were wet with tears. "What do you mean?"

"Haberdashery is all I know."

Marguerite pulled away. "Go, Papa. Save yourself."

Chapter Thirty-Three

People on the Rue Saint-Honoré gave a wide berth to the limping man with the bandaged face. Antoine had done the best he could, even going so far as to borrow a shirt and serge du soy coat from the grandfather, but he couldn't do anything about his nose, or the bloody wound in his side, which now seeped through the rue poultice to stain his clean shirt. He looked more like a ruffian back from an adventure on the high seas than a master marchand-mercier. He tried to ignore the people on the street by focusing on how to get past Monsieur Michel, the younger, so he could talk to Monsieur Michel the elder. He must be business-like. He would not be swayed by requests to leave. He knew his appearance would go against him, but he couldn't waste time; his wife was on the warpath. He must re-establish himself as a man of means and obtaining the vouchsafe was the first step. He spotted the shop, and the alley beyond, ignored the latter and marched straight through the door.

"Monsieur Michel," he barked to the young man reaching up to a shelf, on which lay a bolt of grey Albigeois linen.

The young man looked horrified. "Leclerc," he shouted into the shelving. "Leclerc. He's here again."

"Who's here?" came a disembodied voice. Leclerc appeared, wiping his hands on his shirt front.

The younger man snarled, and waved a kerchief at Antoine. "Get away from here. Go away. Leclerc, do something."

"But it's only Antoine." Leclerc did a double-take. "What on earth have you done to yourself?"

Antoine squirmed. If only his side didn't hurt so much. If only his heart didn't feel like someone was squeezing it tight. If only his nose... if only he had a nose. A gob of mucus caught in his throat and he broke into a fit of coughing. Leclerc pulled out a chair and ushered Antoine into it.

"My dear friend. Come, come and sit down."

"Don't encourage him to stay," said Michel the younger. "Get rid of him."

Leclerc ignored the young man and focused all his attention on the visitor.

"Antoine? What is this? Look at you? What happened?"

"I had an accident. I'm fine. Well, I'm not fine, but I must speak with Monsieur Michel. Not this one." Antoine thumbed at the young man and lowered his voice. "I have a matter of great urgency to discuss."

The floorboards overhead creaked. Leclerc shot a glance heavenward.

"It is the same as before? You want him to vouch for you? If so then it's not so urgent, surely."

Another creak.

This time it was Antoine who glanced up.

"He's here isn't he? Fetch him down, or take me up there. Either way, I won't leave until the job is done."

"Ah, Antoine…"

"Why haven't you got rid of him yet?" snarled Michel the younger.

"Have some respect," replied Leclerc. "This man has come to us for help, and your grandfather knew his father. He had a shop on the Pont Marie once. He was a marchand-mercier before you were even born."

The young man's mouth fell open. Leclerc placed a hand beneath Antoine's arm.

"Come, I'll take you up." With that Leclerc helped Antoine to his feet and guided him through the stock room at the rear to a narrow set of greyed stairs that wound like a corkscrew to the floor above.

"What just happened?" said Antoine, confused by Leclerc's change of mind.

"That weasel thinks he can order me around like I'm a mouse or something? I'm sick of it."

Monsieur Michel the elder sat on a high-backed chair in the window of the modest room directly above his shop. The older man turned his wrinkled face and bright eyes on his visitor.

"I wondered how long it would take before you returned."

Leclerc gave a little bow. "Monsieur. My apologies, but he insisted." To Antoine he said, "Have you forgotten your manners?"

"No, indeed no. Monsieur Michel. Antoine Montvoisin at your service." He bowed, and instantly wished he hadn't. He felt the poultice on his side come unstuck. He clapped his hand to it.

"I know very well who you are. I've known you since you were a boy, but you're hurt. Come, sit down. Tell me what's been happening since that business with the flood."

Monsieur Michel pointed to a chair by the far wall. Leclerc manoeuvred it closer to the window and stood beside it. Monsieur Michel raised his eyes to meet those of his long-time assistant. "He wants me to vouch for him, isn't that right?"

"That's correct"

"Very well. Leclerc, go now to the corporation and fetch that man Faverolles here."

"He may be busy."

"He'll come."

Leclerc didn't move.

"Go. Now. It's urgent."

Leclerc made himself scarce and Monsieur Michel turned to Antoine. "It *is* urgent, isn't it?"

"It is. Yes, and thank you. Thank you so much. I wasn't sure you'd remember me."

"How could I forget the boy who used to hide outside in that alley while his father haggled over the price of Alamode? But what's happened to your nose?"

Embarrassed, Antoine hung his head. The blood rushed into the wound and stung his face.

"An accident." That was an understatement. "I've had the most terrible run of luck." Oh, but where should he begin? "I shouldn't bother you with it."

"It's no bother. I do very little these days except watch the world pass by. I've been ill and this is my first week back." He glanced out of the window. "There's an old man out there watching the shop. A friend of yours?"

Antoine craned his neck to see. The grandfather stood huddled in a doorway over the road.

"Of sorts."

"A spy. How exciting. Come on, tell me all about it. Aren't I an old friend?"

"Yes, but…"

"But nothing. Tell me. There's nothing more I like than to hear the latest gossip."

"He's the father of my wife's rival."

"Is he now? Ah, and the rival would be?"

"La Bosse." How much to tell his father's old friend? Antoine blurted out, "My wife tried to kill me."

Monsieur Michel shook his head but said nothing.

"It started when I found the babies in the garden." Antoine fixed his eyes on the street, stretching out, merchant upon merchant; a feast of goods and parading shoppers, and the grandfather, watching and waiting. Antoine sighed.

Monsieur Michel patted his knee, and said in a mocking tone, "You married La Voisin."

"She wasn't always La Voisin." Antoine mimicked the other's inflection.

"No, that's true enough, but you chose a woman just like your mother. Well, in some ways, at any rate. In others, not so much."

"Why do you say that?"

"You forget boy, I knew your mother. Oh yes, I knew her."

"Of course you did." Antoine hadn't just accompanied his father to the Rue Saint- Honoré, he'd come with his mother too. That time he kicked a stone against the button merchant's wall, and watched her basket while she supped an ale in the tavern… and what about when she forgot about him and went home on her own, only to send his father back for him later? Antoine had made a nest in a handcart outside this very building and had fallen asleep. His father had only found him because Monsieur Michel had pointed out the boy's hiding place.

"Ah you had a difficult childhood. I always knew that. Your father and I would… well, we would talk. Time was when he wanted to leave your mother, but… what with one thing and another, he couldn't do it. Those whom God joins together, let no man put asunder. It's like you and your wife, I think."

Antoine wasn't sure. His parents had never seemed particularly happy, but they hadn't seemed particularly unhappy either.

"I was the one she hated, not him. My father loved her right enough." Just like he loved Catherine. Just the same.

"It's not easy to escape your upbringing. You learn ways of being in the world. You relive them over and over. Your mother is the first woman you fall in love with and then… and then you find a wife to replace her."

"I hadn't thought of it like that. Do you think my mother was a fortune teller, like Catherine?" He was trying to work out if hatred came with the job. Perhaps his mother had led a secret life; a hidden existence. Perhaps that was what had made her so angry; the fact that she had to pretend to be someone she wasn't.

"A fortune seeker. More than likely. Fortune Teller? No. She was an orphan. Never knew love. Not until your father met her. Practically, scraped her off the street he did. Poor little thing. Desperate for a good hot meal. He called her his little Medea you know, after…"

"After the witch in the Golden Fleece. He loved that story."

"And you know what she did, don't you? After Jason left her to marry Glauce?"

"Who Medea?"

"She gave the new bride a beautiful wedding dress, which burst into flames and killed her." Monsieur Michel gave Antoine a long hard look. "Oh, your father fell for your mother hard, but she couldn't return his love. She didn't know how, you see. It cut him to the quick. He gave her everything and she gave him nothing but sadness."

Tears squeezed between Antoine's eyelashes. He blinked them away. "She used to tell me her grandfather was a man called Helios and her aunt was someone called Circe. I never met either of them."

Monsieur Michel chuckled. "They were Medea's family, not your mother's. Your father taught her to read and write by having her copy the Golden Fleece from a book. You might still have it. Carried it everywhere, he did. A thin volume." He raised his eyebrows in question. "No?"

Antoine shook his head.

"His stories were in his head, not a book."

Monsieur Michel sighed, "Ah well. Tell me about these babies."

"Babies?" Antoine had forgotten he'd mentioned them. "Oh. Unborn. Still born. Unbaptised. Murdered. I don't understand why any child should die. I've tried to. I have. I know that some women... Some men..." He choked on his words. The idea of it still hurt. "I've tried to forget about it, but I can't. She buried them, you see, under the grass. In my garden. Babies that..."

"Bad company ruins good morals. What you have to understand is that some women are so desperate they will do anything, anything at all, to be rid of their problem."

Antoine had heard the same from the grandfather. He glanced out of the window. A boy with dirty feet sat where the old man had once stood.

"The baby. The husband. The mother. The King."

Antoine's eyes widened. "Won't they go to hell though?"

"Who? The women who get rid of their babies? They'll certainly pay a price. They'll weep and mourn and feel guilty, and make excuses and feel more guilt. Some will kill themselves over it. Some will enter a convent or… Would you say your wife had good intentions?"

It was a strange question. Antoine wasn't sure how to answer it. He remembered how Catherine had reacted to Mademoiselle Du Parc's death: her tears; her impassioned words. Life was so fragile.

"I think she cares about them. The women, I mean." Catherine was capable of love. She had to be. "You said my mother couldn't return my father's love because she'd never known it herself. Do you think she had no love in her at all? None, for me, I mean." He'd always thought she'd hated him. Now he wasn't so sure. Monsieur Michel's words had opened up the possibility that the first Madame Montvoisin, Mignonette or Medea, whatever her name was, may have loved him, but been unable to show it.

Monsieur Michel stared out of the window.

"Leclerc has succeeded in his mission. Faverolles follows him. See?" He pointed. "We don't have much time. Understand this. Some women, men too, make a catastrophe of every little thing. A baby is conceived and it's a disaster because the husband was away at war. She has five children, and another mouth will beggar them. She

286

is attacked by a ruffian and the baby will remind her of that moment every single day of her life. There are a thousand reasons. I cannot say if it is good or evil that brings these unfortunates to your wife but come they do. We cannot escape the fact that there is a need, no matter how much we rail against it. No matter how much the Bible states it is a sin."

Antoine heard the shop door open and close.

"But Maman? What about her? Did she love me? Do you know?"

"Of course she loved you. The one she hated was herself."

"It didn't feel that way when she hit me."

"No, it probably didn't, but trust me, she was a lost soul and she hated herself for it, but it didn't mean she loved you any the less. She just didn't know how to show it."

A rumble of voices, then footsteps on the stairs.

"We'll speak more of it another time." Monsieur Michel planted a beatific smile on his face. "We've business to attend to."

"I hope this isn't a wild goose chase," said Faverolles as he stomped into the chamber. He gave Antoine a curious look. Leclerc brought up the rear.

"Monsieur. Welcome. It's been a while since you visited us," said Monsieur Michel, half rising from his chair.

Faverolles doffed his hat with a flourish. "Likewise, I'm sure. What's so important that your man drags me halfway across the city?"

"Monsieur Montvoisin here has asked me to vouch for him."

"Indeed!" replied Faverolles. "Are you sure you have the right man? He looks like a common or garden ruffian to me."

Antoine had no energy to take offense. He sat passively, the words washing over him like silt over bare toes dipped at the river's edge.

"Monsieur Faverolles, if you will take note. I have known this man since his birth."

Antoine looked up and caught the speaker's eye.

"Yes, I have. My boy. I have. He is as honest a man as I have ever met and if he says he is a master marchand-mercier, then that is what he is."

Antoine didn't think the man from the corporation was entirely convinced.

"He's hard to identify," said Faverolles. "What is the problem with his nose?"

"An accident," said Antoine. He touched the bandage. He dreaded taking it off and looking at it. It would be better once he had the new silver nose the grandfather had promised him.

"You say he is Monsieur Montvoisin and he is a master. Do you have any proof?" said Faverolles, addressing Monsieur Michel.

The latter sighed. "Does my word count for nothing? Take yourself back to your office and write in that book of yours that on this day I vouched for this man, Antoine Montvoisin. Now be off with you." He waved his hand and hrumped his distaste for the officious little man standing before him.

Faverolles drew himself up, puffed out his chest and announced, "I will take my leave of you Messieurs. Rest assured the gentleman here will be duly recorded as a master."

He doffed his hat once more and turned tail. His footsteps echoed on the bare stairs. Once he had gone Leclerc broke into a chuckle. Followed closely by Monsieur Michel, and finally, Antoine.

***

The light was fading fast as Antoine took the road down to the river, spotted the Pont au Change and made a beeline across it, heading for Tournier's tiny shop. Standing outside, he congratulated himself on successfully navigating the day's hurdles: his many aches and pains, not least those in his side, his heart, and his absent nose. Then there was his daughter's wrath, though really he couldn't fathom it, and Monsieur Michel the younger's snide remarks, and those of Faverolles, not to mention Michel the elder's revelations about wife and mother both. He would think on those later. For now he had a deal to do and a shop to open.

As before, the interior of Tournier's lair was dark, and redolent of boiled mutton. A solitary candle threw dancing monsters across walls and ceiling. Tournier sat next to the window, the green glass glinting like iridescent algae on the surface of a pond. He looked up as Antoine entered.

"Yes?"

"I've come about the shop. The one you told me about, further along from here, I'd like to take up your offer."

Suddenly dizzy-headed, Antoine steadied himself against the door jamb. He should have waited until he was in better heath. His nose, his absent nose, hurt, and he had a constant gob of mucus in the back of his throat. He resisted the urge to hawk it up and spit it out.

"Yes?"

"It's me. Antoine Montvoisin."

"You're hurt. Hurt. What have you done? Not that wife of yours was it? It was, wasn't it? La Voisin. I met her. Oh yes, I met her. Did I say?"

The floor creaked as Antoine took a step forward.

"I hope my house was to your liking." He didn't want to discuss Catherine. He'd made his mind up. The house was his and he'd use it as collateral against the shop. She could stay there as long as she needed. If his new shop failed, well then she'd have to leave because the house would pass to the moneylender.

"It needs some work, and not in the best of situations, but yes, it's a fine property, if you like that sort of thing. How much did you want?"

"Three hundred livres," said Antoine. He knew he'd never raise that much, but it was worth a try.

"On what terms?"

"What do you suggest?"

"I can't do three hundred, and I'd have to charge you thirty percent over three years." Tournier smirked.

Antoine gasped.

"I could go to two years and twenty-five percent on one-fifty."

"Not enough." And too much. He still had stock to buy. No one would give him credit until he'd started trading and turned a profit. This moneylender was fleecing him before he'd even laid his hands on the cash.

Tournier scratched his head. "Tell you what I'll do. Yes, what I'll do is this. I'll rent you the shop and I'll give you one hundred against the house. Repay me over two years at twenty percent. It's the best I can do. There'll be rent to pay on the shop of course."

"And it's yours? Not someone else's?"

"I own all the property on this side of the bridge down to the second abutment."

"Ah… so, let me get this straight. You'll let me have the shop and one hundred livres against my house, which is worth at least three hundred?"

"A hundred is more than a year's income for a man like you. Don't sniff at it. Take it. Take it."

"And what's the rent?"

"Ten a month."

"Five."

"Seven."

"Deal."

"I'll draw the paperwork up. Come back tomorrow. Tomorrow mind. If you don't, well I might withdraw my offer. You hear me? Come back tomorrow or don't come at all." With that Tournier slithered off his chair, took up the candle and led his new client to the door.

Outside, Antoine felt so weak and feeble that a sudden gust of wind blew him into the parapet. Sandwiched between the old wooden buildings, he hung on tight, feeling a rush of panic. He'd done too much; expended too much energy. The deep dark Seine swirled below, the water thick with effluent. For a moment he was right back in his old shop on the Pont Marie, the flood rising, taking the floorboards and his livelihood. What was he doing renting another shop on a bridge? A small boat bumped against the abutment. The sky glowered, threatening rain. A solitary bird battled against the wind.

Antoine pulled himself off the parapet, walking slowly, every step a struggle. Outside the new shop he stopped to look through the tiny window. It was smaller inside than his old place; a narrow strip of nothing. The door was paper, the window sugar, and walls shimmering treacle. Mon Dieu, but this bridge could be washed away as easily as the other and it certainly wasn't home. He wiped his brow on his sleeve. He was burning up. He needed to lie down.

He crossed the remainder of the bridge, teeth clenched against the pain in his face, hand held close to his side, and fever raging through him like a forest fire. He wasn't sure he could make it as far as La Bosse's. His stomach growled. He hadn't eaten anything in… he couldn't remember how long. It was no wonder he felt as weak as a day old puppy.

He spotted the sweet golden candlelight of a tavern and made a beeline for it. As he did so a man fell in behind him. It wasn't the grandfather, so who…? The idea of being followed niggled him. He glanced round and the man feigned disinterest. Antoine quickened his pace, entered the tavern and faded back into the shadows near the door. Here, he watched as the man came in and scanned the occupants, before going back out again. Antoine waited for a moment, debating whether to risk a drink. No, it would do him no good. He stepped back outside, glanced this way and that, noticed the man waiting over the road, and slipped down a side-street to enter the portico of a rather grand house. Here Antoine hid, back to wall. From deep inside the house came the sound of a dog barking and footsteps.

A voice said, 'Who's there?'

Antoine knew he'd have to risk it. He stepped out into the street and a fist ruined the remains of his face. Another punished his stomach, and then another and another. A face leered close, like death weighing up how much damage had been done. After what seemed like forever, an uppercut laid Antoine out. Seconds later he felt himself being dragged along the ground, grit scraping his scalp down to the bone. He saw the flash of a blade. The dog barked. Shouts.

Night passed; a lifetime of darkness. When he came to there was just the filthy ground, and the grey granulations in a stone wall. It put him in mind of the silt at the river's edge. Barely able to breathe, he gulped in air and sucked up the dirt. He spluttered and coughed, rolling over until he hit the wall and could go no further. Squashed between an overflowing outhouse and the back of a derelict warehouse, he let the darkness drift in. Buried alive! The winding sheet tight! He fought the god-awful sensation. Hands pinned him down. When he opened his eyes two nuns stood over him.

Not dead then. Not dead.

"Nine lives," he muttered.

"What did he say?" asked one of the nuns.

"He's delirious with pain. We should pray for his deliverance," said the other.

Chapter Thirty-Four

Three boys, yelping and laughing, kicked a stone along the Rue Beauregard and shouted back and forth, "Nibble and stitch, nibble and stitch, the cat and the witch, the cat and the witch."

Inside the house, Catherine caught the words as they wandered and worried them down to the bone.

"The witch, the witch? Nibble and stitch? What does that mean?" She flew outside and caught one of the boys by the arm. He yelped and pulled out of her grasp, running to catch up with his friends who'd gone on ahead.

"Nibble and stitch, it's the wicked witch," he shouted. The boys stood some distance away, taunting her with their rhyme.

"Come back here," she shouted. She didn't have the energy to chase after them. This business with Antoine had exhausted her. At least now it was over. He was well and truly dead.

One of the boys picked up a handful of dirt, and threw it at Catherine, screaming at the top of his lungs, "The cat's out of the bag. You tried to kill him but he's still alive," before running off.

Digging deep, Catherine thundered down the street, bellowing at the top of her voice, "Where is he? Tell me or I'll…" Faces turned. Catherine came to a halt outside the church door.

"What?" she shouted at the watching gossips.

"Another failed attempt," said the Abbé Davot, coming up behind her.

"What d'you mean, failed? Antoine's dead as dead can be. Paid that fool Latour. You know him. He promised he'd see to it."

"Latour? I don't think so. I heard Antoine's in the infirmary at the Holy Cross."

"He can't be."

The raven leaned in close. "You're losing your touch."

Catherine's upper lip curled in anger. She'd been so sure. So very sure. "If he's in the infirmary there's still a chance he'll die. He's got to be hanging on by a thread." She could pay Antoine a visit. She was his wife. The nuns couldn't deny her entrance.

Davot smiled slyly. "You're thinking of taking him a curative, aren't you? Something to soothe his aching bones. I wouldn't if I were you. They know who you are. Everyone knows who you are. Better you cast a spell and call up the devil. Make sure of it that way."

Incandescent with rage, Catherine took off at a pace, careening through the winding alleys and courtyards. No one would stop her from visiting her poor dying husband. No one. She stopped at the corner to catch her breath. Up ahead the butcher's stall buzzed with flies, the slabs of meat already putrefying, the ground below it awash with blood and punctuated by islands of fat and old bones.

The priest was right: she could call up the devil. She could envelop Antoine in curses so old and so impossible to break that the only way out was across the River Styx.

"Monsieur," she said, coming up alongside the butcher, taking care not to stand in the blood. A fly landed on the back of her hand, and another in her hair. She flicked them away.

"I'll have that," she said, pointing at a sheep's head shorn of wool, absent of skin, just flesh and sinew, bone and blood. It stared at her from between the various carcasses. The butcher wiped his nose on the back of his sleeve and reached for the head.

"Ten sous to you."

"Five."

"You'll beggar me," said the butcher.

He dumped the head in a burlap sack and twisted it round and round until the blood oozed through the rough weave. Handing it over, Catherine held it at arm's length and walked back to the house, letting herself in by the garden gate and going directly to a patch of thick-grown wolfsbane. With the edge of her petticoat protecting her hand, she plucked a good bunch of it and carried both head and herb deep into the heart of Antoine's laurel by the bottom wall.

"The end comes to us all. As the sun sets. As the babe cries. As the wolf bleeds and the sheep bleats."

She dropped the sack on the ground and plunged her hands into the humus-rich tilth, pulling up roots and weeds, feeling the soil under her nails. She'd have to scrub and scrub after this, but it would be worth it.

"No man is immortal and once sealed up in endless night, a hundred rolling suns and a hundred more, bring down this curse upon your head."

She glanced through the lattice of leaves. The blackbird's empty nest sat mid-bush. How many times had Antoine sat in here and watched the blackbird hatch its eggs? She shook the thought away, opened the burlap sack and rolled the head out into the shallow depression in the soil.

"Stupid. Stupid."

Antoine wasn't a bad man, but he was an annoying one, and now he wouldn't die. Poison would have been clean and quick, but no, he had to go and survive. She'd tried violence, but damn him if he hadn't gone and survived that too.

Catherine spoke to the sheep's head. "Why couldn't you see how important my work is? Why did you have to question it? Why go on and on about it?"

She'd tried to explain. She'd tried to make him understand. The women who came to her in the dead of night, panic-stricken at the thought of bearing a child out of wedlock, or to a husband who beat her, or because she'd been raped, or a thousand and one other reasons – they were the ones she served. The women who couldn't endure any more punishment from father, husband or lover – them too. It was beyond the ken of any man. Antoine would plead for the unborn child; he'd tell her what she did was a sin and that she would burn in hell for all eternity, but that couldn't be so because God had given His blessing. The priest had told her as much and not just Davot, but the others too: Abbé Guiberg, and Abbé Mariette. Catherine touched the crucifix hanging around her neck. The blackbird clutched the edge of its nest with curled claws, flexed its legs and lifted off, out of the bush.

"The Lord is close to the broken-hearted. He lifts up the crushed in spirit."

Catherine forced the wolfsbane into the dead creature's mouth.

"Blessed are the dead who die in the Lord." Scooping up soil she covered the sheep's head until it was completely hidden.

"Maman?" Marguerite called from the kitchen door. "Where are you? Madame Celestine is here."

Catherine, earth-smeared and unkempt, froze.

"Maman? She says it's urgent."

Catherine tamped down the soil and stood back to look at her handiwork. It would do, and by morning, or perhaps a little longer if the weather held fine, Antoine would be dead.

Chapter Thirty-Five

Deep at the heart of the old Monastery of the Grand Augustins lay a quadrant open to the sky. Here, on milder days, Sergeant Desgrez could often be found pondering the many criminal cases he juggled: the murder of an infant, not three years old, the theft of silver from a tavern, an attack on an old woman, and so on and so forth. On this particular day, with the winter sun glancing off the windows, Desgrez's mind had turned to the problem of the poisoners. He needed to break the city's silence. He shaded his eyes and watched a short, stout man approach him from the south cloister. The man had round shoulders and a large belly. He carried a sheaf of papers and a silver-topped cane.

"Sergeant Desgrez?" said the man.

"Certainly. What can I do for you?"

"You are the same Desgrez who arrested the Marquise de Brinvilliers?"

"Yes. To whom am I speaking?"

"Maître Perrin, at your service. I am an advocate with a small practice in the Rue Clery." He glanced across the quadrant. "May we sit?" He indicated a stone bench set against the eastern wall. The frost had lain on it all day. It didn't look particularly inviting, but Desgrez shrugged an agreement.

"If you wish."

Desgrez led the way. The advocate dropped his sheaf of papers onto the bench and sat on them.

"A little bird tells me you wish for information on the fortune tellers," said Perrin.

"Go on."

"Yesterday I dined at a house in the Rue Courtauvilain. You've heard of Madame Vigoureux?"

The name was familiar to Desgrez. "Tell me more."

"She's a dressmaker... which is sometimes a euphemism for..."

Desgrez flexed his fingers. He'd forgotten his gloves and his hands were cold. The tale was long in the telling.

Perrin went on. "The thing is, her friend La Bosse was also with us."

Desgrez's eyebrows shot up. Interesting.

"We drank rather too much and I'm afraid... well, she started to talk about her clients." Perrin sniffed. "Chilly out here."

"Madame Vigoureux? She talked about her clients?"

"No, no. La Bosse. She was the one."

"And?" said Desgrez. Good God if this man didn't get to the point soon he'd have to wring his neck.

"She, La Bosse, said, 'Another three poisonings and I can retire'. Another three poisonings? How many do you suppose she's poisoned already? I couldn't let it lie. I had to come." Perrin pursed his lips. "Did I do the right thing? It's important isn't it?"

A cloud passed in front of the sun and the quadrant greyed. A crow landed on the ridge of the roof opposite, then another and another. They croaked a raucous harmony.

"Did she mention La Voisin?"

"La Voisin? No, no mention at all. She may have been about to, but Madame Vigoureux warned her to be quiet. She'd said too much and she knew it." Perrin leaned in close. "My wife knows La Voisin. At any rate she knows what she does. Tell me, did I do the right thing?"

"Who told you to come to me?"

"Ah, that would be telling now, wouldn't it? Let's just say, it was an elderly gentleman and leave it at that."

"An elderly gentleman? Where did you meet him?"

"Does it matter?"

"Not really."

Perrin touched the tip of his hat, jumped down off his papers and shoved them back under his arm.

"Mon Dieu, but you must act. Another three murders is three too many."

"We may need you to testify to what you have told me." Here was a perfectly good advocate; a man used to giving testimony; a man whose word could be relied on in court.

"No, no, I can't do that. What if one of these… these 'fortune tellers' comes after me, or my wife. Think of it."

"But it's your duty."

The advocate didn't reply.

"I could have you arrested," said Desgrez. "Force you to tell what you know to my superior."

Perrin gave Desgrez a piercing look. "Sergeant, you may act on what I've told you or not, but don't think I will stand before the good judge and attest to it. Not unless you can guarantee my safety."

"And your wife?"

"Her too."

"If we arrest them all? Will you make a statement the?."

"Will I be safe?"

"As safe as anyone."

"When they are all in custody, then I will stand before whichever judge you chose and make my statement, but not until. I bid you adieu." With that Perrin disappeared back the way he'd come.

The crows took off, one by one until the roof's ridge was bare. Desgrez pondered on the problem. The advocate was a solid witness right enough, but it still wasn't enough. Especially, as Perrin would say nothing in a court of law until such time as the perpetrators of these foul poisonings were under lock and key.

The cloud passed. The sun lay fingers of warmth across the quadrant and Desgrez's knees.

An idea came to him: he would obtain the material evidence himself, or at least, he would send someone to obtain it. He wondered why he hadn't thought of it before. All it would take would be for a young woman to suggest they needed to rid themselves of their husband; someone convincing and he knew just the person: Madame Vert, the wife of one of his archers. He hurried to his office, stopping only to tell a gendarme to fetch her to him. The woman arrived cherry-cheeked and wiping her hands on her apron.

"I was making bread, I was. What d'you want?" she said.

"You work in here? In the kitchen, I believe?" said Desgrez.

"What of it?"

"I've got a job for you."

"I've got a job."

"Another. I want you to go to La Bosse."

Madame Vert gasped. "Her?"

"You know her?" said Desgrez.

"I know of her."

"Good. Then I want you to go to her. Tell her your husband is a drunk who ill uses you. Say you want to get rid of him. You understand what I mean by that?" Desgrez gave Madame Vert a pointed look.

"What's it worth?" she said.

Desgrez dropped a draw-string leather purse in her hand. She weighed it, her auburn curls bobbing with her nodding head.

"I understand sir. He hits me something terrible. I can't live with it no longer. No sir. I wants him dead. I wants to poison him, I do."

"Don't make it so obvious," said Desgrez. He'd been tempted to send her to La Voison, only it might seem too obvious a ploy. La Bosse would do to start with. The other would follow soon after.

"It's her business, it is. Everyone knows that," said Madame Vert.

"Her business. Yes, well you would do well to remember what our business is… Use some of it to pay for a remedy. She must think you genuine."

"You wants to catch her in the act. I understand."

Madame Vert curtsied and slipped the purse down the front of her bodice. Desgrez watched her leave, then turned to his books. Hours passed. Endless hours, marked by the city bells and by the threading of the sun, in and out of the darkening clouds. Desgrez stoked the fire in his office and wondered if he'd done the right thing. Perhaps the archer's wife had failed to persuade La Bosse of her terrible need. Perhaps she'd run off with money, or given it to her husband so he could get drunk. Archers were a rum lot. In spite of his misgivings, at a little past sundown, Madame Vert returned. Desgrez was fast asleep, the ashes cold in the hearth.

"She gave me this." Madame Vert held out a phial of liquid. "It cost all the money you gave me. I reckon you owes me."

Muddy-headed, Degrez tossed her a coin. "Have a drink on me."

Chapter Thirty-Six

The infirmary was all sighs and groans, the sweet smell of incense, cool light and stillness. Voices drifted in song, the old walls echoing distant chanted prayers. Pain laced Antoine to his cot, his mind meandering like a thread, his injuries healing slowly. Each day unfurled like a new leaf opening to the sun; gently and with care. The rhythm repeated unchanged: Matins, Lauds, Prime, Terce, Sext, Nones, Vespers and Compline. Each came with its own distinguishing cadence. The nuns were all whispers and soft swishing skirts. Antoine learned to distinguish each by their footsteps: Sister Marie had a limp, Sister Jeanne tippy-toed, Sister Claudine was flat-footed. For a long time, he thought of nothing and everything in a great melee of fractured feelings. One moment desperation carved into him, and in another he gave thanks for his survival. Slowly, as his wounds healed and his mind cleared, he took to replaying old conversations, particularly those of the grandfather, and Monsieur Michel.

"Bad company ruins good morals," the old haberdasher had said. "Your mother was an orphan. Never knew love. Scraped her off the street. Little Medea."

Evil hearted from the very beginning that was his mother. She wasn't to blame. No one had ever loved her, not in the early years at any rate. Mignonette, that's what her name had been, not Medea, but yes, his father had been partial to the Greek myths.

"She's not the only Angel Maker," the grandfather had said. "Believe no evil, 'til the evil's done. Other days, other ways." What had the grandfather wanted with him? Why had he followed him around day after day after day? And La Bosse, the old man's daughter, as bad as Catherine, and yet she'd shown him kindness when he'd needed it the most.

The days looped soft and slow and soon it was as if Antoine had never lived anywhere but with the Daughters of the Charity of Saint Vincent de Paul, as the nuns were called. His thoughts calmed. The idea of a new shop faded. The horror of the babies in his garden dwindled to a speck of almost nothing. His concerns for the King's safety dwindled. Only his desire to see Catherine smile remained. Some days he lay abed and imagined nothing more than a disembodied smile, pulsing in and out of his consciousness.

One morning Sister Jeanne came to him and, leaning in low, the wings of her cornette like a dove's spread wings, said, "There is someone here for you."

Antoine caught her soft smile and, reflecting it dreamily back to her, raised himself cautiously on one elbow and peered down the length of the infirmary. Who knew where he was? No one. No one at all.

A familiar face stared at him at the door.

"You." Antoine might have known.

"Taken your time," said the grandfather.

"Taken my time? What d'you mean?"

"I've asked every day about you. Given them a donation too, by the way. They wouldn't let me in until now. They said you were too ill. I couldn't let you go and die, could I?"

"Why not?"

The grandfather's eyes moistened.

"You look like your father, you know."

No one had ever told Antoine he looked like his father, and now this, from someone who couldn't possibly have known him.

"How?"

The grandfather said, "Did I tell you we're related?"

"We are?" It seemed impossible. Antoine couldn't ever remember meeting any relatives. Neither a grandparent nor an uncle, an aunt nor cousin. No one.

"I should have told you before."

"Something that momentous? I should think so. Who are you then?"

"Well now, your father was my cousin. Or, at least... our grandmothers were sisters. Can you believe that?" said the grandfather.

Thunderstruck, Antoine exclaimed, "No. No, that's not true. I would have met you, wouldn't I? I would have known. No. I don't believe it."

Why had the old man come? It had been so peaceful here. So quiet. He'd been thinking he might take holy orders and become a monk, and now here was the whiskery grandfather come to confuse him with a story about being a long lost cousin.

"We were estranged. Happened when he married your mother. Found her on the street, he did. Took her in."

"Have you been talking to my wife? How d'you know this?"

"I told you. We're cousins. I should have said something sooner. I shouldn't have been so... so enigmatic. The philosopher in me took over. He came from a good family, did your father. We both did."

Antoine closed his eyes. Perhaps if he ignored the old man, he might go away.

"His parents wouldn't have her in the house you know. She had no family of her own. No dowry, nothing, and it pained your grandfather so much he banished them. Told them never to come back. So, your father took up on the Île Saint-Louis, and then later…"

"On the Pont Marie."

"I was just as bad as everyone else. I thought Titou was damned fool and I told him so."

Antoine hadn't heard anyone call his father that for a long time. It was short for Antoine; his own name.

The grandfather continued, "I took the family's side and your father said he never wanted to see me again. I took him at his word. I've regretted it ever since."

"But you followed me. You followed me everywhere. You… she… your daughter wanted me to spy on my own wife. She wanted me to steal secrets. To take Catherine's business."

"Oh that was nothing. Friendly rivalry. I followed you because I wasn't sure who you were. I thought you hated what your wife did for a living. I thought you were in need of moral support, love even."

"Love. Pah. So what do you want?"

"Nothing. I don't want anything. Just that, when I saw you… well, it stirred up old memories."

"Old memories. I don't believe you." The grandfather was inventing it all.

"Ah, I don't expect you to understand it." The old man squeezed away a tear.

Antoine chewed over the new revelation. A cousin. Mon Dieu, but he wished he could turn time back. A nun's quiet footsteps pressed into the silence along with a whisper of prayer and the smell of slow-rotting rushes.

"Another week and you'll be well enough to leave," ventured the grandfather.

Antoine couldn't wait another week. What about the shop? Damn it, but he'd forgotten all about it.

"How long have I been here?"

"Three weeks."

"Three weeks!" Antoine stood up. The world spun. His legs buckled. Misery piled on misery. The shop would be gone; someone else would have taken it. There were other shops, of course, but he'd set his heart on that one. He couldn't say why, when he'd never even been inside it. It was just… well, the shop had offered hope. Hope for a new future. Hope for Catherine's love, and hope that he'd stay alive long enough to enjoy it.

"I wish you hadn't come," said Antoine.

"You still need a new…" The grandfather fished in his pocket and pulled out a small object parcelled in burlap and tied with twine. "Here, take it. Take it."

Antoine pulled the twine loose. Inside the package lay a small silver nose.

"I'll look like a Linnet with that." He tried it on, secretly pleased. "What do I look like?"

"Fetching. Very fetching." The grandfather reached into his pocket for a second time. "The shop," he said, and he held out a roll of parchment. "It's yours if you still want it. Go and see that fellow Tournier."

Antoine stared in disbelief.

The grandfather explained. "When your father needed me, I turned away from him. The least I can do is be good to his son."

"Ah, I don't know what to say. Thank you. Thank you so much." The grandfather's generosity overwhelmed Antoine.

"Just make a success of it. It's what your father would have wanted for you."

"And what do I call you now?"

"What have you been calling me?"

"You never told me your name."

"You never asked."

"True enough. I've always thought of you as…" He'd never met his real grandfather; never met anyone in his family. …as the grandfather."

"Then call me that."

"Come with me when I go to the money lender?"

"You don't need me to do that."

"All the same."

The grandfather shrugged. "If you want."

***

From a distance the palace at Saint-Germain-en-Laye seemed to float on a sea of trees. The carriage jolted and bumped, jolted and lurched, throwing Catherine and the other passengers from side to side, and up and down. The woman opposite had been sick out of the window. The man next to her waved a kerchief and complained in a loud voice that "the King would be better advised to remain in the city". Catherine clutched her purse tight and offered up prayers that they would soon be safely delivered to their destination. The carriage descended into the forest and some little time later pulled into the town square. The woman who had been sick offered Catherine a fawning apology. The man who had waved his kerchief walked off into the gathering crowd with nary a glance behind. Today was petition day. Today was the day Catherine would deliver death to the King. The trouble was, there were too many people: young women with babes in arms, old crones, men with diabolical diseases, and a smattering of merchants.

Romani climbed down from his place beside the coachman and guided Catherine through the crowd. All was noise and dust and the smell of sweat and foul breath. It was almost impossible to reach the palace gates for the mass of humanity in all its disguises.

"Where have they all come from?" said Catherine.

Three guards stood by the gatehouse and another across the square. It was well known that the King received each petition separately. This was the reason Catherine had travelled here herself, rather than trust the petition to Romani alone. Since his botched attempt at murdering Antoine Catherine no longer trusted her daughter's beau. She pushed through the throng of people.

"We'll bribe a guard to let us in. Over here." Romani pulled Catherine to one side, out of the melee.

"There are too many of them," Catherine said. "The guards. Can't you see?"

Romani scanned the square. "No more than usual."

"No, there's something wrong," Catherine said. "I don't like it."

Romani caught the eye of one of the guards.

"Monsieur, our petition is very urgent. If you let us through, you won't be sorry." Romani put his hand into a pocket and half pulled out a drawstring purse. The guard shook his head and shouted out over the heads of the mob.

"Won't do you no good. The King's not taking petitions today."

"What?" said Catherine. "Not taking petitions? But we've come especially. We've come from Paris."

The guard shouted, "There's folks come a lot further than that."

"What are we supposed to do then?" said Catherine.

"Put 'em on the table."

"On the table?" Catherine couldn't see a table.

"We've been instructed. No petitions will be handed to the King today." The guard pointed. By the gate stood a low table, on which lay piled petition upon petition.

Catherine whispered to Romani, "They know. We have to leave. Now."

Someone had talked and Catherine had a good idea who. It could only be Antoine. She shoved her way back to the line of carriages.

"Who will take me to Paris?" she bellowed.

***

Boots sounded loud on the old cobbles. A window banged back against a wall and a voice shouted, "Some of us are still sleeping". A contingent of gendarmes, all grunt and determination came to a halt outside La Bosse's house. At their head, Sergeant Desgrez. At their rear, De La Reynie. Desgrez consulted his list of suspects. They would go for La Voisin next, then Lesage. He pounded on the door.

"Open up."

Nothing from inside.

Desgrez stepped back. "Break it down."

The burliest man put his shoulder to the wood. The jamb splintered. The door fell and the gendarmes flooded in.

Chapter Thirty-Seven

The grandfather was supposed to meet him on the steps of the infirmary, but as Antoine walked the long hall towards the sallow daylight, he couldn't see his saviour anywhere. He trailed a glance back down the way he'd come, but the end of the hall had already disappeared into the gloom. All that was left of his sojourn was an echoing chant. He adjusted his new nose. It would take some getting used to. The ribbon holding it in place annoyed him. All the same, it was better than no nose at all.

Outside, he scanned the street, wondering if he should wait, wondering what could have happened. Antoine leaned against the wall and watched the world go by. Since the grandfather's last visit, he'd unpicked and rethreaded the news that they were related several times. He'd sifted through his memories for clues about the family's origins. His grandparents had lived in a village somewhere on the outskirts of Paris. Montvoisin senior had brothers, but they'd either died or dispersed to the four corners of the world. Antoine wasn't sure of their names. Perhaps a Philippe, or a Raymond. Once upon a time, the family had money, but they lost it. His father used to take Antoine on trips sometimes into the vast countryside. Once they passed a small chateau and his father said, "Uncle Guillaume gambled it away." Antoine had only been six at the time and had been more interested in flicking flies away with a switch of willow, than in his father's stories of fortunes lost. Now though, he wished he'd paid more attention.

What was it his mother had said? "Your father doesn't know how lucky he is to have a family." Antoine had always thought she meant the three of them, but what if she'd been talking about the entire gamut of unknown Montvoisins? Antoine retied the ribbon keeping his nose in place and took off down the street. The grandfather, who was no grandfather at all, but a cousin of sorts, was very late.

Turn and turnabout; this road, that road until Antoine reached the Seine, which was all breeze-flecked ripples and scudding river traffic. The sight of it thus reminded him of the day he'd told his father he was going to marry Catherine. He'd been standing at the window watching the sails on the water merchants' boats crack and ease with the wind, while his father wrestled with a length of linen and muttered under his breath, "What are children good for if not to help their fathers." Antoine had thought if he didn't ask Catherine to marry him soon, she'd drift away and find someone else. Probably, she'd run off with a ship's captain, who'd offer her a life on the high seas in exchange for a chest of jewels. Almost no one married for love.

So it was that Antoine blurted out, "We're going to be married," and Montvoisin senior dropped the end of the linen and trod on it.

"Damn it, now look what you've made me do. She'll be the death of you. She has no dowry. Nothing. Just like your mother." Antoine's father had pointed a quick-bitten finger. "She's after your money, and you don't have any.

Not 'til I'm gone. Then I suppose you'll inherit the business."

Not long after that Montvoisin senior had died of a strange malady, which Antoine knew now had been instigated by his own dear Catherine, but which, at the time, had been put down to a surfeit of drink.

The bridge. Such memories. Such fears. It wasn't the Pont Marie and not strictly 'home', but it was almost as good as.

The idea that Catherine might be lured away by the promise of wealth had always worried Antoine and now, Lord above, she probably thought he was dead and the house all hers. He should go home. Show her he wouldn't be killed so easily. So easily... ridiculous. She'd tried how many times now? No, he couldn't go home. It would be more of the same. Catherine would never stop trying to kill him and he'd never stop pining for her smile. No, the only way he could go back to the house on the Rue Beauregard would be to tell her he was a successful merchant once more, with money aplenty and the opportunity of expansion. She couldn't help but smile then. She'd fall in love with him all over again.

Antoine drew up level with the little shop, cupped a hand and peered through the slats in the shutter.

"I wondered how long... yes how long it would take you," came a voice. Tournier stood behind Antoine, key in hand. "That old gent said you were indisposed. We can sign the papers inside. Inside, yes?"

Chapter Thirty-Eight

Desgrez had positioned himself square on to the church of Notre Dame de Bonne Nouvelle, so he could watch the closed door, and listen to the drifting lilt of muffled voices coming from inside. He'd come for La Voisin. The maid had told him she was in church. He didn't want to make an arrest in the house of God, but here on the street she was fair game.

He waited.

And waited.

The door opened. A huddle of people came out. The Sergeant knew only that La Voisin was short and fat. Abbé Davot stood on the step, watching his flock disperse. Desgrez caught his eye. The raven went back inside and closed the door. A couple of women walked the length of the church wall, the rest of the congregation melting away. Desgrez started across the road. The women reached the garden wall. The fatter of the two turned to wish the other goodbye. She put her hand to the gate and Desgrez stopped it.

"Madame Montvoisin?"

"Yes? Who enquires?" She looked him up and down. It made him feel very uncomfortable.

"I am here to arrest you in the name of the King," he said.

***

Lesage, squatting in his own muck, heard the rattle of the keys in the lock and looked up, half expectant, half fearful. De La Reynie and three gendarmes entered, filling the cell with threat.

"I don't... I can't..." Lesage cowered, hands over his head.

De La Reynie boomed, "You would be best advised to confess your sins. You won't receive a second pardon. This time it will be the executioner's block."

"No. No. I... I haven't... I can't... I have information. Yes. Information."

"Go on."

"I can give you names." Lesage scratched his head. "Ah yes, but you have names. Names aplenty. Abbé Davot? Do you have him? Yes, you do. And La Bosse? I'll bet you haven't arrested her yet. Yes, what about her?"

"You're wasting my time. We took them all." De La Reynie said.

Horror-struck, Lesage begged, "Please... I don't want to die. I can tell you all about La Voisin. I can tell you how she plotted to kill the King."

"I'm listening," De La Reynie said.

***

Gossip ran through Paris like floodwater: the King's life had been threatened; someone had tried to poison him; arrests had been made; the poisoners had been rounded up and thrown in prison. Not a witch left. Not a single fortune teller.

Entrenched in his new shop, Antoine heard, but didn't comprehend. The King was alive and that was enough for him. He didn't dare think whether his own darling Catherine had been taken, never mind his daughter,

Marguerite. Some might have said he was only doing what he was good at, which was turning a blind eye to the awful truth, and later Antoine had to admit, there was something in that. So enamoured was he with the shop and all it entailed that he forgot about everything else.

Several days passed where all he did was place orders for stock, running about the city like a madman, inspecting cloth, selecting the best wool, and worrying the silk merchants with his constant demand for the brightest colours and the softest fabrics. Back in the shop, he counted his purchases the door and marked off the days to his grand opening. He wanted to throw a party and invite all his old clients. There'd be Monsieur Michel the elder, and Leclerc too. He might even invite Faverolles, from the corporation. Then there was the grandfather and La Bosse. How annoyed his wife would be at her rival's presence. No point in running to tell Catherine before he'd arranged it all. She'd just pour cold water on it, but after the shop was actually open, well then she'd see the sense in it. She might even smile. If she did, he'd be ready. Oh, how he longed to see that glint in her eye. He'd decided on Thursday week. On that day the shutter would go up and he'd be open for business. Antoine was so busy with the arrangements he didn't even realise that the grandfather hadn't visited him. In fact, he hadn't seen anything of the old man since the conversation in the infirmary.

Two nights before his opening party, Antoine piled up bolt after bolt of bright silk, ran his fingers over the rippling stack, closed his eyes and breathed in the dry cloth aroma. He was almost ready. This was the life he was meant for: the textured feel of slub silk, the soft touch of wool, the way the cotton flexed when rolled out, and the deadened sound of the water against the pillars below. In that moment, he was as happy a man as he'd ever been. He listened to the watermen shout to one another beneath the bridge and the voices transported him back to his childhood. He saw his mother, threading cotton by the light of a candle, while his father got quietly drunk, and always there'd been the noisy watermen. Ah, but it hadn't been all bad.

He froze.

Catherine had been arrested. La Bosse too. And the grandfather? Had he fallen prey to the gendarmes, and what of Marguerite? How could he have been so blind, so foolish? What was he thinking, stuck here in this shop, while his family, his whole family, were arrested and sent to the Bastille or, God forbid, that fortress Vincennes. He had to go home. Home, to the house on the Rue Beauregard. There wasn't any point in building a vast empire of haberdashery if the woman he loved with all his heart lay festering in prison somewhere… and Marguerite… her too.

Antoine half ran, half walked, taking the shortest route he knew. He ignored the drunks pouring out of the taverns and the whores at the river end of the Rue St Denis. Briefly, he considered turning into the road where lay La Bosse's house, but he thought better of it. Time enough for that. He had to get home. Turning into the Rue Beauregard, he noticed the way the house stood in silhouette against the night's country sky, beyond the city wall. In a few of the other houses he glimpsed candlelight through the shutters, but not his. He banged through the garden gate, crunched a snail underfoot and slammed in through the kitchen door. The house lay silent and dark.

"Catherine?" shouted Antoine. "Marguerite? Are you here?" He knew they weren't.

He left the way he'd come, and ran the length of the street in a lather. At the crossroads he bent, hands to knees, to get his breath back. An old drunk, singing softly, sat under the eaves of a house on the corner. A cat, tail erect and twitching, meandered across the road. The crescent moon hooked a dark cloud and tossed it aside just as quickly. The grandfather would know where they'd been taken.

Minutes later Antoine banged on La Bosse's door and didn't let up until the maid answered, candle in hand, eyes blurry with sleep.

"Don't you know what time it is?" she said.

Antoine pushed past her. "Where are they?"

"Who?"

"Your mistress. The old man. Where are they?"

"Taken to the Bastille," said the maid.

"Both of them?" Antoine could barely comprehend it.

"Madame, yes, but Monsieur is asleep."

"Asleep? Where? Where?"

Antoine grabbed the newel post and shoved off it, up the stairs. "Are you here old man?" he shouted. "Are you here?"

The grandfather stood in a doorway. His bare feet showed white against the dark floor, where the pale moonlight seeped through the window behind him.

"What's all this noise?" said the grandfather.

"Why didn't you come and tell me?" said Antoine.

"Tell you what?"

The old man shuffled back to his bed. Antoine followed him. The room was small, the bed no more than a cupboard set into the wall.

"That they'd been taken? Do you know where they are? Are they in the Bastille? We have to get them out."

Antoine's words tumbled over one another. It was all his fault. If he hadn't told about the plot to kill the King, then the letter wouldn't have been sent via the Jesuit, and the gendarmes wouldn't have arrested Catherine.

"That was weeks ago. Where've you been?"

"Where've you been?"

"Begging for my daughter's release." The grandfather got back into bed, lay down and pulled the covers up over his head.

"What about my wife? My daughter? Are they in the Bastille as well?" Antoine said.

"No." mumbled the grandfather.

Antoine tore the cover off the old man's face.

"Where are they then?"

"Vincennes. They won't let you near it. God knows I've tried. Go away." The grandfather grabbed his cover back.

Antoine paced. The floorboards creaked.

"What are we going to do? What? We have to do something. What are we going to do?"

The grandfather let out a big sigh. "There's nothing we can do. Not unless you've suddenly come into a fortune."

"I've spent everything I had from Tournier on the shop, but you... why didn't you come and tell me? Why? When it happened. What were you doing? Where were you?" Antoine said.

"Hiding. Praying. Waiting for the danger to pass. It was a good thing you weren't at home. They took my grandson too. They would have taken me only I know how to make myself invisible. And since then…"

"And you couldn't make them invisible too?"

"You know my daughter. She's not one to hide. She's outspoken. They all are. That whole coven."

"You should have told me. You should have come for me. Aren't we family? You told me you were my father's cousin? Is that even true?" said Antoine. "Were you lying to me?"

"Of course it's true."

"Then you should have come and found me."

"There isn't anything you could have done. Me neither. You knew this is what would happen. You were part of it. The King is alive because of you… because of me. Go home."

"We could go together. We could petition the King. We could… there's got to be something we can do. I'm not sitting around waiting for… for…"

"For nothing. All we can do is pray their end comes swiftly."

"Their end? You mean execution don't you? I know you do. I never meant for this. Not for anyone."

Antoine struck the wall with his fist, bounced across the room and hit the door jamb, thundered down the stairs and out of the house. In the street he yelled at the top of his voice and doubled up as if in pain.

Chapter Thirty-Nine

It was dark in the prison cell. The air was thick with the smell of dung, the floor awash with urine and vomit. Catherine curled up tight in her corner and tried to keep her toes out of the worst of it. If she had her time over, she knew she would do it all again, and change nothing. Until recently, six others had occupied the cell with her, but one by one they'd been taken until she was the last one left.

Day upon endless day they questioned her, the man De La Reynie and another called De Bezons, threatening her with all kinds of torture and once even forcing her mouth open and filling her belly with water until she begged them to stop. They wanted to know about her clients: who they were and what they wanted. They were particularly interested in anything the King's mistress, Madame De Montespan, might have instructed her to do. They regaled her with tales of how they had questioned the Countess of Soisson and the Countess of Roure.

"There's nothing you can't tell us we don't already know," De La Reynie told her one morning. Four guards stood behind him.

Catherine had been tempted to say, "then why are you asking me all these questions?" but she didn't. She knew it wouldn't do any good. They dragged her out by the hair and left her in the middle of a subterranean chamber with a vaulted ceiling and lit by flickering torches. Around the perimeter stood a circle of stern men. Whispers echoed around and around, making Catherine feel quite sick.

"Madame Montvoisin, let me introduce you to your accuser," De La Reynie said.

The door opened for a second time and La Bosse was pushed forward.

"What is this?" said La Bosse. "Why have you brought me here?"

Catherine said nothing. It was a trick to get her to divulge her secrets. Well, she wouldn't fall for it.

"Mesdames," said De La Reynie. "You stand accused of murder by poison, of abortion and sacrilege."

"Not I," shouted La Bosse. "Not I. She is the poisoner. She tried to kill her husband so she could marry a magician."

"Not so," Catherine said.

La Bosse spat out, "Lesage, that's his name. I'll bet they have him locked up already."

"Him," muttered Catherine.

"She sells inheritance powders and she doesn't care who to," La Bosse said.

"You accuse me because you think they will be easier on you. You know nothing."

Nothing. Nothing. Nothing. It echoed.

"Your husband is my cousin. What do you think of that?" La Bosse snarled.

"You lie."

"You wish."

"You used him to get to me," Catherine said.

"You tried to poison him and when you failed you set your dogs on him, but they failed too."

Catherine thought of the sheep's head and the incantation in the bush at the bottom of the garden. Antoine couldn't have survived that.

"You think he's dead don't you?" La Bosse laughed. "He won't die until he's good and ready."

Ready. Ready. Ready.

Time slowed.

Catherine flew at La Bosse like a rabid dog and brought her to the floor, kicking and punching, biting and gouging. Instantly, the guards pulled the women apart.

"Justice to prevail," said De La Reynie. "You will both make a public apology before the Cathedral of Notre-Dame. Take them away."

***

The winter tested Antoine's mettle by sending torrential rain and the threat of flood. The river tortured the bridge and more than once sent him scuttling back in fear to his shore-bound home on the Rue Beauregard. He was grateful when spring came with a burst of cherry blossom and breezy sunshine.

Antoine had all but resigned himself to Catherine's fate. He walked out to the fortress of Vincennes every Saturday, hoping to be let in; hoping his very presence would be enough to turn the wheels of justice in Catherine's favour, but every time he was turned away.

"It would cost more than you've got," said the guard at the fortress gate.

"How much?" Antoine asked.

"I told you. More than you've got. Piss off out of here."

"What about my daughter? Is she here? You can let me see her, at least."

"It'll cost you," said the guard.

Antoine sighed. "How much?"

"You know how much."

It was an exercise in futility, nothing more. Despondent, Antoine shuffled back to the Pont au Change. He had to be up early the next morning for a delivery of Fontainebleau wool. By the time he reached the shop the sun was stretching pink across the waters of the Seine and birds were settling along the roofline He made up his cot in the corner of the shop and crawled under the covers. He'd just fallen asleep when the banging started. For a moment the sound blended with the ebb and flow of his dream: a noisy affair where he was chopping wood with a thwack, thwack, thwack and got distracted by the raven priest sitting aloft the apple tree, only to look down and see Catherine's head on the block. Antoine tumbled out of his cot onto the cold board floor.

"Where... what... Alright, alright."

He still hadn't got used to living in such a small space. He'd thought it would be easy; as if the flood had never happened, but the Pont au Change was a different bridge with a different feel to it. He might go home for good soon. He missed his garden.

Antoine opened the shop door. It was the grandfather. His face was wet with tears.

"Naked she was. Naked as the day she was borne."

"Who? Who are you talking about?"

"Marie. My daughter. They put a noose around her neck and... and a candle in her hands. Oh, but I couldn't watch. I couldn't... but I had to." The grandfather snorted back his sobs, and wiped his nose on the back of his sleeve. His hands shook like an old drunk's.

"They hanged her?"

"No, not hanged, burned at the stake. They said… they said they were delivering her to Satan to mortify her body, so that her soul may be saved on the day of judgement."

"And Catherine? Did they burn her too? And Marguerite?"

"No." The grandfather sank to his knees.

"I told you we should have done something. I told you," Antoine said. He helped the old man up.

"Death isn't anything. Just part of the journey of life," the grandfather said, but he didn't sound convincing.

"That's why it hurts so much, is it?" said Antoine. "You are full of shit, old man. Full of shit… I'm sorry though. I'm sorry La Bosse had to die like that."

The grandfather patted Antoine's hand. "You're a good boy. Your father would have been proud."

Antoine wasn't so sure.

***

Summer threw up wildflowers between the cracks in the Rue Beauregard. House martins nested beneath the eaves, and in the laurel at the end of the garden the blackbird built a new nest, while a cat lolled in the splattered sunlight by the kitchen door.

Success had forced Antoine home. He needed his shop for stock. There wasn't room for him to sleep there as well. With his return, he'd taken to looking in on Catherine's mother. The old woman didn't seem to comprehend that Catherine was in prison.

"My daughter's coming to see me this afternoon," she said one afternoon, curling a finger and beckoning Antoine come closer. Her breath stank to high heaven.

"Her husband is a rum sort. She'd do well to knock 'im off. I told her more than once." She sat back in her chair and cackled.

After that, Antoine didn't visit again for a whole week, but then guilt got the better of him. She was old and didn't know what she was saying. Her daughter was locked up and she'd probably never see her again. Come to think on it, he'd never see Catherine again, not to mention Marguerite. At this he almost choked on his own tears. He could afford to be kind.

As a peace offering, he took a dish of day-old garbure to her, walking through the alley between the houses and across the road. He knocked on the door and waited. An old man shouted through the window, "No need to stand on ceremony. Come in. Come in."

Inside, the stale smell of unwashed bodies mingled with that of burnt onions. The old man shuffled out of his room, craned his neck and sniffed long and hard.

"More there than she'll eat," he said. "What you done to your face?"

"Nothing."

"You got a... a... silver is it? Got the pox?" He grimaced, exposing toothless gums.

"No," muttered Antoine. He touched his silver beak. The flesh beneath was still tender and the ribbons tying it on still bothersome.

The old man grabbed the newel post with a gnarled hand and called up, "She hasn't been out this morning. It'll stink in there. It stinks everywhere. What was it took it then? Your nose."

"Never you mind," said Antoine.

Madame Deshaye's room was shuttered and dark. The fire had burned out in the grate and the smell of urine and something of questionable origin hung in the dead air.

"Maman. I've brought you dinner."

He set the dish down on the table and opened one of the shutters. The light struck a glancing blow over the deathly white face of Catherine's mother. Antoine sat down with a 'hrump' on the bed. He watched a fly buzz against the window for longer than he intended. He'd meant to be in and out. Now he'd have to arrange a funeral. It never rained but it poured.

"Why'd you go and die Maman?" he whispered.

His eyes filled with tears, but not for the newly dead Madame Deshayes, but for his own mother; long since passed and gone to hell. It had been a growth, they'd said; the gossips and their endless suspicions. A growth on her breast. Antoine had caught two women chewing over her demise like crows picking at carrion.

"Open and fungus," the physician said. The speaker had a shawl of delicate pale blue, and a hat that framed her blotchy face.

"Oh, how terrible." The second woman had silk embroidered shoes that were too small for her puffy feet. Antoine had imagined them exploding greasy flesh and had hung back. The old crones perhaps hadn't known that he'd been the one to find his mother… or perhaps they had and were deliberately salting their conversation with its horror.

"Ate away at her until it reached her heart."

"No! I can't believe it. A buboe?"

"A cancer. Black-hearted she was. Black-hearted. The devil took her. I always said as much."

In his mind's eye, Antoine put the length of the bridge between himself and the gossips. His mother hadn't been perfect, but she'd been the only one he had. He snatched a look at Madame Deshayes, all crumpled and caved in. Love strikes where it may.

He stood up too quickly and felt the blood rush to his head. He grabbed the bedpost to steady himself and kicked something. Not the pot. Something wooden. He bent down, head all thump-thump, blood rushing to a nose that wasn't a nose, and pulled out a small coffer. He expected it to be filled with nothing more than worthless trinkets, but instead he found a stash of tarnished coins. He held one to the light and scrutinized it.

"Now what have we got here then?" He wasn't sure, but... "Well blow me. A Louis D'or." He picked up another, and another, and another. He counted thirty-three all told.

"The old witch is as rich as Croesus."

Antoine flipped the lid shut. Wouldn't do to leave them here. Not with a funeral to arrange and people coming and going. Did Catherine know about the money? Must do. Couldn't have escaped her notice. Antoine pulled the sheet from the bed, wrapped the coffer in it and tucked it under his arm. He'd take it home for safekeeping. No need for anyone to know about it.

Chapter Forty

Versailles was a magnificent building site and had been for many years. On this particular morning, with a light mist hanging over the lower gardens and the sun struggling to make itself evident, His Majesty paraded, entourage in tow, through the parterre, taking in first one damp vista and then another.

"Walk with me," said the King, waving his hand absently. As his entourage was already following in his wake no single person stepped forward. This forced the King to stop. The comedy of errors stopped with him. Madame De Montespan gazed out over the parterre. The Queen pursed her lips in annoyance. The King glared at De La Reynie, who took up the rear of the party. De La Reynie pointed to himself and gave a look that said 'me?'

"Yes, yes, you. You." The King sounded annoyed.

De la Reynie stepped forward and bowed long and low, sweeping the gravel path with his hat. Someone giggled.

"How goes this investigation of yours? The poisoners?"

Madame De Montespan coughed. The Queen silenced her with a look. De la Reynie's stomach rumbled. He'd hurried from his *petit déjeuner*. He'd been kept waiting for another two hours while the gentlemen of the court fussed over protocol and grumbled about who should and who shouldn't attend their Monarch that morning. De La Reynie had been promised a private audience and yet here he was, court jester.

"Your Majesty, this is not the right place or time to discuss such matters as I would broach."

"And why not?" the King said.

"The ladies, Your Majesty. These things are not for delicate ears." He glanced at Madame De Montespan.

If the King caught his inference, he gave no indication of it. "But I am asking and you will give me an answer."

"Your Majesty." De La Reynie dipped his head.

"So tell me." The King began to walk. De la Reynie had no option but to fall in step.

"We have interrogated most of the prisoners to the point of death," De la Reynie said. In fact, he'd found much evidence to suggest that the King's mistress was as guilty as any of those presently under lock and key. He couldn't however say so in present company.

De la Reynie lowered his voice. "Central to our investigation has been the testimony of this man Lesage. He has told us many things in exchange for his life. Only recently his accomplice La Voisin has begun to squawk. She implicated the playwright Racine in the death of his mistress, the actress Mademoiselle Du Parc."

"Is there anything in it?" the King said.

"It a seems woman suffered the loss of her child at the hands of a midwife, which this La Voisin arranged. Racine says La Voisin poisoned the Mademoiselle. "

"The child was born dead?" The King appeared horrified at the thought.

"It was, how shall say? Unborn, Your Majesty."

"Ah." The King watched Madame de Montespan, whilst leaning in close to De La Reynie.

"You are being cautious aren't you? I wouldn't want anyone to uncover some distasteful truths."

De la Reynie lowered his voice to match that of the King's. "We have uncovered the existence of a gang of alchemists, coiners and magicians, all of whom have extensive ties to the court. Some, we know to have had treasonous plans, but you know this already."

De la Reynie hesitated to explain further. He feared there were those in the King's entourage who had used the services of La Voisin and her many associates.

"And what should we do with these rogues, eh? Burn them all at the stake?" The King laughed. Everyone followed suit, save for De La Reynie.

"There have already been several executions. Others have been sent to the galleys." De La Reynie stopped, allowing the King and his entourage to continue without him.

"You've arrested the lady in waiting I hear?" the King said, loudly.

"Madame Des Œillets. We have. It was hard to track her down at first. She had taken up with a mysterious Englishman and…"

A slight gasp went up from Madame De Montespan, which did not go unnoticed by De La Reynie.

The King waved a gloved hand. "Take care you do not overstep your mark, Monsieur."

De la Reynie bowed. "But of course, Your Majesty. The last of the prisoners will be executed soon and that will be an end to it."

***

Later that morning, with the early mist burned off, a latticework of sunlight patterned the ground beyond the gates at the fortress of Vincennes. The birds sang brightly in the trees overhanging the walls surrounding the grounds, and a squirrel foraged in the undergrowth, turning over last autumn's mulch and testing each find with sharp teeth. The air was warm with the last heat of late summer. Antoine watched the guardhouse from a dip in the road, where the carriages, taking the corner at speed, had thrown up dirt onto the bank beyond. Every now and then the guard walked the length of the path that led from gate to fortress. When he did the second guard came out of the guardhouse and stood with his back to the gate. Antoine approached.

"Monsieur," he said. "I'm here to visit a prisoner."

He'd spoken to this man on several occasions. The conversation was always the same.

"It'll cost you."

This time Antoine was prepared.

"I have ten Louis D'Or. They're yours if you let me in."

"Ten what?" The guard turned round. His face was red, his eyes piggy. Behind him the other guard was making his way back towards the gatehouse.

Antoine put his hand through the bars on the gate. He held the five Louis D'Or in a pile between pinched fingers and thumb. He gave a little jerk and the guard held out his own hand. Antoine dropped the coins into the man's palm.

"There's five more if you take me to the prisoner Catherine Montvoisin. Do we have a deal?" Antoine pulled his hand back. "Her or my daughter, Marguerite. Or both."

The guard felt the weight of the coins and smiled. "Can't do both, but you have a deal." He threw back the bolts and opened the gate just enough for Antoine to slip through. The gate clanged shut behind him. The other guard nodded and took up his post at the gatehouse.

Antoine followed his man from the gatehouse to a flight of sunken steps by the leeward wall of the fortress. Down these steps and through a small door, which, once closed behind them, shut off all sounds of the outside world. Along a corridor that grew increasingly darker and danker with every step. They reached a heavy oak door.

"In there. You don't have long." The guard held his hand out. Antoine gave him the remaining five coins and waited while the door was unlocked and opened. Antoine stepped inside. The door closed behind him. The key turned in the lock.

Darkness, save for a slit window, through which a narrow shaft of light penetrated and hit the wall opposite. A cold, damp smell of decay and an echoing silence. Antoine waited for his eyes to adjust. At first he thought he was alone and the guard had played a dirty trick. He felt for the door and banged on it shouting, "Oi, open up. What's this?"

Someone moved in and out of the shaft of light. Antoine froze.

"Who's there? Catherine? Is it you?"

She turned her eyes on him, the sunlight shaft slicing through her, catching one side of her face, her bosom, her body, one leg and out through a toe to pierce the floor. Antoine lunged forward, meaning to scoop her up in his arms, but something about her stopped him.

"I can get you out. I have money now." He thought of her mother, dead in her chair, and the stash of Louis D'Or. Guilt washed over him. "It wasn't my fault. You shouldn't have agreed to kill the King."

Catherine said nothing.

"Have you seen Marguerite?" Antoine said.

Still nothing.

Antoine took a step forward, and another. He stood so close to her he could have leant in and crushed her against the wall. Catherine glared up at him from beneath a matted fringe of hair. He smelled her foul unwashed body odour and rotting teeth.

"I love you," he said. "I only wanted to make you happy. I thought the shop would do that. I thought if you saw I could earn a decent living and... I just wanted you to be happy. I thought if you... if you were happy then you'd love me. Why don't you love me? Why did you try to kill me?" Antoine felt tears welling up. He couldn't stop now. "I have the shop now on the Pont au Change. Did you know that? It's only small, but in time... I love you Catherine. I'll do anything for you. Anything. Just tell me what it is you want and... I can buy you passage out. I can." He clenched his fists. He wanted to touch her, but it wasn't right.

"Are you alright? What have they done to you? Are you hurt? What? Talk to me."

Silence.

"It doesn't have to be this way." Antoine fell to his knees.

The key sounded in the lock. The door opened.

"Time's up," said the guard.

Antoine didn't react.

"You hear me? Time's up."

"Alright. Alright," Antoine said, struggling to find his feet. He stood close to Catherine and whispered, "I love you."

"Enough of that," said the guard. "Come on."

As Antoine passed through the door Catherine said, "Tell them I'll give them whatever they want. Names. Deeds. Everything."

Antoine would have rushed back to her, but the guard grabbed him and pulled him through the door.

"What about my daughter?"

"What about her?" replied the guard.

"Can I see her?"

"No," and with that the guard pushed Antoine back down the subterranean corridor towards the steps leading out.

***

"Are you here?" The grandfather shouted through the kitchen and up into the echoing house.

A rumble overhead.

Footsteps on the stairs.

A grunt as Antoine pressed through the door and stood there, jug in hand, hoicking the phlegm from the back of his throat.

"'Scuse me," he said and he spat into the jug.

Antoine had hidden the remaining coins in his linen chest. It had washed up on the shore after the flood. A miracle really. The chest had been his mother's. He'd been glad to find it, just lying there between the beached river barges. He was going to use the rest of the money to buy Catherine's freedom. He just wasn't sure who he should speak to. He was glad the grandfather was here. He'd know the best thing to do.

"You've got to come quick," the grandfather said. "They're taking her to the Place de Grève." The old man's face was as red as a cherry.

"Who? I've got to go to the shop. I can't… You've been running. Taking who? Where?" Antoine peered into the jug and pulled a face. There was blood in his spit and in the back of his throat. He suspected it had trickled down from the back of his nose. His silver beak still rubbed.

"Your wife, that's who. The Place de Grève means …" The grandfather mouthed the word 'execution'.

"Now? They're taking her now?" Antoine said. "They can't do that. I've got money now. I told her I would…" He had to stop the execution. He had to get there quick. He practically threw the jug onto the table and muscled past the old man. The grandfather caught him by the arm.

"Sanguine today are we?"

"What?" Antoine had no time for cryptic conversations.

"Blood is nourishment. The vital force. She's about to die and you've survived."

"Let me go."

Antoine snatched his arm out of the grandfather's grasp. They couldn't kill Catherine. They couldn't. She hadn't done anything. Not really. Not anything to be executed for. Okay, that was a lie. She'd done plenty. She'd murdered babies. She'd murdered husbands. She'd tried to murder him. She deserved all she got, but all the same it wasn't right. He loved her. He'd told her so. He'd buy her freedom. He ran upstairs, fished under his bed, pulled out the linen chest, opened it and dug deep. The coins lay in a wrap of wool, bound with a thick silk ribbon. He pushed the bundle under his shirt, next to his heart and ran back downstairs. He ran out of the gate, across the road, into the alley, and out the other side into the Rue de Clary.

Hadn't the Lord Jesus said 'Suffer little children, and forbid them not, to come unto me: for of such is the kingdom of heaven.'? Yes, He had. Antoine knew that much. A fist of pain tightened in his chest, his poor missing nose throbbing and throbbing. He couldn't stop. He had to get there.

HE

HAD

TO

GET

THERE

He ran the length of the Rue de Clary and onto the Rue Montorgueil. Catherine had helped women whose husbands had been curmudgeons and drunkards, wife beaters and… not him, no he'd not been a wife-beater. There'd been no reason to kill *him*. God damn it but why did his heart have to pick today to give in, and what the hell was he doing running into the wind with no nose?

No nose.

He ran and ran, afraid Catherine would be killed before he got there. Afraid that *he'd* die before got there. So she'd peddled inheritance powders. What of it? She'd told him herself on many occasions: people die. People die, but not her. Not Catherine. She couldn't. He'd not seen the smile, the longed-for smile, and he had to get there, only now his legs hurt as well as his heart and his nose. He tore the silver nose from his face and grabbed at his jerkin front, fist clenching and unclenching. If he fell down dead right now, he'd deserve it. After all, he'd tried to take the house away from her, and all because of the shop – the stupid, ridiculous shop, and oh damn it but his invisible nose hurt so much; wind to the raw skin and puss draining down his throat, bringing tears to his eyes. No, he cried for Catherine, not for his own pain. Not for that.

He ran past the end of the Rue Beaurepaire.

Oh, but *she'd* conspired against the King. *She'd* committed treason. *She* was the one that deserved to die. Lord, but she hadn't meant it. It was a mistake. You couldn't execute someone for a mistake, and that's what they were going to.

No air. He couldn't breathe. He coughed up a great gob of crimson sputum and spat it out onto the damp cobbles.

"A mistake," he shouted, and ran past the Rue Monconseil and all the way down to the Mansion with its creaking cage and loathsome pillory.

A pile of faggots and the marketplace awash with people.

And what of the babies? The dead babies? What of them?

Antoine slowed his pace, his chest burning, his legs aching, his breath shallow and quick, his nose, his bloody not-nose, throbbing away. He glanced behind, half expecting the grandfather to be there at his heels, but he wasn't. Of course he wasn't. The old man couldn't have possibly kept up.

"Never forget... never forget, she tried to kill you eight times. Eight." Maybe the grandfather had... Antoine stopped in his tracks. "Eight times," the voice came again. He spun. People everywhere, but no one he knew. He started towards the pyre.

"Eight times? Seven." Had he counted wrong?

"Eight times she tried to kill you. She deserves to die."

Where was the voice coming from? Antoine struggled through the crowd: unwashed labourers, the pig-man, an assortment of wives, a wine merchant, and a baker carrying his bread on a huge board balanced precariously on his head, street urchins weaving in and out of the growing push of people and the smell as high as... and there, the grandfather. Yes, it was him.

"Nine lives you've got and nine you've had," said the old man as Antoine approached. "You know that don't you? Still, you're sanguine today. That's good. That's very good."

A soft rain had started up. It prickled Antoine's bloody face and dampened his jerkin.

"How did you get here so quickly?" he gasped, pressing forward. He stood on someone's foot, elbowed a woman in the ribs, and shoved aside a small boy standing on tippy toes to crane a look over the heads of those in front of him.

"Begged a lift on a laundry cart," said the grandfather. "You need to get your nose seen to."

But Antoine wasn't listening. His attention had been drawn to the approaching tumbrel. Catherine half sat, half stood in the back. Her hands were bound behind her back, her eyes covered with a dirty rag. Her clothes were stained and torn, her hair wild. A cabbage, thrown from the crowd, hit her on the side of the face.

Antoine blinked his tears away. "My dear sweet love."

His own pains were nothing compared to how he imagined hers must be. He reached into his shirt and pulled out the wool bundle, feeling the coins inside. The crowd melted away even as it held him back. Hands grabbed and pulled. Antoine was borne away. He dropped the parcel of money and lunged for it. The silk ribbon snagged under someone's foot. The wool rolled open, the coins shone bright. Someone shouted 'gold' and everyone dived for it. Antoine was kicked in the groin and kneed in the head. He fell back, money lost, heart broken.

"My heart," he gasped, and was about to disappear beneath the melee for good, when the grandfather bore him up, pressing forward with his friend so that they reached the front of the throng in time to see Catherine dragged down from the tumbrel by her guards.

"No," shouted Antoine. "No. Catherine. My love. I'm here."

The grandfather held onto him. "There's nothing you can do. Nothing anyone can do. If there was, my own daughter would be here now, and she's not so…" The old man sniffed back his tears.

The executioner forced Catherine to climb the faggots and perch indelicately on the crossbeam. Her hands were untied and then retied around the central post. She sagged at the knees and the rag covering her eyes caught on a knot in the post and exposed her bloodshot eyes. A priest stepped forward, his hand to his crucifix, his lips intoning barely heard prayers. Desolation ripped through Antoine. As more faggots were piled up around Catherine's feet, he imagined she searched for him and shouted, "My darling, I'm here. Here. Look."

Someone lobbed a turnip and then another. A volley of rotten vegetables followed, along with the sound of a braying mule and trumpet blown by someone who had climbed to the lower reach of the Mansion's rotating cage.

"She's my wife. My wife," but Antoine's voice was lost in the noise of the crowd as a hundred or more voices barked and bayed for Catherine to 'burn in hell'.

"Do not repay evil with evil or insult with insult." Catherine's words were borne on the soft breeze to carry over the heads of her accusers.

And then the fire was set and the crowd surged forward like a wave, only to take a step back as the flames burst out bright and hot, the splintering wood barking and crackling.

Antoine screamed, but nothing came out.

Catherine struggled against her bindings and called out, "Repay evil with blessing, because to this you were called so that you may inherit."

The priest shouted out, "You have done all this evil; yet do not turn away from the Lord, but serve Him with all your heart."

Catherine screamed as the flames bit into her feet and seared the skin on her ankles, ripping up through her petticoats to set her bodice on fire and scorch her tormented torso. Antoine broke through the cordon and clawed at the closest faggots, burning his hands in the process. The thugs behind him picked him up and threw him away like an old sack of grain. Antoine scrambled to his feet, but the priest, soft-skinned and young, was right there, pressing his face to Antoine's own, whispering Biblical incantations: "Woe to those who call evil good and good evil, who put darkness for light and light for darkness, who put bitter for sweet and sweet for bitter."

"Catherine!" Antoine shouted, but the crowd had turned on him now, bearing him away, pummelling and prodding, kicking and punching him, until he didn't know which way was up or what day it was.

"Take me!" he shouted. "Take me instead," but it was no use. Somehow, he found the strength to force his way through the hateful mob, and reached the burning pyre just in time to see the flames lick around Catherine's lips and blister the skin on her cheeks. Her eyes burned bright and for a moment Antoine imagined she looked straight into his heart, his soul, and his very being.

"My love," It came out as a whisper. No more.

Catherine's mouth assumed a rictus grin. Antoine sank to his knees as the inferno razed all to bone-white ash.

He had seen her smile. She loved him.

Chapter Forty-One

The garden opened its heart to the warm summer. The lavender put out its fragrant violet spikes. Apples blessed the old tree and roses wandered across the ancient, crumbling pigsty. A warm, soft evening breeze ruffled the quivering grass and Antoine's hair as he took himself from kitchen door to the well. He threw the bucket down, the rope snapping taut, the echo deep.

Catherine had been gone five months… nay, six this Friday, and Marguerite? She'd begged for mercy and promised to tell all. The Sun King had blood on his hands, but at least Marguerite would live to tell the tale. There was gossip that more than sixty prisoners still languished in the prison at Vincennes.

Antoine pulled the bucket up and set it on the wall. He thought back to that momentous evening when Catherine had dropped the dead baby and he'd thrown up against the gnarled apple tree. Beneath this very garden lay a patchwork of bones. Did they bleed into the walls of the house and thence upward to the roof? Did they fly across the rafters like so much newly braided and twisted lace? The whole world was naught but death.

Antoine took himself to the bottom of the garden and hid beneath the laurel to watch the blackbird in its nest, beneath which, in the humus-rich soil, lay the remains of last year's fallen chick. More bones. More death. The devil had the power to kill both body and soul. He glanced up at the church. At least that interfering raven Davot had been executed. Then there was Lesage. Tittle tattle had told him no one could stop the snake from hissing out his endless drivel about this priest and that courtier. They daren't execute him, for fear they may miss a juicy piece of gossip.

Antoine toed the skeletal hatchling; lace in the dirt; beak like pincers. The Comtesse de Soissons, the very same woman who had once graced this garden and asked about having her husband killed, had gone into exile. Romani had been sent to the prison at Château de Besançon and Marguerite... A fat tear rolled down Antoine's face. He missed his darling daughter. He couldn't bear to think of her locked up. They wouldn't let him visit her, not now she'd been moved to the Belle-Île-en-Mer.

He left the laurel bush and went to sit on his bench beneath the kitchen window. This was where it had all started. If he had his time over again, he'd make the same choices, no doubt about it. He'd loved Catherine; loved her with all his heart and always would. It was the same with his mother. He'd not been able to change her either, but it didn't matter. Really, it didn't. His mother had found peace in the arms of the Lord, and he had to trust that Catherine had too.

Catherine. It had been so long since he'd taken her in his arms. So long. He'd sacrifice everything just to have her return to him. Well, perhaps not Marguerite. No, he'd not give up his daughter, but this business with the shop: he'd been arrogant. Ah, he shouldn't have pursued it at all. He should have just left well alone. Perhaps then his own dear Catherine would still be alive.

The smile.

He'd seen it.

Absently, he rubbed his chest. These days the cold bit into his bones and he suffered with his feet. He scuffed one shoe on the side of the other and cracked his knuckles. Despite everything, the garden looked nice. He fancied the lumpy grass wasn't as lumpy as it used to be. He closed his eyes.

***

The grandfather lay awake all night, worrying over whether he'd been a good enough father. Perhaps he hadn't paid enough attention to his daughter. Perhaps he should have married for a second time. He'd never been wealthy, or a nobleman, or a lawyer. His life though, had been full of opportunity. He wondered if he'd squandered his time. It was true, he'd been a martyr to philosophy. He turned over and watched the wall; a blur of nothing.

Outside, the black night gave way to a grey morning. The grandfather stopped worrying and waiting for sleep. He got up, ruffled his hair and pulled on his beard. He slipped his feet into his well-worn boots and hitched his breeches up. He'd been so wise at the start of it all. So very wise. Now he was nothing but a bag of old bones. He was ready to die. He'd like to see his daughter again, whether in heaven or hell. He grabbed up his jerkin and his hat, and let the door bang close behind him. Pitching a nod to the heavens – rain threatened, he felt sure of it - he took off for the Rue Beauregard.

The sluggish daylight draped a melancholy haze over the city. An old woman threw a bucket of slops out of her window. A boy chased a kitten into a culvert with a stick. Last night's early morning drunk pissed up against a wall. The grandfather took little notice of any of them. Street gave onto alley. Alley onto another street. Losing a wife was one thing. Losing a daughter? Something else again. Life was full of surprises. From cradle to grave, it promised one thing and gave another.

He turned a corner and spotted Antoine's house. Head down he made for the garden gate, pressed his hand against the splintered surface and pushed it open. At the corner of the house he spotted a mottled spider in the centre of its web, sailing this way and that between wall and leggy rosemary. The path lead round the house and there on the bench beneath the window sat Antoine, head bent, hands on knees, eyes closed.

"Hope you haven't been there all night," said the grandfather. He sat down next to his friend. Antoine remained silent and still. The grandfather nodded; he understood.

"Life is a beautiful lie, and death the painful truth."

The old man listened to the rustling leaves on the apple tree and watched a bee flirt with the last of the lavender. He patted Antoine's deathly cold arm. "Rest in peace my friend. Rest in peace."

Epilogue

Ten thousand nights, or more, passed in the blink of an eye, and Antoine's house, like the church next door, fell into disrepair. Losing its centre of gravity, the floors fell through: second to first, first to ground. The walls bulged out into the street, threatening to explode stone and mortar, lath and plaster onto the cobbles. Brambles found entrance through broken windows and the tiles slipped from the roof and allowed the rain to seep inside.

The garden gave itself to nature: the lavender unruly, the apple tree gnarled, the grass, like summer hay, uncut and luxuriant. The earth erupted, musky and rich. A mole nosed the air briefly and threw up a mound of soil that sank, very slightly, as the creature returned to the depths.

Atop the mound lay a tiny bone.

END

ABOUT THE AUTHOR

Angela Elliott has been an artist, an engineer, a counsellor for victims of crime and a scriptwriter on documentaries and films. She lives in London.

OTHER BOOKS BY THE SAME AUTHOR

Some Strange Scent of Death
The Remaining Voice
The Finish

www.angelaelliottbooks.com

Printed in Great Britain
by Amazon

60704381R00210